# MONTANA STAR

# MONTANA STAR

•

# DeAnn Smallwood

*AVALON BOOKS*
NEW YORK

Published by Thomas Bouregy & Co., Inc.
160 Madison Avenue, New York, NY 10016

Library of Congress Cataloging-in-Publication Data

Smallwood, DeAnn.
  Montana star / DeAnn Smallwood.
      p. cm.
  ISBN 978-0-8034-9916-4 (acid-free paper)    1. Women
physicians—Fiction.    2. Montana—Fiction.    I. Title.

  PS3619.M358M66 2008
  813'.6—dc22

                                                        2008017331

PRINTED IN THE UNITED STATES OF AMERICA
ON ACID-FREE PAPER
BY HADDON CRAFTSMEN, BLOOMSBURG, PENNSYLVANIA

To my husband, Marvin, who never gives up on me
and is always there to listen, love, and encourage.
Thanks for loving me through all my writer's ups and downs.
You're my very own Star.

Thanks and gratitude to Janet Zupan, fellow author, who so generously gave of her time and expertise. You're a wizard with all those pesky punctuation things.

And a special thanks to our daughter, Myria, and son-in-law, Jim, for all your behind-the-scenes support and love. You two are special.

## Chapter One

The scrap was creased and wrinkled, the small print barely discernable, but that really didn't matter . . . she knew it by heart. She kept it folded and tucked away in the small beaded purse hanging from her wrist. The words held the only proof she had, the only link that assured her there was an end, a destination.

She lay her head wearily against the rough fabric of the seat, closed her eyes, and took a deep breath. Then, silently to herself, she repeated the words of the newspaper ad, her Aladdin's lamp, her way out. She refused to fall prey to the "what if's," of what waited for her at the end of this journey. She concentrated on the words. *WANTED . . . WIFE . . . WOMAN TO WORK BESIDE ME ON RANCH IN MONTANA. CAN'T BE AFRAID OF HARD WORK. SEND ANSWER TO BEN, GENERAL DELIVERY, WISE RIVER, MONTANA.*

The boy, sleeping with his head on her lap, stirred and repositioned his small body. Automatically, she put her hand to his head and gently smoothed the dark curls matted with sweat. She glanced ruefully at the damp spot on the dark blue satin

1

dress, made by his small mouth, a wrinkled thumb stuck securely in it. It was so hot and airless in the railroad car. Still, she envied him sleeping. He was tired and had been uncharacteristically whiny before he'd given in and let the lull of the wheels rock him to sleep. He had tired, at last, from the excitement of the adventure of riding on a train for days, then getting to live on a ranch with real live horses. Had she been wrong in painting such a pretty picture for him? Telling him he'd have a horse of his own? And land, lots of land for him to roam and grow in? He was so trusting; her heart filled with love for him, and she vowed again that nothing would ever hurt him. She would always be there, looking out for him. She always had, and no . . . no ranch in Montana was going to change that. And no rancher either. She squared her small shoulders and tilted her delicate chin, an unconscious gesture that those who knew her recognized as her back-against-the-wall-fight-until-death stance.

Still, she wished she could arrive looking a little less wrinkled, a little less tired, and . . . what, she thought. A little prettier? Would it matter? "The ad hadn't said anything about pretty," she chided herself. It asked for a woman. Well, she was that all right. It asked for a hard worker. Well, she was that as well. Still. . . . She absently patted the boy, then gently drew the wet thumb from his mouth and laid it alongside the wet spot. She sighed. "You can't make a silk purse out of a sow's ear, Aries." The voice whispering from the grave was her father's. "Make the most of what God gave you, girl." Well, wasn't that what she was doing?

She stumbled across the ad in a month-old newspaper. She was using the paper to wrap china figurines that had been her mother's pride and joy. They were one of the few things of value she'd been allowed to keep after the house and furnishings were sold to pay her father's bills. Bills she wasn't even aware of until his death. She'd grabbed the page of old news-paper and was angrily wrapping it around the Dresden shep-herdess when her eye caught the words: *WANTED . . . WIFE.* Her fingers had trembled as she smoothed out the paper and poured over the ad, reading it several times, butterflies start-ing in her stomach. Then she'd gently, reverently laid the pa-per on the desk, and reached for a sheet of paper. "Please, God," she'd prayed. "Don't let the ad already be answered. Please let this Ben person still be looking for a woman who isn't afraid of hard work, and please," she'd added, "please, please, let it be me. If this isn't the solution for Timmy and me, then I don't know what is. I don't know what we'll do."

Aries really hadn't lied in her response. She'd omitted a few things, and perhaps embellished a few others, but the impor-tant issue, her ability to work hard, was true. She was a hard worker. It was just . . . well, she'd never done anything re-motely close to the kind of work she supposed a woman would do on a ranch. But she could learn fast. She was smart. Her fa-ther had always praised her for her keen sense of memory and ability to do something after being shown how only once. She'd work hard for this Ben. She'd learn how to be a ranch wife if only . . . if only someone would show her how—just once. But none of this was shared in her letter to Ben, General Delivery, Wise River, Montana. Instead, she'd written about how strong she was, how healthy she was, how she loved the outdoors, how she loved animals, and that she was alone in the world and wanted very badly to live in Montana on a ranch. She said she was alone, but she really wasn't. There was Timmy. Would Ben mind that she was bringing her little brother with her? She'd been trying so hard to sell herself she didn't want to tell him that she would be bringing with her an additional re-sponsibility. What if he'd responded that she could come but he didn't want a small boy to feed and clothe too?

Another thing she hadn't shared was . . . well, there was more than one thing, that was for sure. But what she should have shared and hadn't was Timmy. She'd left the house quickly and practically ran the few blocks to the post office to send the letter before she lost her courage, and before she'd taken the time to realize the magnitude of what she'd done.

Aries hurried back home and finished wrapping the figurines. Then, setting aside the shepherdess (her mother's favorite), she took them to Mr. Mueller and, gulping back her embarrassment, she asked him if he'd be willing to buy them. He had; she suspected he'd felt sorry for her and had given her as much as he possibly could for the beautiful, wrapped figures, resting in a row along the bottom of a wicker basket. She blinked back tears as she left the store, clutching the money in her hand. She shut out the memory of the marble mantle that had been home to the figurines for as long as Aries could remember. The beautiful woman who let her young daughter carefully hold them, tracing their fragile beauty with a child's hand. The figurines were gone, and in a few weeks the marble mantle that graced the elegant home where she'd been raised would also be gone. She only hoped the money rolled up in her hand would last her until she heard from Ben in Montana.

Ben. She'd thought of him so much, she felt warmer just saying his name. Foolishly, she had elevated him to the rank of guardian angel, and had even gone so far as to imagine what he looked like. He'd be tall, but not too tall, slim and elegant, with good manners. His blond hair would blend with hers, and his big brown eyes would shine when he first saw his wife-to-be step off the train in Broken Arrow, Montana. Of course he'd love her . . . and Timmy. He'd be patient, and he'd teach her how to be a ranch wife.

In the weeks that followed, Aries quieted her rising fear by vacillating from praying she'd get a positive answer, to praying the ad had already been answered and filled by a woman who knew all about being a ranch wife. She watched the days go by and knew time was running out. Aunt Georgia, her father's maiden aunt pressured Aries to accept the offer, for her and Timmy to come and live with her in a small town outside of Philadelphia. She was in need of a companion, a woman to care for her, and for these services she would give Aries and Timmy a place to stay and their meals. Of course, they would be expected to earn their keep. Aunt Georgia let Aries know immediately that Timmy wouldn't be coddled as he had been by her and her father. He, too, would work for his room and board. Aries knew that their lives would be miserable under the pity and charity of God-fearing Aunt Georgia, a woman known for her rigid beliefs and stern interpretation of what was moral and immoral. She also had made her feelings clear over the years of what she had thought of the delicate, beautiful woman her brother had taken for a wife. Aries knew that her aunt also disapproved of her, and that she felt her father had been too lenient in her upbringing, particularly for allowing Aries access to knowledge improper for a decent woman. Aries knew that she would have to bite her tongue and curb her independent nature every moment she lived in her aunt's house.

Then the reply came.

*Dear Ma'am,*

*I would be willing to have you as my wife. I am sending you the money for a train ticket to Wise River. I will pick you up at the station the fifth of June. Ben*

She read it over and over, trying to find some clue to the man Ben. She wished he'd shown some warmth or let her know that he was anxious to have her come join him on the ranch. The word *willing* left so much to be desired. Still, maybe he was a man unused to showing his feelings, and not at ease with a paper and pen. She'd help him with that, perhaps in return for what he'd show her about the ranch work. Again, she felt a stab of guilt for not telling Ben about Timmy. Surely he wouldn't mind a little boy. Not the Ben she had idealized and created in her mind.

Smiling, she'd quickly penned a thank-you-but-no-thank-you note to her aunt. Aries told her she would have to decline her generous offer; but she and Timmy had made other arrangements. She felt lighter than she had for days, despite the niggling fear that tickled at the bottom of her stomach.

The few days before the trip were spent packing a large steamer trunk. When she figured in the ticket prices to Montana with the cost of taking the trunk, she realized it would be cheaper if she sent the trunk on a freight train instead. It was an easy decision. There would be precious little money left after buying Timmy's ticket. She would just have to pack for their immediate needs. She knew they might wait weeks for the trunk to arrive in Montana.

She squeezed clothes into the two carpetbags her parents used when traveling to her father's medical seminars. She would also take her father's black leather bag containing his instruments and some emergency items. She then turned her attention to the serious business of filling the trunk. She had refused to sell her father's medical books and instruments. They were her old and trusted friends; they were her life. She carefully packed the apothecary bottles, filled with pills of different colors and shapes and labeled in her father's neat hand. Beside these, Aries put her father's catalogs for medicines and herbs.

As Aries touched the jars and bottles, she was overwhelmed with longing for the short, heavy-set man who had the natural ability and the medical knowledge to diagnose and treat his patients. People had come from all over to see her father. He was known throughout Philadelphia as an outstanding healer and physician. He was also known for his love of gambling. But Aries had not known of her father's enjoyment of a "good game of cards." Upon his death, she discovered the addiction and the high stakes. It was only because of high respect and genuine liking for her father, that his marks had not been called in. But they had been left due by his surviving daughter. She knew her father never would have willingly put her and Timmy in this position. She knew he honestly thought he would pay off his debts . . . the next week, the next month, the next year. No matter, that with each card game, the figure on the markers grew higher and higher. Card games, the worry of the increasing debt, late nights, fatty foods, and the thick, fat cigars he stuck in his mouth first thing each morning and took out just before he closed his eyes at night, took their toll, and one night James Burnett suffered a massive coronary. The housekeeper found him, when looking for the good doctor who wasn't downstairs, sitting at his usual place, enjoying his favorite breakfast of fat Polish sausages, eggs, fried potatoes, and hot cakes dripping in butter and maple syrup. Aries was lost in grief. Her father was her life. He understood and supported her love of medicine and healing. He stuck up for her when, as a young girl, Aries rebelled against learning to cook, clean, and sew. He did nothing to hide his pride in Aries, as she demonstrated, time after time, that she had inherited his astute perception and abilities to treat the ill. Finally, her mother gave up the battle, compromising by demanding that Aries must learn to sew. From then on, Aries joined her father each day in his busy practice. She woke when he did, stood beside him during office hours, home and hospital visits. Her days ended when his did, and except for his card games, the two of them were inseparable. When she was younger, he carried Aries in from his buggy, fast asleep where she'd curled up on the seat next to him, exhausted from a long night through a difficult delivery, or any one of a number of medical emergencies that sent them traveling throughout the city to the homes of his patients. She became his accepted shadow and, indeed, people knew that to benefit from Dr. Burnett, they must accept his daughter. At the hospital, Aries took on the role of nurse, never daring to appear as learned as the men who dominated the medical profession. She knew it was only because of her respected father that she was allowed the courtesy, in an arena few women had penetrated. She saw how the nurses were treated, how they jumped to attention whenever a physician entered the room. She watched as they kept their mouths shut, never volunteering an opinion or offering any advice, even when it was obvious they knew as much or more than the doctor in charge.

Over time, Aries' knowledge deepened past the browbeaten nurses. In fact, she was often superior to the physicians who made their way to the city to study under the renowned Dr. Burnett. When they complained about his high standards, his barking questions, his attention to cleanliness, his love of preciseness, she knew only too well what they were talking about. Many times, her lamp had burned long after her father had fallen into bed to prepare a paper to submit to him the next day. She had learned to keep a sharp mind, ready always for the bark of the one word that would put fear on the faces of the interns. The pause in action, and then the question shot out: "Opinion?" His bushy eyebrows raised, his small eyes would fix on the face of the recipient. He pursed his lips as he waited impatiently for the answer. Aries had learned to respond quickly, succinctly, and with accuracy. She gave the medical opinion and then waited, her breath held, for a sign of success or failure. Often, the sign was so subtle that she would not know she had been inaccurate until after supper, when her father would say, "Aries, it would be beneficial for you, and for the patient, if you would prepare a paper on the putrescent of wounds."

The raise of an eyebrow, and two words, "Thank you," was highest praise when an "opinion" was delivered correctly.

She looked now at the half-filled trunk and realized she was packing enough medical paraphernalia to stock a physician's office. She sat back on the cane-bottom chair and rubbed a hand across her face. *Why am I doing this? Why am I packing medical items when in all likelihood, I'll never again be able to use any of them?* She moved from the chair back to the floor and, on bended knees, she continued the task of wrapping and fitting everything into the trunk. Aries lacked only the certification from the medical examinations stating that she was a physician; this took nothing away from what was her birthright, her inheritance. She may not have the paper, but she had the knowledge.

Fitting the last bottle into place, she arched her back and rubbed the ache that had grown increasingly worse over the past few hours. There was still plenty of room in the steamer. She glanced at the odd assortment of dry goods on the oak kitchen table. Her cheeks flushed as she recalled the fierce bargaining and bartering, when she traded her exquisite silks and satin dresses, her stylish hats and parasols for the bolts of calico and cotton material. Surprisingly, she found she had a natural ability and tenacity for wheedling prices down, and for convincing store owners that they, not she, were the recipient of the bargain. She knew they would have no problem selling her gowns and other items. Many of them had never been worn.

Aries had tackled her new adventure as she would a medical

question. At the Franklin Library Company of Philadelphia, where her father was a paying subscriber, Aries read everything she could find on Montana. It was precious little.

She now knew that Montana was bounded on the north by Canada, on the east by North and South Dakota, on the south by Wyoming, and on the west by Idaho. The land area of Montana was more than three times larger than Pennsylvania. It appeared to be a spectacular region of high mountain ranges, separated by valleys. It became the forty-first state on November 8, 1889. As she read about Montana, she realized she was taking Timmy into a western frontier, turbulent and still largely unsettled. She looked for mention of Wise River, but found nothing. She pinpointed it somewhere in the Bitterroot and Rocky Mountain region. According to the map, this was an area of the state where rivers and lakes were in abundance. Rivers had Indian names that rolled off her tongue in a halting manner. Kootenai, Flathead, Blackfoot. Then came names like the Musselshell, Milk, Marias, and Clark Fork Rivers. There were drawings and mention of a lake stretching across the area close to where she was headed. The area had been inhabited by the Flathead Indians. If she thought the names of the rivers were strange and somewhat frightening, the mountain names only added to her distress. Bear Paw Mountains, the Little Rockies, the Sweetgrass Hills, and the Little Snowy and Big Snowy mountains. She read on, wanting and needing to know more, yet dreading each word. Still, when she read about the wildflowers and their abundance in Montana, she felt soothed and she smiled as she read the list: balsamroot, shooting star, mariposa lily, bear grass, and bitterroot. Aries gradually formed an image of the land. She read about the trapping and white-tailed and mule deer, Rocky Mountain elk, black bears, antelope, moose, and mountain goats. The waters of Montana teemed with fish. Aries knew that Timmy would grow up fishing and hunting. Being a part of a cattle ranch was a good life for a boy. As for her, well . . . it wouldn't be Philadelphia. And sadly, Aries would be far from the new Women's Medical College. Her hopes for attending had died with the man who had given her such a deep love for healing. But, perhaps, there was a place for Aries in this untamed land. Certainly, there was a man named Ben who thought she had something to offer. She vowed that she would do everything in her power to become a part of Montana, this man's life, and his cattle ranch in a valley called the Big Hole. It was with this determined frame of mind that Aries made her next decision.

Mrs. Ellis had been Aries Sunday School teacher before the demands of accompanying her father had interfered with going to church. She remembered how on many Sunday mornings, the well-meaning lady had drifted away from a Bible story and into stories of her life on a small farm in Nebraska. In her childhood and as a young bride Mrs. Ellis had lived a farm life. Then she adapted to life with her husband in a bustling city. But her fondest love and memories came from her ranch years.

The very next day, Aries called on Mrs. Ellis, and over a cup of tea served in an egg shell cup, she took a deep breath and spilled out her story and dilemma.

"Mrs. Ellis," she started, then stopped, at a loss for words. How could she tell someone she'd lied and sold herself and invented talents to a strange man in Montana? This man who would be waiting on the train platform in a town she'd never heard of, in a state that was largely undeveloped, unsettled, untamed, and wild. She cleared her throat and tried again, "Mrs. Ellis."

"Aries, I've known you for many a year," the kind woman intervened. "I've seen you develop into the lovely young woman you are now. What I've never seen is you sitting still for so long, sipping a drink you don't really want, and trying to make social talk. Now, honey, you've got something to say, and in my experience, the best way to get something out, is to just say it. Go ahead. I'm listening." Her blue eyes twinkled above her powdered cheeks. She reached out and took the cup from Aries, and set it on a small table. She sat back, her eyes fixed on the petite blond sitting across from her. She noticed the perfectly fit gown, set off by a stylish hat on a cascade of corn-silk, blond curls. Her small frame, her expensive outfit, and her good manners could easily lead someone to cast her in the role of a wealthy socialite, a young woman whose only thought was the latest styles, fancy balls, and male attention. They would be very wrong. Mrs. Ellis knew Aries as fiercely independent, totally unaware of her striking beauty, and quite able to hold her own in any situation. Aries was no simpering, dependent female. Mrs Ellis had never known Aries to seek out, or enjoy, male companionship other than her father's. She gave the girl a nod of encouragement.

"Mrs. Ellis, I need your help," Aries managed to blurt out. "I'm afraid I've done something terribly wrong, something that can't be reversed." She reached into the satin reticule hanging from her wrist and extracted a folded piece of newspaper. Without saying another word, she handed the paper over. Then, when she thought adequate time had passed, she reached in again and handed Mrs. Ellis her carefully penned reply.

"Oh." The word loud in the hush of the room. "Oh, my." Then Mrs. Ellis chuckled, and then again, louder. "Oh, my, Aries. You've certainly done something quite unusual, to say the least. I don't know about the wrong part, and whether or not it can be reversed. But I suspect there's more to this, so let's hear it. One thing I can tell you right now: you've managed once again to behave in a most independent, some might say, unlady-like manner. Still, I must say it's the most exciting piece of news to come my way in some time. Now, tell me, why did you do this, and what do you need from me? I know you're not sitting there on the edge of that chair because you've decided to pay me a much-overdue visit." She smiled at Aries.

Aries took a deep breath and began her story. She told the woman her financial dilemma and of Aunt Georgia's offer. (Which was acknowledged by a sniff of disgust and the response, "The sanctimonious old bat.")

"So you see, I'm quite desperate. I have to make accommodations for Timmy and me and I'm running out of time. I believe this ad is an answer to my prayers, yet I've misrepresented myself to this poor man. I sold myself as a woman quite able to meet the demands of a ranch in the wilds of Montana"—she raised her dark blue eyes to the woman "—you know that's a lie. You were my mother's dear friend. You know I haven't the vaguest idea of how to run a home, much less a ranch. I might manage to direct servants on running a home, but I don't believe that will do me much good in Wise River, Montana."

"No," Mrs. Ellis chuckled again, "no good at all, Aries."

"Well," Aries paused, forcing a small smile to her lips, "that's where I hope you'll come in. Mrs. Ellis, can you teach me what I need to know in . . . in four days?"

"Me?"

"Yes. Don't you see," she rushed on, "you can help me. You know how to cook, clean do . . ."—she waved her hand around the room—"do all those other things that women do to make the house run smooth, to make it a home. I have four days before I board that train. Four days, Mrs. Ellis, to learn what my mother couldn't teach me in twenty-four years. Will you help me? Can it be done?"

"Land's sake, child, no!" The older woman shook her head emphatically, yet her eyes twinkled at the challenge asked of her. "No, not even in four months. Oh, Aries, you do manage to create a whirlwind wherever you go. Still . . . this is exciting. Aries," she uttered the name into the still of the room, "is this what you want? You'll be going into an untamed country to link yourself to a man you don't even know. Child, anyone else but you would be scared to death, but even though you sit there and tell me you've possibly done something wrong, and you're worried about misrepresenting yourself, I suspect you're secretly thrilled by the adventure, and wouldn't really want to reverse Ben's offer, his claim that he is willing to take you for his wife—would you?"

Aries delicate face flushed pink. "No." Her one word was low. But she raised her eyes, and there was a distinct light in them. "Mrs. Ellis, my father's death devastated me. I thought my life was in order, that I would follow my destination of working by my father's side, maybe even, by some miracle, entering medical school and becoming a physician. That was my dream. I never considered marriage a part of my life. I knew no man could take Father's place or my love for medicine. I've never desired to be some man's property." She sighed. "But that's not to be. Fate stepped in and now I have to think of Timmy. I haven't many resources to draw from, certainly not financially. To be blunt, this ad is a godsend. I feel this ad has given me an opportunity to do something more in keeping with my nature. Something that fills me with a sense of purpose and excitement, more than marrying some washed-out excuse for a man who wouldn't allow one original thought or opinion. A man looking for a genteel woman, delicate, given to vapors, and ready to present him with a passel of children, all in his image. On the other hand, I could live a life as dear Aunt Georgia's poor relation, her meek, grateful companion."

"Aries," the older woman interrupted, "how on earth do you know this man Ben won't be looking for the same kind of woman you just described?

"I don't," she murmured. "I don't know for sure, but something"—and she placed her hand under her breasts "—something here tells me that any man who is willing to carve out a ranch in the wild state of Montana isn't looking for a socialite. He will be looking for a wife. No, he'll be looking for a helpmate. I believe, Mrs. Ellis, that he'll want a strong woman, one who can stand at his side and take whatever that land throws at them." Without realizing it, a light crept into the blue of her eyes and an animation filled her face. Her head was tilted back and her shoulders squared with conviction. "Mrs. Ellis, I am a strong woman. I can be that woman. Oh, I'm fearful. Please don't think I'm not. I'm not fearful though of the land, the wilderness, or my abilities. I'm fearful of the man, Ben. I . . . I've never desired a man. Rarely do I find them attractive, and those who are appear to be more aware of their attributes than anyone else. No, I've yet to find a man who would fill my father's mold. So, I'm fearful of Ben. But I remind myself that he must be strong, able to stand tall and make solid decisions. A rancher in Montana would have to have those qualities. I assume there is a shortage of marriageable women in Montana. I only hope," and she lowered her voice, "that he is kind and patient. I'm going to need some time. But I will do it. I've done harder things, Mrs. Ellis. Being a wife can't be that hard, can it?" she asked fearfully.

Mrs. Ellis didn't answer. As the silence grew, so did the knot in Aries stomach. Perhaps she was wrong in thinking Mrs. Ellis could help. Still, she knew that if someone tried to teach her these elusive skills, she would apply all of her being to learning them.

Mrs. Ellis drew in a deep breath and stood up. "Aries," she

said, "come over here." She led the way to a small, Queen Anne desk. From the narrow drawer, she pulled out a sheath of paper and laid it next to the pen and inkwell resting on the highly polished surface. She pulled out the small chair and waved Aries toward it. "Sit down, my dear. We don't have much time."

Aries gingerly sat down in the chair and looked expectantly at the woman standing next to her. *How on earth was this going to help me? Hadn't I made myself clear?*

"Aries, there is no way in the world you can learn everything you need to know in four days. No, I believe the best way to proceed is for me to tell you what I think most pertinent about running a good ranch home. You take notes. You're a scholar, and their use as reference should appeal to you. There's too much swimming around in that lovely head of yours right now, and it would be ridiculous for us to think you could remember it all. I'll talk, and you'll write. It will be rambling, to say the least, but I'll try to be concise and share the pertinent details. There is one other thing."

"Yes?" Aries question was hesitant.

"Cooking. The way to a man's heart is through his stomach. Especially a rancher's. And, we don't know if you'll be cooking for a few ranch hands as well."

Aries groaned.

"We'll start with cooking lessons, but I'll expect you here early tomorrow morning to start copying down my recipes. I don't share these with just anyone, but I think, in this case, you're going to need all the help you can get. Are you ready? Can you start now, and plan on staying here late tonight?"

"Yes . . . yes. Oh, Mrs. Ellis, thank you. I know I can do this, I know I can. Why, why this will be just like learning how to mix the powders and herbs for Father. I have his books on how to crush the . . ."

"Aries," her tone was sharp. "You are not learning how to

be a doctor. You are learning something that, for you, is much harder. You, young lady, are learning how to make yourself a wife and live up to whatever abilities you misled about yourself to that man in Montana."

Aries was subdued; in a contrite voice, she said, "I apologize, Mrs. Ellis. Yes, I can stay here late tonight. Timmy will be looked after by our housekeeper. She has agreed to stay on and prepare the house for the new owner after Timmy and I leave. She'll give Timmy his supper, and see that he's tucked in for the night. Now, where do we begin?"

"Very well, we'll start on how to draw a chicken."

"Draw a chicken?" There was surprise in Aries' voice.

"Oh my. It's worse than I thought. Aries, when you draw a chicken you remove its innards prior to cooking it, of course. Now, you will have to enlarge the natural opening. Write this down, Aries. Don't just gaze at me as though you were attending one of your father's lectures."

And so it followed for the next few days. When Mrs. Ellis was busy elsewhere, Aries copied recipes. Then, when the busy woman was free, she reviewed what Aries had written down, and added a few lines of explanation to each recipe. Along with the recipes, Aries wrote down household hints Mrs. Ellis passed along, as she thought of them. Milk would remove ink stains. A wet cloth under a bowl would hold it steady when whipping eggs or cream. By dipping a broom into boiling soapsuds once a week the straw stayed tough and pliable and it would last longer. Flour, water, salt, vinegar, and kerosene mixed together then boiled until stiff, rolled into balls, and kept closed in a can would clean the wall paper in an average room. There was so much she didn't know, and by the end of the four days, she was filled with admiration for the housewife keeping house without the luxury of a dry goods store, a cook, or a housekeeper to assist her.

"Aries," Mrs Ellis interrupted the writing one day, "what have you packed in that trunk? Do you have room for some essentials I think we'd better add? I believe you and I had better take a shopping trip tomorrow morning to Wilson's Emporium and Dry Goods. I know of several items you need, and you can get them easier here than in Montana."

"Uh, I've packed, uh . . ."

"Oh, Aries, let me guess. You've packed most of your father's office into that steamer trunk."

"Yes," Aries answered with an embarrassed smile. "And please don't think me rude, Mrs. Ellis, but I'll not leave a thing behind. There is still quite a bit of room. What do I need?"

"Timmy needs at least two pairs of those wonderful Levis."

"Levis?"

"Yes. They're heavy denim trousers made by Mr. Levi Strauss. They'll withstand the hard wear Timmy will put them through out there on a ranch. Why, they're reinforced at the seams with small copper rivets. He'll outgrow them before he'll wear them out. Mark my word, your Ben and the ranch hands will all be wearing those Levi's. And you. You, honey, won't want to try and attend to the chores wearing one of those beautiful silk gowns. Take a few for something special, but we need to buy some yardage of cotton calico. Thank heavens we're not trying to teach you to sew in these four days too. At least your sweet mother won that much of the battle."

Aries eyes danced, "Calico, Levi's, what else, Mrs. Ellis? Perhaps I just need a bigger steamer trunk, and can I coax you into hiding in it and coming along with me?"

"Don't you know I would if I could, child. Lordy, I do envy you. You'll be seeing country I'll never get to see, and you'll be making a difference out there, Aries. You have the opportunity to help settle a piece of the western frontier. If I were younger, I just might take you up on that offer." She smiled over at the young woman who had worked so hard and faithfully the last few days. There was steel in this young woman. She was someone to cross the river with. *I just hope the man waiting for her there on that train platform is man enough to handle this one. She'll give him a merry dance, that she will. He'll have to be strong or she'll never respect him, and, lord help him, she'll run right over the top of him. She has no idea.* The woman shook her head. *She may know doctoring, but she knows little to nothing about men-their needs, wants, and, hopefully, their love.* Mrs. Ellis felt fearful for Aries, whom she'd come to love, but she also felt a measure of pity for the unsuspecting Ben.

Too soon the day came when Aries closed the lid to the steamer trunk and had it delivered to the station for the first freight train going to Montana. She and Timmy kissed a tearful Mrs. Ellis good-bye and boarded the train. Aries had not cultivated any other friends, having neither the time nor the patience for the young women of her social class. And, to be perfectly honest, the other young women found Aries unfriendly and strange. What kind of woman would allow herself to be a part of such indelicate knowledge? Aries, their mothers warned, was not the type of girl ladies socialized with. She was a prime example of a young woman unschooled in the appropriate feminine role. "Her poor mother," was the frequent lament. Then there was the matter of Timmy. Certainly Aries had demonstrated love for the poor little tyke, but between her and Dr. Burnett they spoiled him. As for male friends, there were those who found Aries attractive. But there were few who made it past her cold reserve and disdain. And, heaven help the man who tried to show Aries her proper place in the world. He didn't return to court her again. She was pretty, beautiful in fact with long, curly blond hair, delicate features, deep blue eyes, and a lush figure. But she wasn't worth the effort. She may look like she needs protection, and a man to hold her close, but don't try it.

So Aries and Timmy boarded the train with no one but an old woman to see them off. She settled Timmy in his seat and sat down next to him, then turned her eyes away from the train station and Mrs. Ellis, toward another direction. In another area of the city lay the two people who had loved and understood her. She mentally whispered another good-bye, knowing she'd never visit their graves again. Aries leaned back in her seat. She was ready. She'd done all she could to prepare for this new life in Montana. The rest would be up to a man named Ben.

Aries shut her eyes, tired of the past days of train travel, tired of worrying, tired of anticipating the reaction and the reality of Ben, and tired of remembering the sequence of events that brought her to the final stages of this long trip. She breathed a sigh of exhaustion, and gave herself up to the wheels and their clickety-clack. Wheels that sung out the words . . . can't go back, clickety-clack, can't go back.

## Chapter Two

"Miss. Miss." A tall, thin man stood in the aisle, in a black suit, a round cap, and a gold watchchain dangling from his vest pocket. "Miss. Best be waking up now. We're about to pull into the Wise River station.

"Yes," the word a whisper. "Yes, thank you. I'm awake."

"Won't be a long stop, just taking on water and another car of wood. You're the only passenger. Don't get that many going out this far. Nope, you're the first we've had in quite a spell. Hope you got someone meeting you. Wise River ain't the place for a young woman and a small boy to be alone in. Still, town's growing up right nice. Got a few more stores than the last time I was through here."

The man moved on down the train, and Aries turned to the window, anxious for her first glimpse of her new home. "Timmy." She gently shook the small boy. "Timmy, we're here. Look, let's see who can see Wise River first. Let's watch for Ben. He said he'd meet us at the train station. Are you awake, honey?"

The small boy uncurled and sat up. The nap had worked its

magic, and all the tiredness and fretfulness brought on by the long train ride was gone. He moved quickly to the window and pressed his small nose against the glass. "I don't see anything but grass and trees, Aries."

"You will. Just keep watching." She turned her attention from the window and tried to do something with her hair and her hat. Finally, she put her tortoiseshell comb back into the reticule, and gave her attention to the window and the scenery. There was only so much she could do. What she really needed—and desperately wanted—was a bath, a change of clothing, a hot meal, and a real bed.

She smoothed her gown and joined the small boy, and two sets of blue eyes peered anxiously from the window of the train. Aries saw the first outline of a building before Timmy, but didn't say anything, wanting to give him the pleasure of being the first to call out.

"Timmy," she said. "I believe you have a frontiersman's sharp eyes. You'll make a good hunter one day."

"Will I, Aries?" he asked, proud of the fact that he'd glimpsed Wise River first. "Ben will let me shoot a real gun, won't he, Aries?" He asked the question again as he had over the past days, while Aries entertained him with promises and stories in an effort to alleviate the fears he had in leaving Philadelphia and going on this unknown journey. He'd asked over and over about the horse Aries had promised him he'd have, about the ranch, the hunting and fishing, and the man Ben. Aries gulped down the rising lump of fear as she saw the town come closer, and felt the train slow down. She squared her shoulders, tilted her chin, and touched the three bags at her feet. She could do this . . . she didn't have a choice. There was no sense in uttering any more prayers.

The town crawled into view. The train station was a small weathered building, with an outdoor privy behind it, and a wooden platform reaching out to the tracks. There was a large water tower with a wooden arm next to the track. It was a far cry from the brick building, tiled floors, and oak benches of the Philadelphia train station. Behind the station, basking in the shimmering waves of midafternoon sun, lay the town.

The train came to a slow, lumbering stop in front of the building. A hiss of steam and vapors blocked the view from the small window. Then the vapors receded, and the conductor came by once again and reached for the bags under the seat. "I'll carry the black one," she told the man. "Timmy, you follow the conductor, but when you get outside, you stand right there on the platform and do not move from my side. Do you understand?"

"Yes, Aries." His small voice was filled with fear.

Aries felt a pang of love and understanding for Timmy and what he was feeling right now. Wasn't she feeling the same way? She swallowed back the rising panic, and said firmly, "I know you will, love. Why, if I didn't have such a big boy by my side helping me, I would be sorely afraid of getting off this train."

"You would?" Timmy's voice was unbelieving as he raised his eyes, "You ain't never afraid, Aries."

"Yes I am, Timmy, but not when I have you. Together, you and I can handle most anything, honey." She reached down and gave his thin shoulder a squeeze. "Now, lead the way, Timmy, and let's take our first look at Wise River, Montana, and see if we can spot Ben."

"Is that the person coming to get you, ma'am?" The conductor's voice held concern for the young woman stepping onto the small steps he'd placed at the car's door. "Ben who, ma'am?"

"Mr. Ben McCabe. He owns the Big Hole Valley Ranch." She glanced at the conductor and noticed the look that had crossed his face.

"Do you know Mr. McCabe?"

"No, ma'am. Can't say as I do. But I've heard of the ranch. One of the first started in this part of Montana. I believe it's a big 'un."

She wanted to ask the man more, but there was no opportunity. They stood on the platform of the train station in Wise River, Montana, with two carpet bags at their feet, and a black doctor's bag in her hand. She, Timmy, and the conductor. No one else was in sight.

The man pulled out his watch and checked it carefully. "Right on time, ma'am. You sure you have someone coming for you?" He looked nervously at the woman, and then back at the train he needed to board as soon as it had taken on water and wood.

"Yes, please don't worry about us. You've been most helpful. We'll be just fine. I'm sure Mr. McCabe just got delayed. Really," she smiled, in what she hoped was more reassuring than she felt. "Really," she repeated, "we'll be just fine." Aries started walking toward the wooden building. "If you would just set the bags over there, I would be most grateful. Timmy, come here." She cast a fearful eye toward the small boy, whose natural curiosity had taken over. He was standing on the edge of the platform watching the arm swing down from the round water tower with the words WISE RIVER painted in white around the middle of the wooden staves. His eyes widened at the hiss of steam erupting as the train filled with water.

The conductor set the bags down, tipped his cap, and said, "Well, if you're certain, ma'am. I best be getting back on the train." He nodded toward the barred ticket window in the wood building. "The ticket master there can mebbe help you. Ain't too many folks in these parts, so he ought to know something about Ben McCabe. Good luck to you, ma'am."

"Thank you," Aries said softly.

Timmy had moved back. He intently watched the train as it gave a convulsive rattle, as though shook by a giant hand, then a lurch, the wheels creeping forward by inches, pulling out of the station. Aries eyes clouded with tears as she watched it slowly pull from the desolate station. She felt as though her only link with the world was deserting her. She longed to run after, shouting that she had changed her mind. She was pulled back from her anguish as the train rounded the curve out of Wise River, and out of her sight, by a small hand tugging at her skirt.

"Aries," the little boy whispered. "Aries, I gotta go."

"Wha . . . what?" she stammered.

"I gotta go, Aries. Real bad."

"Oh Timmy," she glanced around. "Can't you hold it just a little longer. I need to stay here and watch for Ben."

"No." Timmy's response left no doubt that his need was urgent.

"There," she said, spying the outhouse at the back of the station. "There's a toilet, Timmy. You go and I'll wait here in case Ben comes." She saw his fearful look. "Go ahead, Timmy. It'll be all right. I won't move from this spot. You can call out if you need me. I'll hear you." Of that she had no doubt. The silence hung heavy on the small town stretched out behind the weathered train station. It was broken only by the occasional ringing out of a hammer striking metal, which she assumed came from a blacksmith's building down the street. The lazy buzz of a bee moved past her, made sluggish by the warmth of the Montana sun beating down on the shadeless platform. She felt sticky and hot under her heavy traveling outfit.

After watching Timmy's small back as he slowly walked toward the weathered structure with a half moon cut in the door, Aries walked to the edge of the building and scanned, looking for a man who would, hopefully, be looking for her. There was no one in sight. The fear she'd held at bay threatened to engulf her. Aries turned around and walked back to the edge of the platform near the tracks where she could see clearly the curve that had swallowed the train. *I wish, oh how I wish, I was back on that train heading . . . anywhere but here* she thought. *Anywhere.*

She was nearly startled off the tracks by a voice. A hand shot out and grabbed her arm. "Sorry, ma'am. Didn't mean to scare you. I said, you wouldn't be Miss Aries Burnett would you? Course, I'm sure you must be. We don't get many women as pretty as you stopping off here. Matter of fact we, ain't had any. Least ways, none that I know of. You are Miss Aries, ain't you, ma'am? If'n you are, I sure owe you a measure of apology. I meant to be here, standing right here when that train'd pull in, ready to say howdy, when you stepped down the steps. But my horse threw a shoe, and I had to take it over to the blacksmith's," he gestured in the direction where Aries could still hear metal striking metal. "I lost track of time and didn't realize the train had pulled in and left, until I heard it whistle." He bent over and peered closer at Aries. "You are Miss Aries, ain't you?"

The man standing in front of her had to be Ben McCabe. But, oh lord, he wasn't the Ben McCabe of her imagination. Not even close. This . . . this man, if you could call him that, was really a boy of, at best, nineteen years old. Oh how, Aries felt herself cry, how would she be able to marry and respect a boy? How could he possibly care for and provide for her and for Timmy? He hardly looked old enough to take care of himself much less . . . She closed her eyes and willed herself to answer him.

"Ma'am, you okay? You look a bit peaked. Here." He took

her arm and guided her over to the bench, "You best sit down. I expect the sun's been a mite hot for you standing there right out in it, you all delicate looking like. I expect you don't get much sun in the city, Philadelphia, is that right, ma'am?"

"You . . ." she moistened her lips, ignoring his questions, "you," she started again, "must be Ben McCabe from the Big Hole Valley Ranch?"

"Yes, ma'am. That's me." He tipped the brim of his big hat to her.

"Uh, yes, in answer to your question, Mr. McCabe. I am Aries Burnett. I'm here in response, because of . . ." she stammered, not able to finish the rest of the dreadful statement.

"Because of my ad in the paper for a wife." His voice boomed out and hung over the town. Aries cringed and then looked around, hoping the area was still deserted.

"I placed that ad myself. Boy, was I relieved to get your answer. I was getting real worried. You see, ma'am, yours was the only answer I got. So, naturally like, I didn't have no problem making a choice. I just had to send you the money for a ticket, and, and well here you are." He smiled broadly at her from underneath a thatch of brown hair held in place by the big, white hat. He was tall and thin, not yet grown into his gangly arms and legs. One day, he would be. One day, he would be the nice-looking man he showed promise of being. But it wasn't now. Now, he was all arms and legs, and mouth. His mouth dominated his face as it talked and smiled directly at her. His smile stretched from one side of his face to the other, and, against her will, Aries found herself smiling back at him.

"Yes, here I am," she said quietly, absorbing the fact that she'd been the only one foolish enough to respond to the ad. "Now what, Mr. McCabe?"

"Ben," he said. "I'm might uncomfortable with that Mr.

McCabe name, ma'am. Makes me think you're talking to my daddy."

"Uh, okay, Ben. Then please, no more ma'am for me. My name is Aries. Please call me that."

"It's a real pretty name, ma . . . uh, Aries. Darn." His face lit up. "I sure didn't expect to get me someone as pretty as you in answer to my ad. You're gonna be a real surprise when we get to . . ."

"Aries . . . Aries . . . Aries, come quick!" A call shattered the air. "I dropped the catalog down the hole, and it's far down there, and it smells real bad." The door to the privy slammed open and Timmy burst out clutching at the front buttons of his pants. He ran across the space between the outhouse and the wooden platform, suspenders dragging in the dry dirt, to where an astonished Ben and an embarrassed Aries stood.

"Aries," he said, stopping in front of her. "Them outhouses smell. And I can't get the top button to go through the hole. And I dropped that catalog." Timmy was breathless. "Here." He stuck out his small waist. "You button it."

Aries glanced at Ben's dumbfounded look, then bent down to button the contrary button on Timmy's pants. The small boy glanced around Aries shoulder and noticed, for the first time, the man standing behind her. He wiggled, trying to get a better look.

"Wow, you must be Ben. You sure are tall. Ain't he, Aries?"

"Sshh, where are your manners, Timmy?"

"Sorry, Aries," he said quietly, ducking his head.

She slipped the button in its place, straightened up, and placed a protective hand on Timmy's shoulder. She took a deep breath, then plunged forward into the introduction. Best to get it over with. Nothing was going as she had planned in her mind, why expect his first meeting with Timmy to be any different.

"Ben, I'd like you to meet Timmy. Timmy, this is Mr. Ben McCabe from the Big Hole Valley Ranch. He's come to pick us up, and take us . . ." Aries faltered over the next word. She stammered on. "To, uh, to the ranch," she finished lamely.

"How do you do, Mr. McCabe," the small boy said to the staring man. At a nudge from Aries, he held out his small hand. Ben made no response, and the boy's hand hung suspended in the space. Finally, Ben broke out of his spell, and another smile opened across his face.

"Well, I'll be damned," he said, glancing up at Aries, his face a bright red, "uh, begging your pardon, Aries ma'am, I ain't used to having a woman around to talk careful in front of."

"That's quite all right, Ben." Oh, this is terrible, thought Aries. Now I feel like his mother. I feel like I have two boys to look after, not a man . . . a husband, and a small boy. How can this be happening? She looked at Ben, who was reaching out for Timmy's outstretched hand.

"Timmy, huh? You come all the way from Philadelphia with Aries?"

Timmy nodded his head as Ben pumped his hand enthusiastically.

She broke in quickly, appalled at the assumption Ben seemed to be making. "Timmy's my brother," she blurted. "And I owe you an apology. I, uh, I neglected to mention him in my letter. To be honest, Ben, I wasn't sure you would agree to my bringing him along. Timmy and I are all that's left of our family. I hope you understand and forgive me for this omission."

"Well, I'll be," he said again. "Two for the price of one." He rubbed his hand across his face. "This will take some explaining," he said to himself. "But, hey, looks good to me. Yeah! Timmy," he said, "you look like you're a real helper. Are you?

Cause we've got lots of work to do on our ranch, and I sure could use another set of hands."

In that moment, Ben won over Aries, and any of the doubts and reservations she had harbored toward the young man were swept away and dismissed. The small boy stood upright, his chest puffed out. "Thank you, Ben," she whispered silently to herself. "Thank you for accepting him and making him feel needed and wanted. He so badly needs that."

"You bet, Ben. I'm real good at helping."

"Well, then, why don't you start helping me right now. See that wagon?" Ben pointed to a wagon that, until this moment, Aries had not noticed.

So much had happened in the last few minutes, so much had changed, been decided, she felt disoriented and not herself at all.

"Well, if you put your hand right here on the handle of this carpetbag, you can help me carry it over to the wagon. Course," he said quietly, just to Timmy, "I believe I can just take the other one in my other hand, cause it's so much lighter looking. Then, we'll come back and get that black bag there. You got anything else, ma'am? These three little bags all you brought with you?" he asked, puzzled.

"No. And it's Aries, please," she said, smiling. "There's a steamer trunk, but I had it sent freight. It should arrive in a few days." She glanced around again at the desolate town and the expanse of land surrounding it. "Will it be difficult to get it out to the ranch, Ben?"

"Nope," he said, smiling good-naturedly at her, his brown eyes warm and full of kindness. "I have to make the trip back here next week to pick up some supplies coming in on that same train, and I'll just pick it up then. If you'll excuse me for a minute, uh, Aries, I'll put these bags in the wagon, then I'll just go tell Mr. Jenkins, the station master, to store the trunk if'n it comes before I get back to town." He walked toward the waiting wagon, taking a carpetbag in one strong hand, and sharing the handle of the other carpet bag with Timmy. Aries slowly followed them, clutching the black doctor's bag. She drew courage from the familiar feel of the leather handle in her hand. She would be okay. She would make it be okay. He wasn't what she had expected. Not at all. He wasn't what she was looking for in a man, a husband, that is, if she'd been looking. But he was kind, and pleasant. Watching the small boy look up at the tall man, chatting and unafraid of his new acquaintance, made Aries smile her first genuine smile of the day.

Ben effortlessly dropped the two bags over the side of the wagon, shoving them under the plank seat; then, he turned and walked back toward her, his long legs making short work of the space between them. "Here, Aries, let me take that," and he gestured to the black bag.

"No!" At seeing his startled look, Aries forced a smile and said, in a kinder voice, "Thank you, Ben, but this bag has a special significance to me. It was my father's. It's not heavy, and I'm used to carrying it."

He looked at her for a moment, and then said, "I understand. Your father, he's, uh, he's dead isn't he? You said you were all alone." The young man asked the question with kindness and compassion.

"Yes, he's dead," she said with a sad smile.

The young man nodded. "I'll help you up to the wagon seat, and go tell Mr. Jenkins about the trunk. Then, we can get started. We've got a ways to go. Before we leave town, though, I have to stop by Wise River General Store and pick up a few supplies, but that won't take long because I'll be getting the big order next week. We, uh . . . I expect you'll have some things you'll want to add to that list, housekeeping supplies like."

Before she could respond, he placed his big hands around her waist and effortlessly swung her and the black bag onto the hard seat. He turned to the small boy waiting beside him. "You want to come with me, Timmy? We'll go tell Mr. Jenkins to watch for your trunk, then you can sit beside me and help me get Belle and the wagon headed out of town." He leaned down to the small boy and said, in a conspiratorial whisper, "Belle's in a cranky mood since she threw her shoe and had to have it replaced. Standing on three feet in front of the other horses was down right embarrassing to her." He grinned down at Timmy, and like two boys, they shared the joke, laughing at the thought of Belle standing in such a precarious manner.

Aries watched them walk to the station. *It could be so much worse*, she thought, trying to get a measure of consolation from the meager assurance as she glanced around the small town. *He could have been mad about Timmy, and my 'forgetting' to mention him. He would have had every right to be. Yet*, and she gave a tired sigh, *he seems to be the kind of boy, no man*, she corrected herself emphatically, *man*, she emphasized in her mind, *who will be patient. I have that to be thankful for.* Aries smiled to herself. *He thinks I'm pretty . . . that's something else I was hoping for. I just wanted, hoped, it would come from someone that I . . . well, that's not important. Now, if I can just manage to get by with the few recipes I put into my bag until that trunk arrives with the rest, I might just have a chance of pulling this off. Face it, Aries, you weren't thinking or every recipe you copied would be with you right now and you would have one less problem to face. What made me think I could memorize them? Mrs. Ellis tried to warn me that memorizing something to do with medicine and memorizing recipes are two different things. Medicine is my love. Cooking sure isn't. Okay,* she took a deep breath, *no more beating up on myself. I'm sure they will all come back to me. I'll keep it simple, that's what I'll do. Simple meals, until that blasted trunk arrives.*

She shifted on the wooden seat and reflected about how far she'd come since boarding the train in Philadelphia. Her comfortable home, the city with all its amenities, Mrs. Ellis, and her parents, all seemed to be a part of another lifetime and world far away from Wise River, Montana, with the big sky stretching for miles, the mountains shimmering blue in the near distance.

## Chapter Three

They had only gone a short distance when Aries realized there wasn't one spring in the wagon. She would be black and blue by the time they reached Ben's ranch. She glanced over at Timmy, but the bone-jarring bounce of the wagon wasn't bothering him or Ben. He and Ben were talking so much, they didn't notice. It wasn't until they hit a particularly deep rut that caused the wagon to lurch and throw Aries against Ben's arm that the man realized how badly she was being tossed around on the seat.

"Sorry, Aries," he said as he pulled back on the reins, slowing Belle's trot to a slower pace. "I ain't used to having someone else riding beside me. Look," and he motioned to his feet braced against the front of the wagon, "put your feet up like this. It helps."

Aries stretched her legs out in front of her, but they missed the front panel of the wagon by a good foot or more. "Guess I'm not quite long enough, Ben," she said, with a smile. "Don't worry about me, I'll just hang onto the seat. Will it be this rough all the way to the ranch?" she asked.

"Naw, once we hit thick grass it'll be like you was riding on that train that brought you here. Streets here in Wise River are pretty bad. We've had some heavy rains this spring. Hard on the town, but it sure makes it nice for those cows looking for mountain grass to make them fat and sassy. This will be a good year for us, Aries. We already got the cows and calves driven to the higher pasture. They'll stay up there until we bring them down first part of September, before the snow falls."

"You mean there's calves, Ben, baby cows?" Timmy broke in.

"Yep. Not real little ones, Timmy; they're bout three months old now. Born in March. That way, they have time to eat and put some weight on before we drive them to the loading pens outside of Butte. Say," Ben said, looking at the small boy, "maybe you'll be able to go on the roundup this fall. Would you like that?"

"Wow! Can I, Aries? Can I really go, Ben?" Timmy bounced around on the seat looking first at Aries and then to Ben. His face was filled with excitement and longing.

"It's up to Aries, Timmy. But you'll have to be a pretty good rider by then. You can ride, can't you?" Ben asked the question as if it would be unthinkable for a boy of four not to be able to ride.

Timmy hung his head, eyes full of disappointment.

"Ben," Aries offered quickly, trying to spare Timmy more embarrassment and hurt, "Timmy has lived his entire life in the city. There wasn't an opportunity for him to ride."

"You didn't have any horses?" Ben asked, puzzled.

"We had one, Ben," Timmy said quietly, "but it was my father's and I wasn't allowed to touch her."

Aries reached over and covered Timmy's hand with her own, wishing she could take him in her arms and hold him tightly enough to squeeze out all the hurt and pain inside him. She knew he wouldn't welcome her embrace in front of Ben. She would have to be careful not to coddle him, but it was hard; he'd been through so much. Once again, she felt a wave of thanksgiving for stumbling onto this new life. She vowed again that she would make it work, no matter what she had to do. Nothing or no one must take this chance from Timmy. She would do whatever it took to see that he grew up here in this beautiful valley where he could forget his first four hurtful years.

"We did have one horse, Ben, but, our father didn't want anyone bothering her." Then, rushing to the man's defense, Aries added, "He used her daily; we depended on her to pull our buggy. You see, she couldn't be used for anything else. She had to always be ready and rested for use, anytime, day or night. Timmy wasn't allowed out in the stables; he might get hurt, and . . . well, the horse had to be rested." She sounded lame; she couldn't understand why Timmy couldn't at least touch the horse. How could she expect Ben to understand? He had probably been on or near horses since the day he was able to walk. There was much no one could understand about the last four years—so much hurt, it defied understanding.

"Yeah," Ben offered slowly, his brow furrowed. "Well, that don't matter none."

"It don't?" Timmy raised his head hopefully.

"Naw. Shoot, we'll put you up on old Buck and you'll be riding before you know it. It'll be real safe," he added to reassure Aries. "Why old Buck'll just nursemaid you."

"Is he, uh, old Buck, is he a baby horse? I . . . I mean, is he a horse for babies, Ben?" Timmy watched Ben's face, looking for any sign that the man thought less of him.

"Heck no! Why old Buck's about the most dependable, easy gaited horse on the Big Hole. He stands seventeen hands high. Big ole buckskin. Why, them legs of yours will barely reach across his back. But he'll be real fine for you to learn on, Timmy. He'll be like riding in a rocking chair. Ain't a contrary bone in his body. Buck, he wants to please. He'll teach you what to do. That's what I meant by babysitting. Sure didn't mean to offend you, Timmy, cause you sure ain't no baby. No sir. Not by a long shot." He glanced over Timmy's head to Aries, meeting her gratitude. He offered a nod and at that moment the two of them joined in a mutual cause. The man knew that beside him sat a boy who, for some reason, hadn't had an easy time, and Ben knew the woman held the story of those four years.

"Will old Buck be my horse, Ben? Aries said I'd have my own horse."

Aries flushed, wishing Timmy had waited before asking Ben to fulfill promises she had no right to make.

"No, sir," Ben went on, "old Buck'll do fine for a teacher, like I said, but he can't be your horse. See he belongs to someone else. Nope, you learn on Buck, but then, well, you'll need a horse of your own. Aries is right, if you're going to be a Montana cowboy, you gotta have your own horse."

"And you'll get me one, Ben?" Timmy's face turned up to the young man beside him; his newfound love and admiration shown.

"Well," Ben stammered, "I probably won't be the, uh, it'll be up to Jar . . ."

Ben didn't finish his sentence. The peace and calm of the sleepy town was suddenly shattered. Ben swung around in the direction of a shout, ringing out in the silence. A group of men erupted out of the building next to the general store. One tall man in front had another by the arm, shoving him ahead of him. He turned to the men close on his heels and issued a command that was met and swallowed up by angry words, gestures and arm waving. But, whatever he said had an effect because all but one turned and, shaking their heads, went back to stand in front of the door. After a short exchange, the remaining man stepped up and grabbed the prisoner's arm; he propelled him down the street. The tall man watched for a few minutes, then turned and headed back toward the building. Ben quickly turned into the hitching post in front of the row of weathered store fronts lining the street.

There were several buildings, unpainted and in various stages of weathering. The wagon came to rest nearest the Wise River General Store, and the saloon called MAE'S PLACE. It was the biggest building in Wise River, two stories high. Two of the upstairs windows had balconies outside of them. A dress hung over the side of one of the balconies, in a bright yellow that glowed against the building. Two big windows faced the street, and a set of tall, swinging doors filled the door opening. SALOON was painted across one window. The general store looked small, in comparison. Its two windows were filled with lanterns, crockery, a few tools, and a dressmaker's form in a drab, brown dress. Beside it were bolts of blue cotton material, a few baking tins, and a display of brightly colored ribbons.

The loud rumblings of angry words drifted to the wagon. The tall man was doing his best to bring calm to the group, but he was having little success. Suddenly, another man banged out of the swinging doors and ran over to the group. He spoke quickly, and then broke away in a dead run in the direction offered by the tall man. Aries caught the words "hurt durn bad" and "probably drunkern a skunk."

"What is it, Ben?" she asked.

"I don't know, Aries." Ben swung down from the wagon seat, the reins loose in his hands. "You and Timmy stay put here, and I'll go see. Looks like there's been some trouble at

Mae's Place. Don't you worry none," he said, trying to reassure her. "It's probably over by now. Least ways there weren't no shooting." The last was offered over his shoulder as he looped the reins over the hitching rail.

Aries watched him walk to the saloon and the group of men. "No shooting." The casual way Ben had said the words made her eyes widen with surprise. *No shooting! Indeed!* If she needed anything to remind her she'd left the city for the western frontier, those two words brought that fact quickly to reality.

Aries watched as the group opened and welcomed Ben. The tall man talked and gestured. Then the runner returned. This time, Aries heard the words clearly: "You're right. He's out cold. Stinkin drunk, the old coot!"

At that moment, a heavy set woman stepped out and made her way toward the men. She was big, with wide hips, masculine arms, and bosoms high and overflowing the top of her cherry-red gown. Aries had never seen more arms and breasts in her life, and she took in every detail of the imposing woman. A tall white feather stuck out from the side of brassy red hair, and flopped back and forth with every step the woman took. She paused at the edge of the circle of men, put both hands on the wide girth of her hips and bellowed, "Sheriff!"

The crowd fell silent.

"Mae?"

"You get that pipsqueek of a doc yet?"

"Now, Mae, you know we didn't. You know just as well as I do he won't be coming."

"Won't?" she bellowed again. "Won't or can't."

"All in the same, Mae. You know that as well as I do."

"Drunk, ain't he? The darn old louse. Well, ain't he?"

"You should know, Mae. You're the one sells it to him."

"Hmmmpf," she snorted. "Well, now, what you gonna do about this, sheriff? I got me a girl in there," she said, motioning toward the saloon, "bleedin' like a stuck hog. She don't get some help soon, she'll likely die. One uh my best dancers, she is." She narrowed her small eyes at the men. "It's Callie. Ain't one of you fellers standin' there don't know Callie an' admired her high kicks." She squinted at the group of men.

They shifted from one foot to another, some of them looking away, all avoiding direct eye contact with the imposing Mae.

The sheriff cleared his throat, and then said quietly, "Mae, there ain't nothing I can do. Tom took and locked up the guy what did it. Now what else do you expect me to do? I can't help it Doc's stinking drunk. It's gettin' so there ain't hardly a time he ain't drunk. Bill here says he's out cold. Even if we did manage to get him awake, he wouldn't be no good. I'm real sorry 'bout Callie . . . real sorry." He looked imploringly at her. "Darn it, Mae, I ain't no doctor."

"I am."

The words fell softly on the group. One by one, the heads turned to the slight woman standing at the edge. The circle of men parted, opening a direct path between the two women.

"Aries," Ben said, in a hushed voice. "Aries, this ain't no place for a lady. Please, get back into the wagon. You shouldn't be here. This ain't no concern . . ."

"You need a doctor?" Aries ignored the men, ignored the stammering orders coming from Ben. She looked directly at the blowzy woman.

The big woman looked her up and down, her disdain evident. Then she curled her wide reddened lips. Aries felt like what a June bug must feel when eyed by a hungry rooster. She met the woman's eyes and tilted her chin up, squaring her shoulders at the same time. She stood tall and erect, her good breeding evident in every inch of her five foot four inch frame.

"Who are you?" the woman asked, her voice snarling like a whip.

"I'm Aries Burnett." she replied, her eyes never leaving the woman's face. She felt a small hand touch her skirt. Timmy. But she maintained her erect posture, never realizing what a lovely sight she was. The sun caught her blond curls turning them to shiny strands of gold. Her eyes were large and blue as the sky above her. Aries could feel the men's eyes traveling over her trim figure, and it was all she could do to maintain a regal bearing and not flinch. Then she felt a hand grip her elbow. She turned quickly to the touch, reluctantly pulling her attention from the woman.

"Aries," Ben said. "Uh, this ain't no place for you," he repeated. "Please. You and Timmy shouldn't be here."

"It's all right, Ben. I know what I'm doing." She turned from him, dismissing the red-faced young man.

"Ma'am," she continued, looking again at Mae, "you said you needed a doctor. While I'm not board certified, I am qualified to be a doctor. It is my understanding you have a woman inside of that saloon in need of medical attention. We are wasting time, and possibly her life, standing here in the sun. I repeat . . . do you need a doctor?"

There wasn't a sound on the street. Even the insects were quiet. The bearded men stared from Aries to Mae, and then to Ben. The sheriff looked as if he wanted to say something, but just couldn't dislodge it from the back of his throat. It was as if Wise River, Montana, inhaled a large gulp of air and held it.

"Well, I'll be dam . . ." Mae caught herself. Then, she moved forward a few steps. The men quickly parted in front of her, giving her a wide berth.

Aries never moved a muscle, hoping the queasy feeling churning in her stomach would not get worse.

"You know what your uh doin'?" she asked directly.

"Yes, ma'am. I do."

"You ain't . . . well, heck . . . you don't look like no doctor to me." Mae waited for Aries' response to this obvious fact.

"No." She summed it up in one word, and let it hang in the air.

"You lie to me, you make things worse in there . . . and . . ."

Aries stared at the woman, narrowing her eyes slightly. Then, slowly, she turned to the small boy at her side.

"Timmy, go get my bag."

He looked up at her, his eyes big.

"Go on now, honey." She gave him a slight shove in the direction of the wagon. "Hurry, we've got a woman hurt and we've wasted enough time as it is." The last part of the sentence wasn't lost on the big woman, who was standing so close Aries could smell her musky body and strong perfume.

Aries watched Timmy as he ran to the wagon. Then she turned, "Ben," she said quietly, just to him, her eyes dominating her face as they filled with expression, "I'm so sorry . . . I, uh, I know this isn't what you expected. I don't want to start us in the wrong direction, truly I don't, but," she paused, licking her lips, "Ben, I have to do this. Please try and understand." Aries looked imploringly up at him desperately willing him to understand that from the moment she was old enough to comprehend, she had been imbued in the Hippocratic Oath and the standards and ethics of the medical profession. To not offer her medical aide wherever it was needed would be incomprehensible, and so very unforgivable to her father's memory.

"Aries," Ben's words caught in his throat. He looked at her, then glanced at Mae, "I don't think you understand." He paused, searching for the right words. "That's a . . . that's a saloon, and the women that work there . . . Darn it, Aries, the woman inside there, uh, the woman what's hurt . . . she's uh, she's uh . . ."

"She's a dance hall girl," Mae boomed, effectively cutting off Ben's stammering. She glared out at the men as if daring them to disagree. "And a darn good un too." She leaned closer to Aries, her breath warm on the girl's face. "It's a saloon all right, and no place for a lady I agree. An' some of my girls . . ."

"I know." Aries said, her firm words effectively stopping Mae from finishing the sentence and uttering the damning words.

Mae clamped her mouth shut, giving Aries a hard look.

"I know what she does for a living," she repeated to both Mae and Ben. Her words and the way they were delivered stopped either one from making further attempts to persuade her away from her course of action.

Just then, Timmy pushed his way through the men, the black bag heavy in his small arms. The small boy held it as if it were of great value and mystery; as though he were proud of being allowed to touch this cherished receptacle.

"Aries?"

She turned toward him, smiling sweetly. "Thank you, honey. Stay by me now," she ordered, softly.

He nodded, his eyes wide with excitement. His life was already so different from just a few short days ago.

With the black bag clutched in her hand, Aries straightened her back, the tiredness dropped away from her face, and she exuded a presence, strong and forceful. She tipped her head in the direction of the saloon and nodded at Mae.

Before they could move, the sheriff broke in.

"Ma'am."

"Yes?" Aries turned, impatient with the delay.

"Ma'am," he began again, standing tall and imposing, his thin legs planted firmly, "that saloon ain't no place for a lady. I don't know you, ma'am, but it's clear to see you're a lady, and well, well, Ben here'll tell you the same thing. You can't go in there, ma'am."

"That's right, Aries," Ben said, clearing his throat, stronger now with the sheriff's backing. "I can't let you do this, Aries." He lowered his voice, "Aries, if I let you go inside, I'd have some pretty tough explaining to do to Jar . . . uh, to uh, oh heck, you being from the city an all, you probably don't know."

"Ben," Aries said, placing her free hand on his arm, "I do know. I know quite well, and I appreciate your concern. I'm sorry if I'm making things difficult for you. That's the last thing I'd want to do. I don't want to start off this way with us, Ben, but you have to understand, there's a person in there in dire need of medical attention. Of which there is none, am I correct?" She went on, not waiting for his answer. "I am able to provide that need, but not if you men insist on blocking my path with all this . . . this talk." Her exasperation bubbled out.

There was a distinct chuckle from Mae.

"Now, if you, and you, Sheriff," Aries said, "will escort me, we'll just follow, uh, Miss . . . Mae, inside, and I'll see to the patient. I'm sure you men wouldn't want this girl's life to end while you stand there arguing with me." She paused, her eyes moving slowly over each man in the group, daring them to respond. Then, she let her gaze rest on Mae, and she spoke the next words directly to her, biting each one off with emphasis. "As I said a few minutes ago, I'm quite qualified to do what's medically necessary. I'd like to see my patient now."

Mae's face broke into a grin and she guffawed. "She's got you, fellers. I'd say you best step aside. This un's tough all right. She's got a bit in her mouth, boys, and I 'spect she'll run with it. Ben," Mae continued, peering at him, I suspect you're right about that explainin' you'll have to do. If Jarrett causes you any grief, you just send him to me. I wouldn't mind spendin' some time with him, doing some convincing. No siree, wouldn't mind at all." She winked bawdily at Ben, and a flash of red spread up his throat and across his face. "That be okay with you?" She watched him swallow convulsively, while slowly nodding his acceptance. She smoothed her hands down the side of her dress and turned on her heel, leading the way to the swinging doors, her hips rolling under the billowy satin dress.

## Chapter Four

Aries' eyes slowly adjusted to the dark room. She felt the
pressure of a hand on the small of her back, steadying her.
She smiled a shaky thanks to Ben. He might not understand
her need to do this, and he certainly didn't approve, but he
would stand by her. She was grateful for his presence, hoping
her fear was hidden in the dimness of the room.

Whiskey, perfume, sawdust, and unwashed bodies mingled; their scents filled the air. Aries stood, just inside the
room, aware that she halted the procession of men crowding
behind her, anxious to see the show and to be a part of the unexpected excitement brought on by the impropriety of this
city lady.

Mae's bright red dress furled behind her, billowing like
wind-filled sails. She wove her way through the tables stopping at one at the back of the room. Aries got the first glimpse
of her patient, looking small and forgotten, a doll cast aside
by a child. Two dance hall girls stood alongside the table,
watching the strange procession closely.

From where she stood, Aries couldn't see much of the

young woman. Mae's frame blocked out all but a pair of thin legs, black tights, and high heeled, lace-up shoes. A riot of colored slips revealed her legs and thighs.

Aries took a deep breath, trying to get her bearings. At the bar along one wall stood a tall, muscular man in a white shirt with a black garter on his right arm. He held a rag in one hand, and a bottle in the other. Several men stood, frozen, along the bar. All talk and activity in the room ceased. Boots rested on the brass rail running along the bottom edge of the bar. Hands held shot glasses poised in mid-air. Tobacco drool, unchecked, made a path through one scruffy beard leaving a brown trail. Another man sat at an upright piano, curled over the ivory keys, the music forgotten, his body twisted toward the door. He was so small he looked dwarfed by the rise of the piano. The only imposing thing about him was a pair of wide, red suspenders that trailed down over the back of a grey underwear top.

At the table closest to Aries four men sat, a deck of cards face down in the middle of the table, four stacks of red, white, and blue poker chips beside them. The largest chip pile stacked in front of an empty space, the chair pushed to the side. The men had forgotten their cards. A tall women, dressed in a skimpy, pink satin dress stood behind one of them, her hand resting possessively on his shoulder.

Aries took this all in, then moved to Mae and the plank table. She looked down on the rouged face of a girl no more than seventeen. But it wasn't her face that held her attention; she wore a blood-soaked gown. Aries glanced around the room.

"Ben, would you get me that chair, please?"

Ben quickly placed the chair behind Aries and stood, waiting for her to sit down. Instead, she pulled it alongside her and carefully placed the black bag on the seat.

It was worse than Aries had imagined: a six-inch cut ran from her collar bone to the swell of her left breast. Blood oozed, soaking the bodice of orange ruffles. When Aries saw the girl's arm, she sucked in her breath and moved closer to the table, lightly placing her fingertips on the uninjured shoulder. A long gash ran down the inside of the arm, deep enough to lay it open like the underbelly of a gutted trout. A trail of blood ran from the gash, down the arm, past the wrist, and between the lightly curled fingers lying still on the rough wood.

Aries felt overtaken with doubt and fear; this was the first time she had ever practiced medicine without the steadying influence of her father. What if she did something wrong? What if she didn't know enough, or wasn't quick and accurate enough? What if the years of study and experience deserted her? She glanced up and met Mae's eyes. Under the woman's hard stare, Aries wondered if the doubt was written on her face for everyone to see. Then she heard a soft whisper inside her head, the cigar rasp familiar and comforting. "Staunch the bleeding. Then clean the field. You can't assess damage through a bloody field, Aries."

"I'll need some boiling water and clean rags." Her voice became stronger as Aries looked around the room. No one moved to help her. "I can't do this by myself," she said forcefully. "I'm going to need some help."

No one moved. The silence was loud. Then from the shadows on the far side of the table, a voice said, "I'll help you." A man stepped forward. He was clad in black. His movements were quick, as he came to the side of the table. His clothes were clean and the black pants, brocade vest, and black shirt fit his lean body well. They looked tailored. Aries eyes fell to his waist, and a tooled, leather bullwhip curling from a holster. The long tip of the whip was split into several ends. It rested against the man's leg. He wore no other weapons. A long cheroot hung from his mouth, and the smoke curled around his head, making it seem as if he'd just stepped from the fires of hell. A black mustache graced his thin lips. He rolled the cheroot to the corner of his mouth, and spoke around it. "Ain't no one here gonna fight for the honor, Miss," he said, a narrow smile on his lips. "You tell me what you need, and I'll see you get it."

"Thank you, Mr., uh, Mr . . ." she gulped.

"Name's Brett, but I'm mostly know as Whip." He paused, letting his words drift, watching for her reaction. "Callie's my girl when I'm in town." He assessed the room, daring anyone to refute the statement. "What do you need?"

"I need hot water, and rags, clean rags," she emphasized. "If at all possible, I'd prefer white, not colored."

He nodded his head, then turned to one of the girls. "Get it." The words were harsh, bitten out. The girl turned quickly from the table, and hurried toward the curving staircase flanking the side of the room. Her footsteps were loud against the hush.

Aries then gave her attention to the still form on the table. "Callie," Aries placed her hand on the side of the girl's face and turned it to her. A soft moan escaped the pale lips. "Callie, can you hear me? My name is Aries. I'm a doctor, and I'm going to help you, but you'll have to work with me. Can you do it?" Aries repeated the words, while mentally begging her father's forgiveness for daring to refer to herself as a doctor, hoping he'd understand, knowing that he knew her abilities far better than anyone else. "Callie," she persisted.

"Callie." Whip interrupted her, his voice cutting through the room as he leaned over the girl, "Callie, girl, I'm here. Should uh been watching things closer and this wouldn't happened," he muttered to himself more than to the girl. "Callie, you got to help out here. This woman doc needs your help."

There was no response to his words. Then, slowly the young girl's hand inched its way to the man's leg, pressed against the edge of the table. Her fingers brushed against his pants, then rested on the table, comforted by this small touch. He looked down, then awkwardly placed his long, tapered fingers over hers, covering them.

"Brett," she said, in a bare whisper.

He leaned over, his lips close to her forehead. A look of caring washed across his face, banishing for a moment the coldness of the man. "I'm here, Callie girl. Right beside you."

"Callie," Aries said softly. "You've been hurt, but I've got to see just how bad it is. To do that, I'm going to have to wash the blood away. There'll be some pain. I'm sorry, but it has to be done. First though, you're going to feel some pressure on the wound where I have to staunch the bleeding. It's slowed some on its own, but you've lost a lot. Can you take this without flinching or moving? If you move, you'll start the bleeding up again. You must lie as still as possible. Can you do this?"

The girl's eyes fluttered open, and she looked at Aries.

"She can do it." The terse words came from Brett, his gaze never leaving Callie's face. "She won't move."

Aries nodded, then turned back to the bag and popped open the brass snap. She pulled the two sides apart, then turned around.

"Mr. Whip," she said, addressing him as he ground out the cheroot with the toe of his boot, "I'll need another table to place my things on."

He jerked his head, and two men hurried to move one of the tables.

"Thank you," she murmured. "I'd like more light, and two basins for the water." Brett raised his eyes to one of the men standing nearby.

After placing the bag on the table, Aries took out the items she would need. The men crowded closer, vying to see what this woman doc was going to pull out. She felt Timmy's body pressed into her leg. Timmy. She'd forgotten him, momentarily. He shouldn't be here watching this. Still, what was she to do? Every moment was crucial, too much time had already elapsed, too much bleeding had already occurred.

Mae's clear voice cut into her thoughts. "Tess, you take that boy there outta here. Ain't no place for a youngun. Get him over next door to the store." She looked at Timmy and said, "Bet he'd like a sarsparilla and maybe a jaw breaker."

Timmy nodded, but then remembered his manners. He didn't want to leave Aries; he felt safe beside her. But he was thirsty, and no one could pass up a chance for a jaw breaker. "Yes'm, thank you, ma'am, I'd like that a lot," he said, respectfully.

Tess looked over at Mae, then smiled at Timmy. She left her place beside the table and walked around to the little boy. "What's your name, kid?" she asked, taking his hand and leading him out of the saloon.

"Timmy," he said, softly.

"Thank you," Aries said, getting a quick nod from the woman in response.

Aries finished setting out what she would need. She had several rolls of bandages, but she would not touch the wound without first disinfecting her hands. Her father was a great believer in cleanliness.

While waiting for the hot water and rags, Aries hurriedly unbuttoned her suit jacket, and lay it across a chair back. She rolled up the sleeves, exposing her slender arms. Then, putting both hands to her head, she fumbled for and found the long hat pin that secured the blue, felt hat. She removed the hat and placed it beside her jacket. Her brief indecision and doubt had passed, and now every movement was sure and precise.

Her self-confidence and ability had been restored by her father's voice, guiding and advising her. She knew that, from this day forth, her father would coach her, guiding her in death as he had in life.

Aries moved the lantern and noted with relief that the bleeding was slowing on its own. The delay was working for them, instead of against them, and she may not have to apply pressure to the wound to staunch the flow. She had seen, at first glance, that a tourniquet would not be necessary. The blood oozed rather than spurted from the wound. Thus, Aries knew an artery had not been cut. Had there been a trauma of that nature, quick action would have been imperative. Her father's bag was equipped with a padded piece of wood to place over the artery for concentrating pressure and controlling bleeding.

Aries let out a sigh of relief. She had witnessed a surgery, once, where the surgeon had carelessly nicked an artery in a man's leg. Blood shot out into the room, covering the surgeon and nurse. Aries remembered watching in horror as the man's life pumped away in spurts of blood with every beat of his heart.

She felt movement behind her. A bucket of boiling water, and a steaming teakettle was placed on the table. From under her arm, the girl took a small pile of white rags.

"Are they clean?" Aries asked her.

"Yes, ma'am. Fresh off the clothesline. I, uh, tore up one uh my slips. It was an old one," she offered lamely.

Aries knew what a sacrifice that was. She doubted that, whether old or not, the slip was needed. But she said, "Thank you. It's exactly what I need." The girl smiled at Aries' words of kindness.

Aries placed her hand on the handle.

"I'll get it for you, ma'am." Brett lifted the bucket and poured the hot water into one of the basins.

She slipped her father's apron over her head, tying it securely around her small waist. The apron, made for the ample girth of her father, folded across Aries back, and wrapped back to the front. Aries methodically tied it, wearing it for the first time. She didn't give any thought to the symbolic passing of the baton; her eyes and thoughts were on her patient.

She unwrapped a bar of soap, then plunged her hands into the hot water and methodically washed them. Lather bubbled between her fingers, and she worked it around them and up the length of her arms. Satisfied, she rinsed them, using one of the clean rags for drying. Then she motioned to the other basin.

"Please, fill it with water, after rinsing it first," she said and set it to the side. "Please don't touch the inside; I'll use it for cleaning the wound. Then, you'll need to wash up too, Mr. Whip. I don't know if you'll be touching the patient, but in case I need your assistance quickly, I don't want the field contaminated." Her head was down, and she didn't look at him, but instead picked up the basin of dirty water and looked to Mae, "Where do I empty this?"

"Get her one uh them spittoons," Mae said. "It'll hold a plenty and what spills out can't hurt this floor none. Mebbe do it some good."

Aries dumped the basin with soap skim floating on it into the spittoon, then shoved it toward Whip.

Without a word, he poured water from the bucket into the basin for a second time. He unbuttoned the cuffs of his shirt, and rolled them back on his forearms, then picked up the bar of soap and began imitating Aries' earlier motions. When finished, he dumped the basin in the spittoon, sloshing some of the water onto the floor, then walked back around the table, and, like everyone else in the room, stood there watching her.

She picked up one of the rags, dipped it into the steaming

basin, and wrung it out before turning to the girl. "As I said earlier, Callie, this will hurt some. Your bleeding has slowed, and now it's more important than ever that you not move. A sudden motion, a jerk, and the bleeding will start up again. Are you ready?"

The girl gave a slight nod, and turned her eyes back to Whip. She clenched her jaw, and with fear-widened eyes, held the man's gaze.

Efficiently Aries cleaned the blood away from the wound. Within seconds, the basin of water was a frothy pink as she rinsed the blood-soaked rag.

She started with the cut on the girl's chest, knowing that it was the arm that would require most of her attention. With the wound cleaned, Aries was able to see it wasn't as deep as she'd first thought. It would heal without stitches. She would use one of her favorite vulneraries, comfrey, knowing that it would both sooth and heal the wound. It would also assist in the formation of new tissue proliferation, while checking the bleeding. Aries had been well-schooled in the use of herbs and other simple remedies to promote health and healing. While her father insisted she know modern sciences and medicines, he never discounted the healing properties of herbs. To Aries, they were old, familiar friends, used often and wisely. She closed her eyes for a brief second, thanking the man she so missed for his uncommon wisdom, and for his gift of it to her.

Callie lay still, her body rigid, her breath coming in short gasps. But when Aries moved her attention to the arm, the young woman moaned low.

Aries raised from her task and looked into the white, pinched face. The pain would only get worse with the suturing. She left the rag in the basin and removed the stopper from a brown bottle.

"Would someone please bring me a glass—a shot glass will

do nicely." This time there was no need for Whip. A shot glass was quickly placed on the table beside her hand. She picked it up and poured out some of the colorless liquid. She held the glass to Callie's lips and said, "Here. Drink it. It's bitter, but will stop the pain." Callie emptied the glass, grimacing at the bitter liquid. Aries offered, by way of explanation to Whip, "This will ease her greatly, perhaps even induce sleep. She's done fine for us, but I'm going to have to suture this arm, Mr. Whip. The pain will be intense. We'll wait a few minutes for the drug to take effect."

Aries turned back to the bag and unwrapped a packet of dried leaves. Then, she took out a small bowl and pestle. At the sight of these familiar tools, so often used by her father when making house calls, Aries felt her throat tighten. She placed the leaves in the bowl, added one part lobelia, and one-half part of wheat germ oil. It would have been better had she had the comfrey root to grind into powder, but the leaves would have to do. As she was mixing, the crowd pressed closer, pushing her against the table. She looked up, frowning.

"Mr. Whip, I need room."

He looked at the ring of men and scowled, as if seeing them for the first time. He straightened up. "Stand back," he growled. "You're getting in the doc's way. Where were you when he was slashing out with that knife? Huh? Where were all of you then?" His accusation hung in the air and the men shuffled back from the table, their eyes avoiding Whip. "Well, you sure ain't no use now. Give her room, stay outta her light. You're using up all the air Callie needs too." He turned his attention back to the girl; her eyes were shut, and her breathing soft and slow. Her grip relaxed and curled in his hand. He watched as Aries finished mixing the paste, and applied it to the girl's chest.

"We will bind it, Mr. Whip, as soon as I finish with her arm. I don't want to move her unnecessarily. However, I do believe luck is with us. The bleeding has stopped of its own accord. While I regret the loss of blood, it has assisted in cleansing the wound."

Aries dumped the bloody water, then refilled the basin. She began cleaning the arm. The wound was deep, and her sense it needed stitches was correct. When satisfied, Aries rinsed the shot glass and filled it with hot water. She slowly poured it into the wound.

Aries threaded a curved needle. "Mr. Whip, will you be the one removing the sutures? They will need to be removed or they will grow into the skin."

"I'll do it," he said, looking down at the sleeping girl. Her face was relaxed and innocent in sleep. He gently brushed a strand of hair from her face, and said, more to her than to Aries, "I'll be here this time."

"I am taking small stitches, hoping to keep scarring to a minimum. There is no possibility that she will not scar, Mr. Whip. I consider it fortunate that the wound was not deeper, severing a vessel. Had it been so, she might have lost the use of her arm, if not her life. I think a scar is a small price to pay, don't you?" She glanced over at him and he swallowed quickly before attempting to answer. His face had an unhealthy sheen to it, and was damp and clammy.

"Mr. Whip, are you okay? I'm nearing completion if you'd like to step out for a breath of air. You have been most attentive, but the worse is over."

"No," he gritted out, "I'll stay. I said I'd help, and I will."

Aries didn't question Whip, knowing that he would have the strength and determination to last. She did notice that the group around the table had thinned in size, the moment she started stitching the arm. She smiled to herself, remembering the queasiness she'd experienced the first time she'd observed her father suturing a wound.

Snipping the last thread, she lay the needle down and opened a small envelope, filled with a powdery substance. She sprinkled it over the wound. The smell of sulphur permeated the air. "This promotes healing and lessens the opportunity for infection. I'll leave you some, Mr. Whip, but you'll need to use it sparingly. It's possible Callie could show signs of adversity to the drug. A rash may come on suddenly, or it may be delayed for a few days. If this occurs, discontinue use immediately. You will need to replace the bandage daily, using a clean—and I do mean clean, Mr. Whip—bandage." She fixed a hard look on him. He gave a curt nod, and she continued, "This will give you time to observe the wound. Keep it clean and dry, and it should heal nicely. I regret that I will not be able to follow up on its healing, but I foresee no problems."

She turned away from her patient for a moment, and looked for Ben. She had been oblivious to his presence. She desperately hoped he wouldn't be angry and disappointed in her willfulness that he would send her back. *Back to what?*

"Ben," she said quietly to him. "How far are we from town?"

He gave her a perplexed look, making her heart clutch fearfully.

"How far?"

"Yes," she said softly, "the ranch."

"Oh," he said, and gave her a reassuring smile. "I didn't know what you were meaning, Aries. We're about six hours by wagon; course it'd be faster on a good horse." His brow furrowed in puzzlement at the reason for her question.

She turned back to the table. "Mr. Whip, I will be that close, should you need me. Remember, cleanliness is paramount to healing. Don't forget that." She went on, "She will probably sleep for the rest of the day. When she awakes, there will be some pain. I will leave a small amount of the liquid to relieve her pain, but use it sparingly. Give her plenty to drink to assist in replenishing her blood supply. With that and rest, the human body should take over and heal itself. I'll show you how to bandage the wound on her chest, and I'll leave you some of the paste too. Change it at least every two days. Don't wipe off the old paste; I do not want the wound disturbed." She gave these instructions while her hands were busy.

When Aries had replaced her last piece of equipment into the bag, she took off the apron, folded it, laid it on top, then snapped the bag shut. She straightened, only then feeling the muscles cramping in her back and neck. She rolled down her sleeves, and, with quick motions, put back on her jacket and hat. Aries was once again the stylish, young woman who had stepped off the train only a few hours ago.

"I'll be taking her to her room now." Whip looked up to her for approval before he gently scooped the sleeping girl into his arms and held her there for a moment, her face resting against the black satin vest. Then, with little effort, he carried her around the table, pausing in front of Aries.

"I owe you, ma'am," he spoke directly. "I won't forget it." With that, he walked through the open path between the men, and up the stairs leading to the rooms.

Aries picked up her bag, and made her way to the door, knowing that Ben was behind her. The letdown from the crisis, coupled with the growing dread, made her body heavy, her footsteps slow.

"Doc." The commanding word stopped her as it rang out through the room that was humming again, now that the momentary pause in the monotonous normalcy of the saloon had passed.

She turned and saw Mae, bearing down on her.

"Thankee," she said loudly. "You're some fine doc. We sure

are needin your likes. You tell that to that stubborn Jarrett, if'n you have a mind to, Ben."

"Yes'm," his agreement was low.

Mae stepped forward and looked Aries up and down, measuring and somber. "I'm beholden." With that, she turned and lumbered toward the stairs.

It was time for Aries and Ben to gather up Timmy and the supplies Ben needed. Hopefully, the three of them would make the trip to the Big Hole Ranch, the real destination of her long journey that evening.

## Chapter Five

Ben was quiet, speaking only when necessary. They found Timmy at the general store, happily sucking on a large sour ball and chatting to Tess, none the worse for the adventure. Medical emergencies had always been a part of his life, and this was no different. The only difference this time was that his father was not there, barking at him to get out of the room, to stay out of where he wasn't wanted.

Ben picked up supplies he needed. He didn't acknowledge Aries and spoke only once, and that was to repeat he'd be coming in next week for a bigger order, but he said that directly to the storekeeper, and not to her.

When he pulled the wagon up in front of the hotel, he turned to Aries and explained that, because they were getting such a late start, he'd go in and see if they'd pack a few sandwiches to eat on the way. Aries nodded her approval, knowing that she wouldn't be able to swallow past the knot in her stomach.

Minutes later, Ben handed her the pack and she took out a sandwich of thick bread and meat and gave it to Timmy, who was sitting between them. She offered another to Ben; he took it and began methodically chewing, as he guided the wagon out of town. Aries rewrapped the remaining sandwiches and placed them under the seat.

Timmy ate silently; the excitement of the day had caught up with him. He sensed the tension in the wagon and shifted his position to sit closer to the one person he could depend upon. Aries absently patted his shoulder, her thoughts racing ahead to the end of the day and her confrontation with Ben. Surely, he wouldn't be taking her to the ranch if he wasn't going to let her stay.

Ben had been right. After they left the rutted streets of Wise River, the wagon path ran through grassland. Aries still had to brace herself on the narrow seat, but after several miles, she picked up the motion and lent her body to flowing with the cadence of the wagon.

Before long, the town was a faint line of rough buildings and houses disappearing behind them; soon even that was blocked from view as Ben threaded the wagon through the trees. Aries tried to keep her mind from racing through questions and fears, but the longer they traveled, the more she realized how alone she was, and how she had placed her and Timmy in the hands of a stranger—a quiet, brooding stranger.

Timmy had long since finished his sandwich; his head drooped low, his body slumped with weariness. It had been a long day—a long few weeks. And now, when their destination should have brought great relief, an end to a journey, it brought only uneasiness as Aries pondered unanswered questions.

Her increasing tiredness and concern over Ben's silence didn't stop her from appreciating the beauty of the land they traveled through. High grass rubbed against the side of the wagon as it cut a path across it, leaving its mark for only a moment before the grass sprang back up, blocking out their tracks. It was as if there was a wide expanse of green with only the wagon, the horse, Ben, Timmy, and herself—the lone occupants of this vast state of Montana.

The sky covered them with blue that gradually darkened as the day wore down. It seemed as though the sky went on forever, skipping lightly over mountaintops and sheltering valleys. Aries felt safe, as though a quilt covered and warmed her, warding off the night and all the unknown.

They topped a crest and Ben halted the wagon. Aries gave a small gasp of pleasure. Ben turned to her. Her face was alight as she looked over the valley spread below them. Everywhere she looked was lush, green grass. It was crisscrossed by a slow moving river, snaking its way around bends, reappearing again in the distance as it broke free and emerged, only to disappear again in a thick stand of willows or tall quakies, their quivering leaves silver in the last light of the day. In the background, far enough away that they appeared blue, was the outline of mountains jealously guarding this rich valley. Several peaks wore haloes of white, airy clouds. They appeared to shimmer in the distant haze.

It was as if God had paused in his creation of the world, and, with a smile on his lips, scooped out a hole of land. Then he'd completed his masterpiece with a variety of colors, each one so vibrant, they fought for recognition. Aries took in the varying greens of the grass and trees, the silver underside of the ever moving quakey leaves, the blue and grey of the river, and the shimmering purple blue of the distant mountains.

She took a deep breath, wanting to inhale this beauty into her very being, wanting to open her arms and gather it to her.

She looked at Ben, then flushed and said, "I . . . I have never seen beauty like this. Ben, it's the most beautiful land I've ever seen."

Ben nodded, and a smile slowly creased his face, banishing

the seriousness that had held reign since they'd left Wise River. "It is that," he said softly, knowing that homage to the grandeur shouldn't be spoiled by talk any louder than a whisper.

She turned back to the panoramic scene spread out below, reluctant to stay long from its beauty, unaware of the man studying her face, not seeing the conflict of emotions playing across his.

"I, uh, I kinda forget how pretty it is, seeing it every day. It's called Big Hole Valley, and that," he pointed to the silver band of river, "is the Wise River. We, uh, well you see, Aries, this here's our land. You're on Big Hole Valley Ranch land now," he said proudly.

She jerked her head back to him. "This . . . this is all yours? This beautiful valley is yours?" Her voice was hushed. The wonder that anyone could be fortunate enough to actually own this gift of nature was hard to believe. She looked down at the small boy laying across her lap, his eyes closed in sleep, and she filled with joy in knowing that he would be a part of this land, this Big Hole Valley. He would grow here and would become strong and confident as he explored and learned his new home. Oh, how lucky they were. Nothing, nothing must be allowed to take this rare chance, this answer to Timmy's prayers. *And from me too*, she thought. *This is for me too. I need this valley.* A sense of homecoming filled her, surprising her with an unfamiliar rush of emotions and desire.

"Oh, Ben, I . . . I don't know what to say. To own this . . ." She took a breath and rushed on, "I don't know how to thank you for choosing me," she flushed, "uh, for picking me to live here with you on this land, in this valley." She stopped and lowered her eyes from Ben's penetrating look. "What I'm trying to say, Ben, is that I know I'm not what you expected." Aries reached out and placed her hand against his arm, stopping him from interrupting her, "Please let me finish. I know that today, that . . . business," she was fumbling for words, "in the saloon was a surprise also. But if you'll just give me a chance, I'll show you that I really can be a help to you here on your ranch. Please Ben, I know I haven't been entirely honest, and then. . . . there's Timmy . . . but," she rushed on, "if you'll just let us stay, we really will be a help to you. We'll work hard, both of us." She was running out of words, and felt all hope leaving her as she watched his face. "I'm so sorry I was less than honest with you, making my letters more than what there really is, but I will learn, I can, I know I can. Please give me a chance to prove it to you, please." *What else could she say? What other words could she use to persuade him to let them stay here with him in this wonderful Big Hole Valley? He had to . . . he just had to.*

She waited, her eyes hopeful. He didn't respond, first looking at her, then looking out into the valley, the reins of the wagon hanging limply in his hand. His Adams apple moved up and down in his throat as he swallowed with the effort to speak. Still, no sound came from him, and, after several long seconds, she turned away, knowing that she'd lost. Tears filled her eyes and feelings of hopelessness rushed through her, making her slump with despair. She had failed.

"Aries," her name seemed torn from his throat.

She didn't turn, knowing that she couldn't face him as he told her he didn't want her working beside him on this ranch. She couldn't face him as he told her he'd made a mistake in choosing her. There was also some feeling of guilt, as she realized again that her desire to stay wasn't based in the man. No, he wasn't at all what she wanted or desired in a man, but that could be lived with. He seemed kind, and even though he was still maturing, he had displayed actions foretelling the man he would grow to be.

It was this valley and the ranch nestled somewhere ahead of them, that she so desired. And that knowledge, coupled with her dishonesty and lack of feelings for him, made her sick within her.

"Aries," his voice drew her back.

"Yes." She didn't look at him, but kept her face resolutely turned to the valley, drawing strength from its presence.

"I . . . I got something needing to be said, and I been troubling how to say it every since we left Wise River. It just don't want to come out easy, so guess there ain't no way but to . . ."

"It's okay, Ben," she interrupted him. She would make it as easy on him as possible to tell her he'd be sending her back. Why he'd brought her this far, tempted her with this valley of his, and then tell her she would never be a part of it, she didn't know. Maybe he was trying to let her down easy. Maybe he just didn't know what to do with her and Timmy and chose to let her stay long enough to rest and then take her back with him to Wise River next week. Yes, that was it. That would be in keeping with the kindness of this young man.

"I know what you have to say."

"You do?" His brow furled.

"Yes." She turned to him, her face pale in the evening dusk. "It's okay, Ben. I understand. Please believe me, I don't blame you."

"You don't?" he stuttered. "You do?"

"Yes. You couldn't have known. It's all my fault . . . me and those darn letters saying one thing, and not saying another. I left out too much, and now its caught up with me."

"Aries," his voice cut into her blaming speech, "Aries, you've got me plumb confused. I don't see how you could possibly know. I know you're smart and got more education than me, but still I don't . . . well, how could you know?"

It was her turn to be puzzled. She shook her head. "Ben, we're not making sense, either one of us, are we?"

"No, ma'am, we're not. Supposin' you just sit there quiet like and let me get the words out. They're sticking in my craw as it is and dancing all around them like this isn't making it any easier. Begging your pardon, Aries, but would you just not talk or interrupt me until I'm through?" He peered at her with an earnest look. He ran his hand through his hair in a nervous gesture. She was struck again by his youthfulness even more apparent now with his distress.

She nodded her head, not speaking. Then, she licked her lips, waiting for the words to fall.

Ben cleared his throat, swallowed, and cleared it again.

"Uh, you see, Aries, I . . . we . . . well dang it," the words exploded, "you been lied to."

The words fell heavy in the air settling around the two of them. Aries opened her mouth to speak, then remembered her promise to let him finish.

"When I advertised that a wife was wanted, willing to work on a ranch in Montana, I, uh, well, I kinda stretched the truth. I put my name as the person to contact and I made it sound like I was the one looking for the wife, and"—his words rushed out now, as though he was anxious to spill them forth and be rid of the burden—"I made it sound as though I was the owner of the Big Hole Ranch." He looked at her, watching as one emotion after another played across her face. She held herself still, filled with disbelief at what she was hearing. Ben shifted his gaze away from her questioning eyes, letting the silence grow heavy around them.

When he didn't continue, Aries spoke, her voice catching, "You . . . you aren't the . . . you don't own . . ." she couldn't finish the sentence. The thought was too horrible to comprehend.

He was shaking his head no, still avoiding looking at her.

"You tricked me? Ben," her voice full of anguish, "you tricked me? There is to be no marriage, you don't want a wife, you don't own the ranch, there is no Big Hole Ranch?"

"No . . . I . . . I . . . mean, yes! No I didn't set out to trick you. I sure wouldn't mean you no harm. Aw heck, Aries, it's kinda complicated. You see . . ." then he paused again, "Aries, it ain't like your uh thinking. It's gonna take some talking out, but, well, I'm gonna need some help doing it. I didn't plan on someone like you answering the ad, you being such a lady, all pretty and all, then a doctor to boot. Well, you're finer than anyone we expected. That's what's been eatin' at me. I feel right terrible for leading you on thinking that I'm the one you'll be marrying. Darn it all, it ain't that I wouldn't want to marry someone like you, but it's just, well, I'm not ready to be marrying anyone. But there is a Big Hole Valley Ranch. It's real all right! Just a few more miles and we'll be at the house . . . only I ain't the owner." He gave her a timid smile.

"You just work there, Ben?" she asked him quietly.

"No, it ain't like that, Aries. I mean I do work there, but it's my home too . . . darn it all, Aries, I can't explain all this to you myself. Like I said, I need help because it's all coming out wrong, and I can see just by looking at your face, I'm worrying you plenty. Funny, ain't it? You being worried about not telling me you're a doctor and me being worried about not telling you I ain't the one marrying you." He looked hopefully at her, wanting her to agree with him, wanting her to tell him she understood somewhat. Not getting the response he hoped for, he said, "Aries, I know this isn't what you thought, and I know you've come a long ways. Could you hold off a little while longer? It's getting late, gonna be dark before long. We need to get moving, but I promise you just as soon as we get to the house, there'll be some answers for you. Would you mind holding off on the questions until then?" His eyes were wide.

She wouldn't be marrying him. The knowledge filled her with mixed and jumbled up feelings. She felt relief that she wouldn't be expected to live with this boy/man, as his wife and helpmate. But there was also the increasing anxiety over what was ahead, and coupled with this was the gnawing question: Was there a man waiting? Then there was the even bigger worry. What if there wasn't anyone wanting to marry her and give her and Timmy a home? What if this really had all been a foolish ploy on a young man's part, a lie? No, she assured her racing thoughts, no. What little she had seen of Ben McCabe, it was enough to tell her he wasn't mean enough to do that. This was a misunderstanding, and there had been misrepresentation of the truth on Ben's part as well as on hers, that was obvious. Still, there was a Big Hole Valley Ranch. She knew that. She was sitting here looking down over it, and Ben had assured her there was a house only a few miles away. Okay, then. She'd do as he asked. She'd not press him any further for answers . . . she'd wait . . . until they reached the ranch and Ben had the help he needed to assist him in untangling this web. She'd wait, but only until then.

"I'll wait, Ben. But only until we reach the ranch." She gave him a look as firm as her voice, "Then I'll expect answers, Ben. Lots of them." She turned her attention back to the valley opening up in front of her, and shifted her weight as Ben snapped the reins and Belle responded once more to the cluck of his tongue. The wagon moved forward into the gathering dusk, toward the ranch waiting for them, and the answers both feared.

## Chapter Six

The dusk settled over them like smoke from a campfire. Aries strained her eyes for the first glimpse of the ranch house that, hopefully, would be her new home.

As they drew closer, the grass gave way to a well-traveled road. The wagon came from out of a copse of trees, and hungrily took to the road. On one hand, she couldn't wait until they reached the house, on the other, the wagon moved too fast toward a destination she wasn't sure she wanted to face.

In the dim evening light, she made out corrals, a barn, several outbuildings, and, yes, a large and sprawling house. A wide, roofed porch covered the front of it, and stretched around one side. The weathered wood gave the house a good sense of belonging and endurance. The yellow glow of lamps shone in two of the downstairs windows, but the upstairs was dark and seemed to frown down upon them. Several big shade trees spread their limbs in front of the house, and bushes clustered and clung to the porch. A faint breeze carried the sweet scent of honeysuckle. The house beaconed to Aries, calling her to rest; two rockers sat still and silent on the porch.

As Ben stopped the wagon, Aries heard night sounds start-ing up, as the day dimmed. Crickets chirped and chickens clucked, arranging themselves for sleep. She felt as though she had come home.

Ben had no sooner jumped down from the seat, and walked around to gather a sleeping Timmy in his arms, than the front screen door slammed open and a man stepped onto the porch, and pounded down the stairs. The house shadows prevented Aries from clearly seeing his face, but she discerned a quick-ness and firmness in his steps. He was tall and thin. His shoul-ders had a slight stoop, as though he were accustomed to bending down when entering most houses and buildings.

"Where you been, boy? Been looking for you all afternoon. How'd you manage to make a six hour trip take ten?" The man spoke as he took long steps toward them.

"Dad," Ben called to him, "I . . . I . . ."

"Nevermind. I'm just glad to see you made it and you got Miss Burnett. His steps brought him closer to the wagon, and then he stopped short. "Hell's fire. Sorry, ma'am," he said quietly, "who's that in your arms, Ben?"

"Timmy, Aries little brother." Ben replied, brushing past the man. "Please, Dad, help Aries from the wagon, would you? I'm sure she's stiff and worn out from all the jouncing." Ben left the two of them staring at each other as he carried Timmy into the house.

Aries looked at the man. Where Ben was young, this man was old. It would seem that she was to be thrust from one ex-treme to another. She felt tears spring to her eyes as tiredness and frustration combined to bring about a feeling of despair.

"Huh?" the man responded to Ben's back, then turned quickly to her. "Sorry, Miss. Here, let me just swing you on down." Without waiting for her permission, he put two large hands around her waist and in one fluid motion plucked her off the seat and placed her on the ground. She could feel the sinewy strength of his arms. "Shoot, you ain't but a mite of a thing, are you?" Not waiting for an answer, he reached behind the seat and grabbed her bags. Then, before she could tell him she'd carry the black bag herself, he took it from her hand. "I'll just take these on in, you just mind yourself. 'Spect you're tired, like Ben said. Well, I got some hot coffee and some real good stew waiting. That'll fix you up." He bent toward her noting the tears in her eyes, and in that moment, a piece of his heart softened for the young girl thrust into such an awkward situation. "Hey, now," he said, setting one of the bags at his feet. He reached a finger up and wiped away a trickle of tear escaping from one corner. "Nothing could be that bad. What'd Ben call you?"

"Aries," she whispered.

"Well, Aries, welcome to the Big Hole Valley Ranch. Now let's get on inside. You and me, and Ben got some talking to do, I'll bet." And, placing his hand, at the small of her back, he guided her up the stairs, across the porch, and into the house.

Aries paused in the hall, so she could adjust to the light. Wooden pegs lined one wall, holding an assortment of coats and hats. On the wooden floor, a braided rug runner stretched out, faded from many washings. Doors branched off the hall on both sides, and at the far end, a stairway wound up and around to a balcony that overlooked a room Aries couldn't see. Bordering the balcony, was a dark, wooden railing. More doors opened off from the balcony. She assumed they were bedrooms, and knew this must be so when Ben stepped out from one, his arms empty. He gently closed the door behind him, and started down the stairs.

The man he'd called "Dad" disappeared through the door on her left. Ben nodded his head in that direction and said,

"This here's the front room. Let's go on in. I imagine Dad's got some coffee going. That sounds good, doesn't it?" He looked expectantly at Aries and stood to the side, so she could enter the room.

A rock fireplace took up the far wall. A small fire burned in a grate that was big enough to accommodate the trunk of a tree. Ben walked over to the fire and stretched his hands out.

"Still early enough in the summer, a fire feels good in the evenings. Come over here, Aries."

She took in the masculine hominess of the big room, the hides of animals stretched out on golden walls of knotty pine wood. There was the long, black fur of a bear, the yellow-gold of an elk, and the sable, brownish-black of a moose.

Leather sofas and chairs were placed at various angles. In the back of the room was a wooden desk with an arm chair behind it. A lamp sat on the edge of the desk, casting its light across a cluttered surface. Rag rugs of varying shades of color and size covered most of the room, adding a cacophony of color. It was a room that called to Aries to come in and sit down. Inside of this room, a person could forget the world waiting outside.

Aries saw her bags sitting on the floor near two swinging doors. Ben's father came through them, carrying two cream-colored mugs with steam rising from them. He smiled as he walked to her.

"I ain't never seen a situation a good cup of coffee couldn't help. I took the liberty of putting a splash or two of cream in yours. Figured you could use the boost. I set the pot of stew forward on the stove, to warm. Sit down," he said, pointing to a brown, leather sofa. "Ben, grab you a cup, son, and come on back in. Let's get this all talked out before we have something to eat." He turned back to her and asked, "That sound good to you, Aries?"

She could only nod as she took her place on the sofa, accepting the heavy mug, looking up to thank him. She was met by a pair of blue eyes deep with understanding and kindness. The man was tall, his chest broad, and he emanated a sense of strength. His hair black, liberally streaked with grey, and thinning. He had on jeans, a chambray shirt, and boots. His face was leathered and creased with smile lines. He stood there, letting her take her fill looking at him; a gentle smile spread across his face. She flushed, embarrassed at being so ill-mannered.

"My name's Ted," he said holding out his hand. "Ted Mc-Cabe."

"I . . . I'm Aries Burnett, Mr. McCabe. I'm pleased to meet you." She took his hand and felt his strength as he gently squeezed her own.

"Well, take a sip of that coffee, and as soon as Ben comes back into the room, we'll talk."

He sat down in one of the overstuffed chairs.

Ben came through the swinging doors with a cup of coffee in his hand, and took a chair opposite his dad. Looking at the two of them side by side, it was obvious they were father and son. Ben hadn't yet grown to his father's size, but the potential was there. They were both handsome men.

"Timmy's sacked out. He didn't even wake up when I put him in the bed. I'll bet he don't wake up until morning."

"Thank you, Ben." Aries took another sip of the steaming coffee and felt the warmth go through her. She was anxious to bring everything out into the open and settle, once and for all, if she would be allowed to stay. *Not only stay*, she told herself, *but to marry . . . who? Ted?"*

"Uh, Dad, Aries knows I wasn't real honest with her in my ad." Ben plunged into the silence. "I asked her to wait until we got here to explain things. Anyway," he mopped one hand across his brow, as he searched for words, "it's gotten a little more complicated than you and I thought." He swallowed hard. "Dang it all, Dad, would you jump in an' help me here?" He looked with exasperation at the man sitting beside him, calmly sipping his coffee.

"You're doing fine by yourself, Ben. Remember, this was your idea."

"Yeah, but you was in on it too. You thought it was a good one. Don't you try and put it all on me. We both thought it would work."

"I know, I know," Ted said, looking over at the boy, his brow furrowed, "but I was fearful. When you go and do something that wild . . . well, you're just courting trouble."

Aries closed her eyes and took a deep breath. "Would you both please stop arguing who's to blame and tell me exactly why you advertised for a wife, and which one of you is needing the wife?" Her voice demanded an answer.

Both men looked at each other, and identical smiles played across their faces. "She'll hold her own, won't she?" Ted asked his son.

"She sure will. She's a doctor, Dad."

"A what?" the words exploded from Ted.

Ben grinned, pleased with the reaction. "Yep. A lady doc. You should uh seen her. You know Callie?"

Ted nodded, avoiding Aries.

"Well, she got knifed bad. Course, Doc was drunk like always. Callie was bleeding real bad, and probably would have died if it hadn't been for Aries. She went right into Mae's place and sewed up her arm, and . . ."

"Wait a minute, son," Ted interrupted, both men forgetting for the moment the woman sitting on the edge of her chair, a growing look of impatience on her face. "You mean she fixed up Callie . . . she went into that saloon and took care of a dance hall girl?"

"That's what I said."

"And you let her?" The man's voice thundered across the room.

"Hold on, Dad," Ben stammered, "there weren't any way I could have stopped her."

Ted shook his head. "Ben, when you and I get ourselves in deep, we go down well deep. This is gonna complicate things even more."

"I know," Ben agreed miserably.

"Gentlemen," Aries' voice was harsh and cut into the room. "Stop this, please. I haven't any idea what you are talking about and, believe me, I need answers. My being a doctor has nothing to do with the ad I answered." She took a deep breath and plunged on, "I answered the ad for a wife to work on a ranch in Montana. You accepted that you would be willing to take me. I thought it was you, Ben since your name was the one I responded to, but it seems you're not the one. Is it you, Mr. McCabe?"

"No, Aries, it isn't." His reply was slow. "Let's start at the beginning and see if we can make heads or tails of this. Then, when Ben and I finish, sounds like you might have a few things to tell us," he said. "Agreed?"

Aries flushed. "Agreed, Mr. McCabe. You're right, I . . . I have some explaining to do also. Please proceed. I'm tired, and I need to know if I'm to be allowed to stay."

"What do you mean? Stay?" The puzzlement at her words was clear. "You just sit there real quiet like and listen to Ben and me, then we'll listen to you. After that, I don't think there'll be any question of your staying. I think, Miss Aries, you're just what Ben and I were looking for. Maybe a little more than we bargained for, but I believe that will be okay, too. What do you think, Ben?"

Ben smiled over at his dad, and a look of agreement passed

between them. The look wasn't lost on Aries, and only served to deepen the worried frown on her face.

"You see, Aries," Ben began, "you ain't to marry either one of us."

"I'm not?" she said faintly.

"No, Aries," Ted said. "Ben put that ad in the paper, but the man who needs a wife to work beside him ain't either one of us. No, the man that needs a wife don't know he needs one, you see."

She didn't, but at this point didn't know what to say.

"And after meeting you, I'm convinced, more than ever, he needs you."

"Who?" Aries had found her voice, weak as it was.

"Why Jarrett. My son, Jarrett. Jarrett McCabe"

It was too much for Aries, another McCabe, another man to deal with. She laid her head on the pillowed back of the chair and closed her eyes as Ted went on.

"It ain't as though Jarrett couldn't get him a wife on his own. He could. Any number of women would be real pleased if he'd give them a look. Thing is, he won't. Something happened to Jarrett, but that's his story to tell." Aries raised her head and looked intently at him. "Jarrett needs someone to share this life with him, shoulder to shoulder. Ben and I both know that. So, we came upon this plan. Looking back on it now, it was probably the wrong thing to do. Still . . . we decided to help Jarrett find a wife, whether he wanted one or not. Ben advertised in the paper, and we had all but given up, when we got your letter. We didn't know what to expect, but you sounded just like the kind of woman needed on this ranch.

"Ben and me, we work here with Jarrett, but the ranch is really his." He smiled at her, then turned his gaze to the windows, sheathed in the darkness of night. "My wife and I started this place. Both Jarrett and Ben was born here. And my

Sara died here." His eyes darkened with pain. "I deeded most of the place over to Jarrett. He's the one that's always loved it. Gave a small section to Ben here, but he's not a rancher. He's got other dreams, don't you, Ben?"

Ben nodded, looking down at his hands curled around the cup.

"I'm getting on in years, and I want to see both my boys happy and settled. Jarrett won't ever leave here, and, unless someone steps in and saves him from his own stubbornness, he'll live here alone. I don't mind telling you, Aries, that ain't no way for a man to live. I know. I had the love of a wonderful woman, and there ain't anything like it. No," he said softly, "nothing ever will be like it."

The three sat in silence, each with their own thoughts.

"Well, maybe it wasn't the smartest plan. And maybe it wasn't as truthful as it should have been. But we didn't intend to cause anyone hurt. I don't know you, Aries. I don't know your story, but I sense you're hurting. For whatever reason, only you know. But you must have wanted a home of your own, although why someone as pretty as you would have to answer a newspaper ad to find one, is beyond me. Still, here you are, and there's the story. It ain't going to be easy. Jarrett don't know anything about this, and I don't expect he'll take kindly to our interfering. But, if you'll give him a chance, I believe you'll see the real man. Maybe in time, you'll even love him. That's what I want for that boy, and I believe you could stand up to the challenge. Now Ben here says you have a story to tell. We've said our piece, let's hear yours. Come on," he said when he saw her hesitate, "it can't be all that bad. Let's hear it."

Aries cleared her throat. It was that bad. What Ted and Ben had done was certainly meddling, but they hadn't really lied. Oh yes, they'd bent the truth, but not nearly as much as she

had. She met Ted's eyes, and felt his kindness and encouragement. If this Jarrett had any of the kindness and understanding
his father seemed to have in abundance, then maybe her fate
would be decidedly good.

"Well," she started, "I haven't been entirely honest with
you, or with Ben, I should say. What I neglected to say in my
letter was that I don't know anything about being a rancher's
wife, Mr. McCabe. Oh, I'm a hard worker, and I'm very willing to try. I learn quickly, but the sad fact is, I don't even
know where to begin. I've never had to run a house, we . . .
uh . . . we had servants to do that. And what I should have
learned as a child, I refused." She raised her eyes to both men
who took in her every word. "My father was a physician, one
of the finest in Philadelphia. He taught me everything I know
about being a doctor, and I believe I could be very good.
However, I am a woman. If you were advertising for a physician, I would have no qualms about my abilities. But to keep
this house," and she glanced around her, "and cook, and . . .
and . . . well, do whatever else a housewife must do, I am
sadly lacking in the ability. So, you see, I wasn't as honest
with you as I should have been. Then," she continued, lower-
ing her voice, "there's Timmy. He's my responsibility, and if
you decide to accept me, then you have to accept him as well.
I love him very much, and he deserves a chance to have a
home." The longing on her face touched both men. "I will do
anything, Mr. McCabe, Ben, to honor the requirements you
expected, and to be allowed to stay here and live in this
house, in this valley. I know I can do it. Please, give me a
chance to make this . . . my home." She looked away, not trusting herself to hold the tears threatening to spill from her eyes.
She held her breath, waiting. She didn't know what the man
Jarrett would have to say about her. She only knew that if she
was able to convince Ben and Mr. McCabe, then she might be

able to convince him. He would have to respect his father's decision, wouldn't he?

Ted cleared his throat. "It seems we were all a bit short of the truth. Ben, you have anything to say?"

Ben shook his head.

"Okay, then. I have two things to say. Number one, we'd be pleased to have you stay, Aries, and be a part of the Big Hole Valley Ranch. Wait a minute," he raised up his hand stopping her from breaking in. "Number two, you quit calling me Mr. McCabe. If I'm to be your father-in-law, I expect you to call me Ted. And that youngun upstairs will call me grandpa. That all right with you?"

"Oh, Mr . . . Ted, I can't tell you . . . I haven't the words to tell you what this means to me. I promise I'll learn, I promise. I already have a plan. I think I've memorized the recipes. I put some in my bag, not as many as I should have," she said regretfully. But as soon as my trunks arrive, I'll be able to cook, really I will. I'll work hard, and until then, there's lots I can do. Jarrett will be so glad . . . oh my . . . he doesn't know any of this does he?"

"Nope," both men spoke at once.

"Will he be home tonight? I'll talk to him then. I'm sure he'll understand. If it's your desire he take a wife, and I'm here, surely he'll be agreeable." She saw a look pass between Ted and Ben.

"He's not due back for a few days, Aries. He's down to Butte on some business. I'm not gonna lie to you, young lady, he's not going to be easily convinced. Still, I think that if there's a woman strong enough to take on my Jarrett, it'll be you." He rose to his feet. "I think we've said about all that can be said tonight. How about some of that stew and then to bed with you before you fall asleep on your feet? You look plumb tired."

"I guess I am. The trip was long, and I didn't rest at all on the train. I couldn't keep from . . ."

"Worrying?" he asked

"Yes," she smiled, "but at least that part is behind me. As good as stew sounds, Ted, I don't believe I could stay awake long enough to eat. Would you mind showing me where I'm to sleep? Timmy and I will do fine together, if you would just help me get my bags to the room."

Ben jumped to his feet and walked over to pick up her bags. He had a crooked grin on his face, and said, "She thought she'd be marrying me." Then, over his dad's chuckle, he said, "Well, what's so funny about that? I'm a heck of a lot nicer than Jarrett." That remark settled over Aries as she followed him to the upstairs bedroom.

## Chapter Seven

Aries awoke to absolute quiet. Momentarily disoriented, she glanced around the strange room, blinking her eyes at the sunlight pouring through a dusty window. Dust motes danced in beams of light falling in golden circles on the wooden floor. While the room was pleasant and cheery, it was definitely in need of a good cleaning.

She stretched, then wrinkled her nose; even the sheets smelled musty. Ted must have made the bed up in anticipation of her arrival, taking the sheets from stored ones put away. Aries wondered how many years ago that was.

She looked over at the empty indentation next to her. The blankets were thrown back as though someone had jumped—oh my gosh—Timmy. Aries had forgotten all about him. Sleep had overtaken her the moment she put her head on the pillow. All the stress and worry of the past few weeks had taken a toll, and with the relief of knowing she could stay, she had slept deeply.

She jumped out of bed, her feet warm against the cool floor. The morning sun had not yet warmed the room. Opening one of the bags, she withdrew a wrapper and quickly put it on. This wasn't exactly the way she'd planned her first day, and she mentally berated herself for sleeping so late. *What would they think? That I'm not only inept at housekeeping, but lazy as well?* Then, she'd neglected to see after Timmy, something she hadn't done since his birth.

She went over to a small table holding a ceramic bowl and pitcher. Big yellow roses were painted on the outside of both the bowl and pitcher, and inside the water was cold. Aries poured some into the bowl and splashed her face, catching her breath. She dried her face on a small towel she found folded on the bottom shelf of the table. When Aries peered into the oval mirror hanging behind the pitcher, she saw that the dark smudges of weariness and fear were no longer there; the woman reflected back to her was smiling, and looked rested. She felt good, no, better: she felt full of anticipation and excitement. She hadn't had this feeling since . . . well, since her father had died and all the decisions weighed heavily on her shoulders. "I belong here," she whispered into the room. "I just know it, somehow I know it."

Anxious to find Timmy, yet not wanting to make her appearance without at least running a brush through her curls, she grabbed her brush out of the bag and began trying to tame the riot of golden hair loose now from the pins and hat and falling down around her shoulders, framing her face. A ray of sun from the window fell across the heavy mass of gold hanging down her back. She lay the brush on the table, knowing that a few strokes would not be enough. She wished she could wash her hair and then relax in a hot bath. "Mmmmm," the thought made her smile. "I don't think that's going to happen, Aries," she said aloud, "the days of someone fixing you a bath filled with sweet smelling salts are over. Any bath you get, you'll have to draw yourself." But the thought didn't seem objectionable. In fact, Aries welcomed the challenges of this new life, and she was anxious to get started.

Pulling the ties of the wrapper tight around her small waist, she went out of the room, her bare feet making little sound as she went down the stairs, back into the now-empty front room, and through the swinging doors.

Aries stopped short. Across the room Ted stood, his hands in soapy water, his back to her. He turned at the sound of the door, and warmly smiled as he dried the suds from his hands. She felt drawn to him, and knew instantly that with Ted she had only to be herself, and that he would expect nothing more. She smiled back at him, unsure of how she should proceed, regretting now that she hadn't taken time to dress.

He sensed her discomfort, but that didn't stop him from staring at the lovely picture she made, standing there in her bare feet. *Yeah,* he thought to himself. *Ben and I did right. This is the one for Jarrett, just wish I didn't have to be the one to convince him of that. Nope. Don't look forward to that at all.* None of this was in his voice or his smile as he motioned to a chair at the round table dominating the middle of the room.

"Decided to get up, did you? Sit down! Don't stand there like a frightened doe. I won't bite." He chuckled as he reached for the coffee pot on the back of the black and silver range. He poured her a cup, then sat it in front of one of the chairs, poured himself one, and sat down, opposite her. "Go on, sit down. That coffee's been brewing since sunup, so it ought to put some hair on your chest, uh," he gulped the words back in embarrassment. "Dang it, now I've really gone and put my big foot in my mouth."

Aries laughed. "Don't worry, Mr . . . uh, Ted. I've heard the expression. Being a doctor's daughter, I've been privy to more shocking words and conditions than most women. I'm not delicate and given to vapors; however, you probably don't have a very high opinion of me at this moment. I've certainly managed to start out wrong. However, I assure you . . ."

"Aries, honey," he interrupted, "sit down, and drink your coffee. My opinion of you was high last night, and it's the same this morning. If you're talking about you being lazy this morning, well I'd say that if anyone had the right to catch up on their sleep it'd be you. When Timmy . . ."

"Oh my gosh, Timmy! Ted, I . . . forgot . . . where . . ."

"With Ben. He's gonna make a mighty fine rancher if getting up early is any sign. Ben and me was just shaking up the stove there and putting the coffee on, when we heard him come through those doors. He's a fine boy, Aries." He peered closely at her. "He took up with me real quick, and of course, he already knew Ben some."

"Yes, he is, Ted. He . . . he hasn't had it easy these four years. I haven't always been able to protect him from . . . well, that will all change now." The last few words were soft and said mostly to herself.

She took a sip of coffee, and her tongue licked her lips as she blinked her eyes. "Oh my, you weren't kidding. That will put . . ." she laughed at Ted's expression.

They sipped their coffee in silence. Ted watched her from lowered eyes as she looked around the big room.

The round oak table and six chairs reigned but there was still plenty of space for a large black and silver Morning Comfort wood range along one wall. It looked both majestic and comforting at the same time. The tall back held two warming ovens, one of which was open; a plate of bacon and toast rested on the door, half in and out of the oven. On the side of the stove, a reservoir held enough hot water for dishes, baths, and other household needs. The top of the stove had four cast iron lids, with a wire-handled lifter in one. While the stove was black as night, the handles of the ovens and fancy work on the side were shiny silver. There was a space behind the stove where the stove pipe met the wall, a warming spot for boots on cold winter mornings. The stove emanated a welcoming warmth, and coupled with the hiss of steam from a big silver teakettle, gathered Aries in a welcoming embrace.

The window over the sink held a pair of red gingham curtains, hanging limply at the sides. Aries could see tops of trees, their branches green, in the distance.

The walls were covered with wooden cabinets, and a small room opened off into a large pantry, where Aries could see shelves of what looked like enough supplies to feed an army.

She turned back to look at a tall hutch. With a sound of pleasure, she rose and went over to it. The top was beveled glass, behind which cabinets were filled with assorted china that, although dusty and grimy, was of delicate beauty. Below, three small storage binds held cooking supplies. A wide oak top left ample room as a work space; underneath, were two bins for flour and sugar. The grooved and carved wooden legs held the big cabinet securely. An iron coffee grinder was bolted to the side. The wooden arm of the grinder had a ceramic knob; as the beans were ground, they dropped through to another jar held securely under the opening. Residuals of coffee grounds dusted it. Atop the two large bins, two drawers held silverware and cooking utensils. It was sturdy, blond oak, and was a kitchen in itself. Aries ran her hand over the soft, smooth wood. Standing there, she felt part of this beautiful piece of furniture, and knew she'd spend many happy hours mixing and rolling out dough on the work top.

"It was my wife's favorite too," Ted said softly.

Aries reached for a gallon-sized glass churn, and pulled it to her. A metal lid with iron gears screwed on a squat jar. Wooden paddles extended to deep within the jar. Giving the handle a turn, Aries watched them go in and around each other. It turned easily, humming quietly with each crank. She bent and smelled the faint odor of butter. Closing her eyes, she felt an affinity with the woman who had last used this churn, making butter for a family she so obviously loved.

"How long has she been gone, Ted?" she asked softly.

"Ten years." Aries sat back down and picked up her mug. Ted leaned toward her, feeling a bond with this young woman, who only a day ago, had been a stranger. He felt drawn to tell her about Sara; he hadn't wanted to share with anyone for a long time.

"She died in childbirth, Aries. We shouldn't uh had that last one. I blame myself too. She'd had trouble with Jarrett and Ben, and we planned on making Ben our last. He was nine and Jarrett was sixteen. We were surprised when Ben came along, thinking that Jarrett would be our only one. She'd had trouble birthing him, but it got worse with Ben. Then this last one . . ." his voice dwindled off and he fiddled with his cup. "Well," he said hoarsely, "we were right surprised when we found out she was expectin'. Course we were tickled. We both wanted lots of kids underfoot. This one was different, though, right from the get go. Sara was sick the whole time, and it seemed as though the baby sapped her strength daily. She wasn't big enough to have her babies easily, that's what the doc told us with Ben. Told us then not to let her have any more. But . . ." he didn't meet her eyes.

"And the baby?" she asked quietly.

"Died too. I lost my Sara, the baby, and . . . and Jarrett that day."

"Jarrett?" she asked, puzzled.

Ted nodded. "I lost my boy that day. I left here with young Ben, fixin' to go into town for some supplies. I'd be back before night. Jarrett didn't want to go. He was always so serious, took things to heart. Said he had some tack he wanted to mend, and I suspect he wanted to be close, should his ma need him. I left a boy that day, and came back to find a bitter, withdrawn man." He looked up at Aries, "I never got him back . . . that boy. I don't think Jarrett's ever really forgiven me for not being here when his mother needed me. I don't think he's forgiven me for getting her that way, knowing how hard a time she had." His eyes were sad with distant memories. "That's okay. I've never forgiven myself. I lost a lot that day. But Jarrett, well, he lost a lot more."

There was no sound in the room save the whistle of the teakettle, humming contentedly on the big range.

Aries swallowed past a lump in her throat. Her heart ached for Ted and for the man she didn't know, the man she might be joined with. He did need her. She would help him forget, help him live with the memories.

"Shoot." Ted wiped the back of his hand across his face. "That ain't no way to start out your first day on the Big Hole." Ted peered closely at Aries. "I feel something for you, Aries. Strange, isn't it? Until last night, I didn't know you, but deep within me, there's the conviction you'll help mend this family. I'm just sorry you've been thrust into such a tough situation. What brings you to Montana? Other than Ben's ad?" Ted's eyes twinkled. "We know that's what caught your attention, but why would a young woman like you need to answer an ad like that?"

Aries didn't answer right away. Part of her felt a reluctance to share her business; yet, Ted had told her about his loss, sharing feelings still raw with pain.

"My father," she began, "was a very respected physician. I believe I told you that last night. I was raised with all the comforts money could buy. Money, I found out later, we didn't have." She walked over to the stove, and brought back the coffee pot and filled Ted's cup, then hers. As she talked, Ted listened, seeming to understand what was being said, and what wasn't. She told him about her early years, and her rebellion against learning homemaking skills. She told him about her love of medicine, and her father's delight in her abilities and his desire to share in a profession he embraced and lived for. She took Ted through her father's unexpected death, the bills, the worry over what to do, where to go. Aries told him of Aunt Georgia's offer. Then, she described how she came across the newspaper ad. She told him of the desperate plea to Mrs. Ellis for help. He chuckled when she described the pages of recipes and household tips she and Mrs. Ellis had frantically written, racing against time, most of them resting now in a trunk that couldn't arrive quick enough. And, last of all, she told him about herself—how she'd never wanted a man, never desired to marry.

"I've never found anyone who appealed to me, Ted. I've had plenty of opportunity. The young physicians training under my father found me attractive enough, I suppose, as well as other men, until, that is," she looked up at Ted, smiling, "until they got a taste of my independent stubbornness. I confess, Ted, that I can be willful. I don't mean to be, but I can't abide weakness in men, or in women, for that matter. I have known women who are homemakers, like Mrs. Ellis and . . . and your Sara, who are strong—stronger than I'll ever be. I know that a man doesn't have to be a physician to be strong, or," and her eyes twinkled, "to earn my admiration. You're a strong man, Ted, strong in ways my father wasn't. My father," she chuckled, "tended to be a bit pompous and pig-headed. He also could be cruel." She looked away, then started again. "What I'm trying to say, Ted, is there are principles by which I measure a man. And, I regret to say, I met no one who measured up. Few women did either. I, regretfully, had few female friends. Still, I suppose that made it easier to pull up the past and leave Philadelphia."

"And what made you think the man you were going to marry, sight unseen, would meet your requirements, would measure up to your high standards?" he asked, not unkindly.

"I don't really know," she replied honestly. "I feel it. No man could venture into this unsettled land, and carve out a ranch without having strength. That man would have to have standards and ideals to live by, or this country would beat him. He would have to be a man able to stand tall on his own two feet. And, Ted, I have to believe that a man of that nature, and strength, would want beside him a woman of the same caliber. I may not have the abilities—yet—to be of a real help to him, but, I believe I am strong. I know I am. I know I have the backbone to stand up to any task, any challenge, and conquer it. I know it." Her voice trailed off.

"Honey, I know it too."

"You do?" she asked.

"No doubt in my mind. Well," he stretched, "we done bared our souls to each other. Left out some things, though, didn't we?" She nodded. "That's okay, you and me, we got time. Yes, I suspect we got lots of time to get it all out. But right now, why don't you get a piece of that toast and bacon for your breakfast? There's eggs in the spring box if you want to fry a couple." He looked at the quizzical expression on her face and laughed. "Don't know how to fry an egg?"

"No." she admitted. "Not really. I've watched the cook do it, and I expect I could, but, toast and bacon will do me just fine."

"Okay, toast and bacon it is. I'm the cook in this house, Aries. I'll keep right on being the cook, if that's all right with you." He looked at her, unable to hide the laughter in his eyes.

"Ted, it's more than all right. I . . . I can make cookies." she offered, timidly.

"You can?" he asked, surprised.

"Yes," she smiled. "I love cookies, so that was one thing I let my mother show me. I can make fat gingerbread, shortbread, oatmeal raisin full of spices, and . . ."

"Whoa!! You stop right there. You have my mouth watering already. Cookies, hmm? You love em? Well, Aries, seems you and Jarrett already have something in common. He's plumb crazy over cookies, and," he lowered his voice, "cookie dough. I remember him getting his hand slapped more than once, sneaking a hunk of cookie dough while he thought his mother wasn't looking. See there, every cloud does have a silver lining. We may have our work cut out for us in the cooking department, but you've just made a start on a path to Jarrett's heart with them cookies. Now, what do you say you eat, get dressed, and do some looking around? Timmy's with Ben down at the barn. Take him with you, and you two spend the day exploring your new home. It'll be time enough when Jarrett gets back to start the serious business of being his helpmate. You best take what pleasure you can now, cause Aries, we got a tough time ahead of us . . . yep, we do." He turned away from her, the words somberly spoken, hinting at unknown problems and worries, leaving Aries again to wonder.

## Chapter Eight

T he water felt wonderful. She'd had no intention on doing anything else but taking off her shoes and cooling her feet in the deep hole where it lapped softly against the bank, cutting under the umbrella of leaves from the big cottonwood. She and Timmy had found the shady spot while exploring the road they'd come in on last night. They wandered from the road, taking a dim trail that led to the river. They stopped to watch the water as it meandered through the willows past a field of early spring flowers. At first Aries and Timmy had been content to splash and wade in the cool water, but the longing for a bath and an opportunity to wash her hair overcame Aries. Timmy, with a small boy's aversion to water, wanted no part of the bath thing, and he promised to stand lookout for Aries while she slipped out of her dress, wearing only a camisole, she walked deeper into the river. Then, shivering with the sudden shock of the cold water, totally immersed her body. She came up splashing and gasping for breath, the water running in rivulets from her long hair. She shook the water from her eyes, and scanned the bank.

"Timmy," she called.

"Yes, Aries." The small boy's answer came hidden from a stand of cattails. "I'm over here. There's some frogs here, Aries. Lot's uh them." His voice was loud in the still of the sunlit summer day, and full of excitement and happiness.

She and Timmy had taken Ted up on his suggestion that they spend the day exploring their new home. Aries couldn't remember when she'd had a more wonderful time. She felt as light as the summer breeze tickling the drops of river on her shoulders. Aries lowered herself back into the water, and found the river actually warmer than the air.

"Don't you leave there, Timmy," she cautioned. "And, you're supposed to be a lookout for me, remember?" Her voice was full of laughter and enjoyment of Timmy's pleasure in the newly found frogs, and in the beautiful valley she was enjoying so much. Even the air held the taste of honey, and she laid her head back into the river, letting the water flow over her, making a golden fan of her hair as it rippled out behind her.

"I'm watching, Aries," he called faintly from the cattails.

She chuckled, and relaxed, giving into the motion of the water, her body rocked by the current. She hummed softly to herself. Aries was so immersed in the pleasure of the moment, she was unaware of a tall man, sitting on a long-legged black stallion, pulled up under the tree, watching her.

"About six more feet on out there, and the bottom drops off. Unless you're a good swimmer, I wouldn't go out any further."

Aries shot up; a spray of water flew as she scrambled to get her feet in under her. Her heart raced.

The stranger chuckled, towering above her on the horse. He was in the shadows of the tree and Aries couldn't make out his face, only the silhouette of man and horse blended together, larger than life.

At that moment, Timmy came running through the cattails, his eyes wide. "Aries, Aries, there's a man coming . . . there's . . ." He stopped short, staring.

"I believe she can see that—just as I'm able to see her there in the water."

Aries gasped and quickly lowered her body back into the river.

The man scowled toward the small boy, and his voice was harsh. "You weren't doing your job, boy. Weren't you supposed to be watching? Out here, a man does his job without being reminded to do it."

"Yes sir," Timmy ducked his head.

Aries heard the man criticizing Timmy, and the golden afternoon shattered. She saw Timmy, his head down in an all-too-familiar gesture. How dare this man intrude, and then take it upon himself to demean Timmy in that way—in the same way he'd heard all his life.

"This is none of your concern, mister," Aries said, quietly. The man turned sharply back to her. "What he does or doesn't do is no business of yours. It was my decision to take a bath here, and if you were any gentleman at all, you would have made your presence known in advance so that I would have had an opportunity to . . . to . . ."

"To make yourself decent? Little late for that isn't it? As for my being a gentleman, well, whether or not you call me one makes no difference at all to me," he said coldly. "What you'd better be thankful for is that I'm not a renegade Indian or someone who would take advantage of a woman alone with just a small, worthless boy to protect her. Don't you have any better sense than to go exposing yourself where there are men apt to ride by and see you, or don't you care?"

"Oh!" she sputtered, but before she could get a scathing word out, the man turned back to Timmy.

"I heard your ma tell you twice to be on the lookout for her. Where were you? Huh? Like I said, when you're given a job to do, you'd best grow up knowing people are depending on you to do it. Next time, it might not be someone like me that happens on you—gentleman that I'm not." His voice was sardonic; he glanced back at Aries. "Next time, the consequences could be a lot different. Understand?" he barked.

Timmy nodded forlornly, and Aries felt herself growing angrier by the moment.

"Sir, I don't know who you are, but I'll thank you to keep your opinions to yourself. He is my responsibility, and I, and I alone will mete out any discipline."

"See that you do," he interrupted her, cutting off the rest of her angry words, "because a real gentleman might notice that you have little to nothing on, and that you're turning blue hiding there in that cold water." With that, he gave his horse a sharp turn and was out of sight before she could do more than gasp at his audacity.

She waited until she was sure he was gone. All thoughts of enjoying the water, or the remainder of the afternoon, were gone, banished by the imposing man on the tall horse. Aries felt herself trembling and wasn't sure if it was from the cold water or anger. "Oh, how dare he, how dare he," she kept mumbling to herself as she grabbed her dress from a low hanging tree limb, and using her full skirt made an attempt to dry herself.

"Timmy," she snapped, her anger at the man making itself known in her voice, "come over here. Don't you dare cry. Come here."

She bent down and tipped his thin face up, making his eyes meet hers. "Timmy, he's right, you know. I did give you a job, honey. We're not living in the city now. Here we have to depend on each other. But, he had no right to take it upon himself to . . . well, never you mind, it's past. We're bound to meet up with people who are rude and ugly in nature. Okay?"

He nodded, his face still and sad.

"You know, we were having a good time," she said, trying to bring back the light that had been in his eyes all day. "Weren't we?"

Another nod.

"Well, let's just keep on having that good time. Let's don't let that mean man take away our happiness. You know, Timmy, I've got a feeling we're going to have nothing but good times here in Montana. Times just like today."

"You do?" His voice was hopeful, and she was touched by his trust in her.

"Yes, I do. Now, let's go on back to the house, and see if we can help Ted get supper. Sound good to you?"

"Mmm, hmm. 'Cept I'm going to help Ben. He said I could help him milk. He said I was just the right size to learn to pull a cow's . . . a cow's, aw, you know, Aries."

She chuckled. "Yes, I guess I do know." She ruffled her hand through his hair, his head warm from the afternoon sun. "Aw, Timmy," she sighed, "things sure are different here. You and I had better learn quickly because I think we have some catching up to do. What do you think?"

"Uh, huh," he answered her, but his mind was no longer on what she was saying, or the dark man who had spoken so roughly to him. He was thinking about the cow, and if he really did have to crank her tail to get the milk to start, like Ben had told him he'd have to do. He sure hoped not, cause he was scared of that big ole cow, and being next to her tail, and hind legs was one place he didn't want to be.

## Chapter Nine

"Didn't expect you back so soon, Jarrett," Ben said, casting a worried look behind Jarrett's back at his father who was sticking a piece of wood into the kitchen range.

"No, didn't expect to finish up quite so soon either. Tatum was glad for my business, and we struck a deal quicker than I expected. He'll take what horses we can deliver. All he asks is they be green broke. Guess he plans on letting the soldiers do the rest." He smiled to himself as he pulled out a chair and dropped his lean body into it, cradling a cup of coffee in one hand. He tipped his hat off his forehead, letting a curly wave of black hair free. His thin face was the color of bronze from hours spent in the sun, and there were faint lines at the sides of his eyes, put there from squinting into the sun, and not from smiling. His smiles were rare, and when they came, brought a gentleness to his stern face. His eyes were blue to the darkness of seeming black. They ranged from light to dark, depending on his mood, and could change in an instant. They were fringed by long, black lashes, the color of his hair. His was a face that made women look twice. But their interest was quickly dispelled by his cold aloofness.

"Everything okay here?"

Ben nodded, not meeting Jarrett's eyes. Ted coughed and made more noise than necessary shaking the stove grates with the poker, and slamming the lid back in place.

"Darn but I'm tired," Jarrett said, rubbing his hand across the back of his neck. "A few days in Butte makes me glad we don't live any closer to a town than we do. Don't believe I've ever seen a place quite like Butte. You know the Chinese have a whole bunch of stores built right under the town? I went into one of them, and I have to tell you, I was surprised. It was clean and well stocked. They're hard working people. I hired a couple of them."

"You what?" Ted asked, surprised.

"We need a cook and someone to do the laundry down at the bunk house. Ever since Cookie got a wild hair to go to Wyoming, the guys have been taking turns and griping about it too. Speaking of cooks, you got anything in mind for supper? Ben," he went on, not waiting for Ted's answer, "before it gets too dark, I want you to cut out a beef and take it on down by the creek a'ways. There's a family of nesters camped somewhere along there. Like as not, they could use the meat. While you're there, remind them they're on Big Hole Valley Ranch land, and we expect them gone in the morning. Don't let them give you no argument . . . especially the woman."

"The woman?" Ted asked quietly.

"Yeah, caught her taking a bath in the river there. You know the spot Ben, where we used to jump off that cottonwood into that deep hole? Well, she was there—her and a little boy. Pretty as a picture," he said quietly, "but mighty sassy. Lit into me like a tiger over its cub." His eyes flashed and a smile played around his lips. He missed the glances between his father and Ben. "Told me to mind my own business, in no uncertain terms. Anyhow," he said, looking up. The men gripped their coffee cups and looked everywhere but at Jarrett. "I want her and the rest of them gone by morning." He chuckled to himself, "Can't help but feeling sorry, though, for the man she's bossing around."

"Uh, Jarrett," Ben and Ted started to speak at once.

He looked hard at them, sensing their confusion. "Yeah?"

Ben looked over at his father and licked his lips. "Uh, Dad and I . . . We, uh . . . well, we got something to tell you, Jarrett."

A coldness settled around Jarrett. He sensed their reluctance, and dreaded hearing another problem. "Okay," he said tiredly, "let's hear it."

"Dad . . ." Ben appealed.

"Son." Ted began, clearing his throat. "Ben and me did something a bit impulsive, but at the time it seemed like a good idea. It still seems like a good idea. Just right now, I wish . . ." His voice dwindled off.

"Say it," Jarrett demanded, looking from one man to another.

"Okay. We, uh, felt like you needed someone—someone to maybe help ease your pain, your loneliness—you know, to help shoulder this load you're carrying all by yourself, so . . ." he cleared his throat again, and continued in a voice so low it was almost inaudible, "we got you a wife, an . . ." Jarrett exploded to his feet, overturning his chair behind him.

"What the? Did I hear you right? You got me a wife?" he shouted, his eyes black with anger. "You got me a wife? How do you get someone a . . . nevermind that. Just tell me this: what got into you two? A wife? Where? Who?"

"Now dang it all, son, just sit down. Ben put an ad in a Philadelphia paper, and, well, we got an answer. Ben picked her up from the train yesterday."

"Stop right there. Yesterday? Okay," Jarrett took a deep breath, making an effort to control his building anger and frustration. Through clenched teeth, he gritted out, "Where is she? Huh? Well, it don't matter where she is, she ain't staying here. What made the two of you think I needed or wanted a wife? Who gave you the right to make that decision for me?" His voice was loud and came in angry spurts as he picked up the fallen chair and slammed it back under the table. He stood glaring at his dad and brother. "Listen closely," he whispered, enunciating each word slowly, "If I wanted to bring another woman in this house, I would have gotten one myself. Me. Myself. Now, I don't know where you have her hidden, but I can tell you both she's not staying. He raked a trembling hand through his hair, knocking his hat onto the floor. He bent down to scoop it up, then straightened slowly, his body taut with anger. The two men in front of him stepped back, still locked in his piercing gaze. "Now you tell me, what kind of woman answers an ad in a newspaper for a husband anyway, and comes all the way from Philadelphia to take a man sight unseen." He snarled, "What kind?"

"This kind."

Three heads turned toward the sound and Aries angry, cold glare.

She stood in the open door, framed by sunlight. Her wet hair hung down her back, the natural gold heavy and dark. Splotches of wet darkened her dress where she'd used it as a towel to hurriedly dry herself. Even so, there was no hiding her natural beauty. Her face was flushed with anger, and her eyes snapped. She was pale, and held her hands in tight fists held close to her body, rigid with defiance.

"Son, I'd like you to meet . . ."

"We've met!" Both answered at the same time, spitting the words into the air like two cats ready to hiss and show claws.

"Aries and Timmy," Ted said. "And Aries, this is my son, Jarrett."

Neither Aries nor Jarrett gave acknowledgment to the introduction, as blue eyes met blue eyes in an unflinching battle of wills. Aries bent down to the little boy trying to hide behind her. "Timmy, why don't you go upstairs to our room and play with your soldiers for a few minutes?" She saw the look of protest on his face, and said, softly, "Please."

Without a word, Timmy walked across the room, making a wide circle around the tall man whose eyes had never left him.

"He could use a few lessons in minding," Jarrett muttered under his breath, but loud enough so Aries heard.

"Yes, and someone could use a few lessons in manners. The only difference is, one's four years old, and the other acts like he's four years old." She copied him, and muttered it under her breath, yet loud enough he could hear too.

"Huh?" Jarrett raised his eyebrows, his eyes narrowing. "Look, Miss . . ."

"Aries," she said, matching his coldness.

"What?"

"My name is Aries. Aries Burnett."

"Aries? Good grief, even your name is . . ."

"Is what, Mr. McCabe?" She spoke slowly, in a frozen tone.

He stared at her, then said with deliberate sarcasm, "Odd." He waited for a response, then baited her further. "What kind of name is Aries?"

"Not that it's any of your concern, Mr. McCabe, but my father named me. He was a lover of astrology, and Aries is the name of a star, a constellation, it's the . . ."

"Well, it doesn't matter what your name is," Jarrett cut in. "You were brought here under false pretenses, ma'am, and Ben," his eyes flashed on the hapless, young man, "since he's the one responsible for getting you here on this wild goose chase, will be taking you"—he nodded to the door—"and the boy, back into Wise River tonight. You can take the train on outta here and back to Philadelphia. I'm sorry for the misunderstanding, and that you had to make the long trip. Course we'll pay for your ticket back. Ben," he said, turning his back on Aries as he put his hat on his head and walked out of the room, "bring the wagon back around and see that you get them . . ."

"That won't be necessary, Ben," she said, in a voice that left no room for discussion. "I'm not going."

Ben turned from one to the other, his eyes wide. Ted stood by the stove, still and watching. It was as if there were only two people in that kitchen. Two people with lightening crackling between them.

Jarrett whirled back around, his eyes black and smoldering. Aries faced him, her shoulders squared, her hands on her hips. Then, she slowly walked toward him, stopping a few paces from him.

"I'm not going, Mr. McCabe." She gave each word a full measure of voice.

"Oh, yes you are." He retorted, his words hard with conviction. But, for just a second, a flash of admiration flickered in the unreadable depth of his eyes. He had to bite back a smile at the audacity of the petite woman daring to face him down in his own house. Two bright spots of anger colored her high cheekbones, and her patrician nose was tilted up, her small nostrils flared. Unable to help himself, he let his eyes stray to her mouth. He lingered on the sweet fulness of her lips. A frown of puzzlement flared as he banished the unfamiliar feelings.

"No, I'm not. I answered the ad for a wife willing to work on a ranch in Montana. I came here in good faith. You have an obligation to honor that agreement."

"I don't have any obligation to you, ma'am. Just because

my father and brother decided I needed a wife, don't mean I have to accept one. My only obligation is to see you back on a train to Philadelphia. No offense, ma'am, but just as sure as God made green grass, I have no intention of marrying again"

"Well, that's good, Mr. McCabe. Because I don't either." His use of the word again totally escaped her.

"Aries." Ted cut in.

"No, Ted, he's right. He doesn't want me for a wife, and," she threw back his words, mimicking them, "no offense, but as sure as God made green grass, I don't want him for a husband. But I still intend to stay here." She took a deep breath and continued. "Mr. McCabe, you may not need a wife, but you do need a woman in this house. You need a woman to take over cooking," she said the word quietly, "and cleaning, and accepting all the other chores a woman does on a ranch. Since you have no intention of taking a wife to assume those duties, then it only makes good sense to hire someone. You do possess good sense don't you, Mr. McCabe?"

"Yes," he growled never taking his eyes from her face.

"Well then, it's settled. I will stay as your housekeeper."

Ted cut in, the trace of a smile on his lips, "Does seem like the answer, son. You and Ben don't have time to do all that needs done, here in this house, and I'm not as quick as I used to be. We got a young lady here, that is willing to take on the task." He put his hand on Aries' shoulder.

Jarrett looked from one to the other. He was sure he'd been manipulated into a hole he couldn't crawl out of, but he darned sure didn't know how it had happened. Manipulated by a sharp-tongued, spitfire woman whose blue eyes shot sparks at him.

He took several sharp, deep breaths, feeling he needed air. Finally he said, "All right, Aries," emphasizing the unusual name, "you can work for the Big Hole Valley Ranch. Just remember, you take orders from me. Just so we understand each other right from the start. I work hard, and I expect my meals cooked and ready on time, and . . ."

"No." The word hung suspended in the air.

"Huh?" he jerked his head up, a muscle flickering at the side of his jaw "what do you mean, no?"

"Just that, Mr. McCabe." Her answer was calm and gave him no hint of the fear raging inside her. "No. Your meals won't be cooked by me, at least not for awhile. You see," she paused, then threw the remainder of the sentence at him, "Until my trunk comes, I can't cook."

He leaned back on the heels of his boots, a perplexed look on his face. He combed his fingers through waves of black hair, tilting his hat back on his head. Then, he wearily rubbed his hand across his face. His next words were slow and careful. "Let's see. You intend to hire on as my housekeeper, doing the cooking and everything needed to help run this house, but you can't cook, unless you have a trunk, which should come in a few days. Am I right?" He drew the words out, emphasizing each one.

"Yes, I believe that's correct."

"Aries," he said slowly, "just how in the . . . No, let me start over. How are you meaning to . . ." He stopped and looked at the three people looking at him, the expression on his face begging for some sort of an explanation.

"Son, Aries can't cook. Don't know how to at all."

Jarrett looked closely at his dad, daring him to enjoy the situation as much (as his voice suggested he was).

"Not at all?"

"Nope. But she's got recipes memorized and some written down she brought with her. The rest, along with tips on how to keep a house, are in her trunk. Until then, well, I said I'd keep on doing the cooking."

Muttering under his breath, Jarrett walked slowly over to the sideboard and took out a cut glass decanter and filled a shot glass with brown liquid. He looked at the glass a moment, then tossed the drink down in one gulp.

"Mr. McCabe. I will not be present where there is cursing and use of alcohol. My father enjoyed a drink, but not to give him Dutch courage."

You could hear a quick inhalation of air as both Ben and Ted took a worried breath. Jarrett's back was as rigid as a ram rod.

"Aries," the words came, cold as ice, "if your father didn't need a drink every now and then living around you, then by, uh, by gosh my hat's off to him. He was some kind of man. However, you'd be well advised not to push me. Now, very clearly, tell me what you can do."

"I can clean. This is a lovely home, but it's dirty. And while I may not be able to cook your meals, Mr. McCabe, I can serve them and clean up afterward. I don't intend to shirk my duties. I will work hard."

"You darn right you will. Everyone works hard around here, and so will you. Don't expect any special treatment. It's hard work. Just looking at you," he said, turning to face her, "I'd say you haven't done much hard work in your life. You'll be scooting back to Philadelphia before long and the ease of city living."

"Don't count on that, Mr. McCabe." Aries replied, holding his gaze.

He didn't look away for a long moment. Then he said, "Okay. I'll expect you and your boy to pull your own around here. He'll work same as you."

"*No!*"

The word fell quietly into the room, stopping all conversation.

"No, Timmy will not work. I expect he'll have chores. I want him to learn to be responsible. But he's four years old, and he will have a normal kind of life for a four-year-old. He'll work, but he'll also play. He will learn that both have their place in this world. I'll not have him grow up angry and forgetting how to smile, how to laugh, how to treat people kindly, how to take pleasure in things."

"Your son is spoiled."

"He's not my son," she cut his sentence short. "Timmy is my brother. Our mother died in childbirth. I'm the only mother he's ever known. There have been circumstances in his life . . . his, his life has been hard. I suppose that's one way to describe it. That's why I want him to have this opportunity to enjoy being a boy, a four-year-old boy."

Ted had looked worriedly over at Jarrett and caught a hurt look in his eyes before he turned his face away, not meeting his father's look.

"Is that agreeable, Mr. McCabe?"

He nodded. Then he looked over at her again, the distant coldness back in his eyes, his face closed and devoid of the emotions that churned within him. "I'll give you two months, Aries. Not one day more. Understood?" He stood tall, never taking his eyes from the woman. She straightened her body, and tilted her head back. She stood, proud and regal as a queen. He felt a moment of intense admiration for her—admiration and unexpected awareness of her beauty. It washed over him, throwing him off guard.

"Fine," Aries answered and turning sharply around, she walked out of the room.

"Fine," the word was thrown over his shoulder as, simultaneously, he turned in the opposite direction, and walked out the back door, slamming it behind him.

The room was silent. The charged air deflated, leaving a stillness like the aftermath of a wind storm.

Ted looked over at Ben who stood, looking from one door to another. Their eyes met and, slowly, a big grin came across both men's faces. Their eyes crinkled and they stuck out their hands in a silent handshake.

"Two months," Ted said.

"Yeah."

"Wanna make any bets?" Ted asked.

"Naw," Ben grinned, shaking his dad's hand.

## Chapter Ten

There was little talk that evening around the supper table. Ted dished up some day old stew—that and a pan of baking powder biscuits and wild honey made up their meal. Aries had never tasted anything as good.

Timmy came in from milking, proud of getting a thin stream of milk from pulling on one of the teats. He was beaming and chattering to Ben when he walked into the kitchen, helping carry the full milk bucket. When he saw Jarrett sitting at the table, watching Ted's father ladle the stew into a crockery bowl, Timmy's eyes became downcast, and he stood just inside the door.

Jarrett saw him standing there, and scowled, "Go wash." Timmy quickly went over to the sink and stood on tip toe, trying to reach the basin of water.

"Here, honey. It's almost too tall for you, isn't it?" Aries held him by the waist and lifted him up several inches until he could wash his hands and face. She set him back on the floor, and handed him a towel. "Take a seat at the table, Timmy. I'll bet you're hungry, aren't you?" She leaned over and whispered to him. "Ted made biscuits. And there's honey."

"Really?" his eyes lit up.

"Mmm, hmm. And, I plan on pouring you the first glass of that milk you just brought in. You milked it, you get to drink it." She smiled, seeing his sunburn. His face, usually pale, had a red glow to it. His eyes looked heavy, and Aries knew he was feeling the effects of the fresh mountain air, and the miles his little legs had traveled. She would have to put some aloe vera on his face to soothe and moisten the burn. He'd have to toughen up fast, but she was pleased that his tiredness was from spending his time enjoying the out of doors, doing things he'd never been allowed to do in his life. Tired he may be, but he looked happy . . . that is, until he glanced at Jarrett. It was plain to Aries that Jarrett intimidated the little boy. *Darn him*, she thought. *Look at him scowling, watching our every move. Well, I won't let him spoil this evening for us. This is our first day here, and we'll end it happy regardless of what Mr. Jarrett McCabe likes or doesn't like.*

"I . . . I'll wait for you, Aries," Timmy whispered to her.

"Sit down, like she told you. Here." Jarrett pushed back a chair with the toe of his boot, and waited for Timmy to respond. Timmy looked up at Aries, and seeing her nod, he slowly walked toward the chair. With downcast eyes, he seated himself, his chin reaching the top of the table.

"Say, Sprout, you look like you could eat off the table without a plate. How about we get you something to sit on, raise you up a little, huh?" Ted said, leaving the room only to return in a few minutes with a thick Sears Roebuck catalog in his hands. Bending down over Timmy, he lifted the little boy up, and slid the catalog in under his narrow butt. "How's that?"

"That's a lot better, Mr. Ted. Thank you," Timmy said.

"Wait a minute. Who's Mr. Ted?" Ted leaned toward the little boy, an exaggerated scowl on his face, "Huh?"

Timmy giggled at the man's face. "You," he said.

Ted poked him in the ribs causing Timmy to laugh even harder and wiggle away from him, squirming on the catalog. He leaned away from Ted's tickling. Then wiggling on the slick paper of the catalog, he felt himself suddenly start to fall over the side of the chair. Before Ted could grab him, a strong arm reached out and took hold of his shoulder, steadying him. Timmy froze as Jarrett eased him back on the catalog.

"Sit still," he said, yet his voice wasn't as gruff as it had been a few minutes earlier. He felt the boy's thin shoulders. *Darn*, he thought, *he's not much more than a baby*. Then, he banished the tender thoughts and turned his back, not liking the strange surge of feelings.

He noticed the table was set with more care. There were cloth napkins at each plate, and in the center of the table was a small glass jar filled with daisies and blue bells. The honey had been taken out of the five pound can and placed in a small pitcher. The silverware was aligned by each plate, and the lamp had been wiped to a shine.

A silence fell as Aries took her place opposite Jarrett. She looked over at Timmy and nodded, and the two of them bowed their heads. The three men looked at them, then looked at each other. Aries glanced up and saw them sitting straight in their chairs, with only Ted's head bent at an angle.

"Ted," she said, "do you say grace, or would you like me to?"

"Uh," he cleared his throat looking ill at ease, "well, uh, why don't you, Aries? Yeah, you go on and say it."

She nodded, and bowed her head again.

"Dear Lord," her voice rang out clear in the quiet of the kitchen. "Thank you for this lovely meal which we are about to eat. Thank you for Ted that cooked it. And, thank you for the Big Hole Valley Ranch that provided it. Amen."

"'Men," Timmy echoed softly, then raised his head, accustomed to saying grace before his meals.

Aries reached for the bowl of stew in front of her, and passed it first to Ted on her side. It was then she noticed Jarrett and Ben's eyes on her face. She glance at them, puzzled by the looks on both men's faces.

"Is something the matter?" she asked.

Jarrett gave his head a quick negative shake, and looked away. But Ben answered.

"It's just we haven't had a woman say grace at this table since . . ." his voice dwindled off, leaving the sentence hanging.

Aries smiled at him, then risked a glance at Jarrett. He was ladling the stew on his plate, his face closed. Any hint of emotion had been wiped from his face. For a quick second, Aries thought she saw a glimpse of pain in his eyes, but that quickly clouded over.

He took the heavy bowl and started to hand it to Timmy, then seeing his small hand, he placed it near his plate, and ladled a spoonful of the thick broth of meat, potatoes, carrots, and onions onto the boy's plate. Steam rose from the stew and curled around Timmy's face.

"How much?" Jarrett demanded.

"I . . . I don't know, sir. Aries usually . . ."

"Don't you ever think for yourself?" Jarrett cut off his words.

"Another spoonful will probably be plenty, Mr. McCabe," Aries interrupted, giving him a look of reproof. "Thank you for assisting him." She was cooly polite.

She helped herself to the stew, and while preparing her biscuit, she breathed in deep the hot, fragrant smell. "Ted, these smell delicious. Do you think you could show me how to make them? I've never seen biscuits like this."

Ted beamed at her. "Shoot, of course you can make them. Nothing to stirring up a bowl of baking powder biscuits. They aren't anything special to us, Aries. I'm glad they are to you, but I expect you're used to light bread, aren't you?"

"Yes," she smiled in remembering, "our cook went every day to a small bakery just down the street from our house. They baked it fresh daily. A lot of times she brought back doughnuts still warm from the oven. They had sugar and cinnamon sprinkled over the top of them. Mmm," she sighed, "I'd forgotten about them," she laughed, "and my mouth's watering."

"Aries," Ben groaned, "don't. I had doughnuts one time at a church social. I couldda ate me a dozen of them."

She and Ben talked easily then mostly about food, and different likes and dislikes. Ted joined in the conversation, but not Jarrett. He didn't look up from his plate, and seemed to be methodically eating, his mind elsewhere. It was as if he'd removed himself from the companionship of the three other adults at the table, and had isolated himself in a private world, a place where no one else was welcome.

Aries finished her stew and turned to see if Timmy needed anything. She paused, a smile on her face, as she looked at the little boy. He was sitting still on his catalog seat, his shoulders slumped, his eyes closing. His body swayed, then straightened as he fought to stay awake. A forgotten biscuit was clutched in his hand, honey dripping between his fingers.

Aries rose from the table, and went over to the sink to get a wet rag. She bent over Timmy and took the biscuit from his hand and washed the sticky substance from his fingers. Her movements were gentle, and once she brushed her lips across his nodding head.

Jarrett stopped eating and watched her, his eyes dark and unreadable. Then, he rose from the table, and, grabbing his hat, walked out the back door, leaving behind a plate of stew.

He had to have air. He had to get out of the kitchen, away from the table graced by a woman's touch, and away from the memories of his mother and her delicate lips brushing across a tired boy's dark hair. Away from memories of still another woman that never had the chance to . . . he breathed deeply, and knew he'd have no peace that night. "I shouldn't have agreed to her staying," he said to the night breeze. Then, shoving his hands into his pant pockets, he walked slowly to the barn, losing himself in the night as the darkness swallowed up the meager lamp light, filtering through the kitchen window.

Aries watched him go. Against her will, compassion for the man filled her. She wanted to run after him, put her hand on his arm, and . . . what? Offer him comfort he'd only throw back in her face? *Aries*, she chided herself, *he's made it plain he wants help from no one. He's not a broken arm that you can heal. Still* . . . Sighing, she turned back to the table, and the silence left by his departure. Ben helped Timmy to his room, and returned to finish his supper, but there was no more talking, no more laughter and sharing. Jarrett was the catalyst that the two men, the entire ranch, reacted to. Even she felt the loss of his presence, and wondered at his power and strength, his ability to hold this ranch in the palm of his hand.

That night Aries crawled into bed beside Timmy, and, pulling the quilt up around her, lay there, with the events of the day running through her head. She'd cracked her window to let in the sweet night air, and she could hear the crickets, performing an evening symphony. An owl hooted, lending his melancholy voice to the music. She turned on her side, and pulled the quilt up around her ears, wanting to block out those sounds she found frightening and strange. Smiling at herself, she knew she was behaving like a scared child, hiding her head under the blankets so the night ghosts and goblins wouldn't get her. She closed her eyes, and without warning,

Jarrett's face came into her mind. She saw him as he'd looked at the table, and saw the look in his eyes as she'd caught him watching her wash the sleepy boy's hands. His eyes had been dark blue and she thought that, for a moment, just a brief moment, she'd glimpsed longing in them, before the guarded look came over his face, and his dark lashes fell against his high cheekbones. When he reopened his eyes they were again the cold, unfathomable windows into his thoughts. *He has such beautiful eyes,* she thought. Then, realizing what had popped into her mind, she quickly turned over, and told herself to get to sleep. She made her mind go blank, willing herself not to think of the tall man who still hadn't returned to the house when Ted had blown out the last lamp in the kitchen, and had shooed her off to bed.

Aries must have slept, but for how long she didn't know. One minute, she was willing herself not to think, feeling her eyes growing heavy as sleep overtook her. But suddenly, she was jerked from sleep by a sound carried through the open window. Her eyes flew open, her heart jumped into her throat, and her body became rigid, stiff with fear, waiting for whatever had pulled her so quickly from sleep to let itself be known. She heard it again. At first, the sound was distant and singular. Then, it was joined by several more throats, making an eerie, howling wail. *Aaaarooo . . . yip, yip, yip . . . aaar-rooo.* The howl seemed closer and stronger. Had banshees been loosed from hell? Were they coming closer, closer to her window? *Aaarooo . . . aaarooo.* Without realizing what she was doing, Aries threw back the covers, and was out of the bed, and the room in a flash. She had to find help. She had to. She ran into the hall, blinded by fear and into the solid chest of Jarrett.

"Wha . . . what the heck?" He grabbed the frightened woman by her arms.

"Jarrett. Oh, thank goodness." Her face was pale, looking up at him, her eyes wide with fear.

"What is it?" he demanded. "What's the matter?"

"Jarrett. There's something outside. Something, oh, it's so awful it's . . . Aries stopped speaking, and the stillness of the night was split again by the mournful sound. *Aaaaroooooo*. "There," she whispered, her hands clutching at his shirt. "It's getting closer. Jarrett, please help me. We have to get Timmy. We have to warn . . . Oh, there it is again."

"Shhh," he said gently. "It's nothing." His hand, with a will of its own, lightly stroked her head, and he felt the silky curls, tangled from the pillow. "Aries," he said, with a reluctance that surprised him, "Aries, it's coyotes. The sound you're hearing is coyotes calling out to each other. It's a full moon tonight, and they're out hunting. Sure, they're getting closer. They know we got chickens here and if one of those stupid hens isn't inside their house tonight, and shut in, they'll have her for supper." His voice was soft and soothed her.

She raised her head and looked at him, fear still evident on her face. Then she pulled away, reluctant to leave the strength and comfort in the safety of his arms.

"Coyotes?" she asked fearfully. "Coyotes can make that . . . that sound? I've read about them, but," she shivered, "but I never have heard one. It's, it's terrible. There must be hundreds of them out there."

He smiled into her face. "Naw, only a few. Sounds it though. There's a den of them just up on the ridge, back of the house. Every year a batch of pups is born. That same couple comes back here to have those pups and spend winter for as long as I can remember. Pups are cutern heck, but they raise hell with chickens. Course they do help keep the rabbit population down, so I leave them alone. A hen every now and then isn't too high a price to pay, I guess. Come here," he took her by the arm, and led her down the stairs, and out onto the wide porch. He chuckled to himself at her tight grip on his arm; he couldn't have pried her fingers loose from his shirt had he wanted to. And, he wasn't sure he wanted to.

"Look," he said, pointing up to the sky just as another howl split the air and Aries pressed closer to him. The moon was full, and the big Montana sky was alight with stars, filling it with diamonds of white.

"It's beautiful," she whispered. Her face was turned up, and he found himself looking at her instead of the sky. She was beautiful, and he drank in her beauty, hating the need that filled him, hating his weakness.

"Now," he commanded, "listen. They're calling to each other. If you listen closely, you can hear the mature howl of the parents, and the yip of the pups answering them. Hear it?"

She strained. Then, a smile broke across her face. "Yes," she said softly, "I can hear it."

"They're having one of their first lessons in hunting. The old couple are getting them ready to fend for themselves."

"It's not so eerie when you know . . . when you look at it that way . . . but don't they bother your cows, your calves? I've read . . ."

"They hunt to eat, Aries. Everything has its place out here. If they were hungry enough, yes. A pack might pull down a calf. They'd probably go first for a deer or elk weakened with hunger from the winter snows. That's when they're the most viscous, hunting in their pack, driven by hunger. Then it's survival of the fittest, and that's how it is here. Only the fit, the strong survive. You have to be strong, or you're pulled down . . ." His voice dwindled off, and Aries knew he wasn't talking about the coyotes.

She shivered in the cool night air, away from the safety and warmth of the man standing beside her, looking out into the night, pulling his thoughts back around him like a blanket.

He glanced over at her, and watched her rub her arms with her hands, the moonlight's glow bathing her body. He felt something stir within him, and was immediately angry at the ability this woman had to make him feel. "You better get back inside. You're cold." He delivered the statement in a flat voice. Gone was the man who, only a few moments ago, was smiling at her, telling her about coyote pups, and parents teaching them to hunt. Gone was the man who seemed to instinctively know what reassuring words to offer.

He walked over to the screen door and opened it. "Get to bed, Aries," he said quietly. "Mornings come quick on a ranch. You've got a full day of work ahead of you." He walked behind her through the empty rooms, and without another word, left her at her bedroom door.

She stood, watching him disappear into his room, and wondered if his telling her she had a full day of work ahead of her was his way of reminding her she was here only as long as she worked. His reminder that she was here on trial. She heard his door click shut as she climbed into her bed. A gentle warmth filled her, a warmth of remembering. She'd seen him with his guard down. She'd seen the elusive, gentle Jarrett. The howl of the coyote family came again, fainter now as they ranged away from the ranch, still hunting in the moonlight. Aries smiled to herself. Their cry would never be fearsome to her again. Her last conscious thoughts before she fell asleep was how good it had felt to have someone to run to, someone to comfort and reassure her. She realized that she was doing what everyone else did on the Big Hole Valley Ranch: she was looking to Jarrett for strength and safety.

## Chapter Eleven

Aries was up before anyone that morning. The silence of the house was broken only by the creak of the floor as she walked across the cold linoleum in the chilly kitchen. She had never been the first one to greet a kitchen still gripped by the cold of the fading night. There was always someone before her, getting the fire started, warming the room, making her coffee. She looked around the shadowed room, and was glad she was standing there, shivering, but filled with a peaceful aloneness.

Glancing out of the window, she saw the first streaks of pink and pearl grey start across the sky, as the sun made a valiant effort to banish the night. She heard the crow of a rooster, and she smiled. Morning. She had always loved it, always enjoyed rising early to meet the day, but nothing she had ever experienced had prepared her for this moment, as morning gave birth to the new day on this ranch, in this beautiful valley. She stood at the window a moment, drinking in the beauty just outside her door. The delicate rays of morning caught her face, and made her ivory skin shine. Absently, she brushed her hand down the dress she had on and felt grateful to Mrs. Ellis for helping her choose something practical to wear for everyday chores. The dress was simply cut, a soft grey bodice and skirt, with a scooped neckline edged by a narrow band of lace. It pulled into a V at her waist, emphasizing her trim figure, and fell in folds around her. Plain cut and serviceable it may be, but on her, it was transformed into a gown.

Reluctantly, Aries turned away from the window, leaving the morning sky, and stepped over to the stove. Picking up the cold coffee pot, heavy with last night's remains, she carried it over to the sink. Two galvanized buckets rested on a small table; Aries picked up the dipper hooked over the lip of one. Dipping out enough water to rinse the coffee pot, she realized that while one bucket was full, the other only had a few inches of water left in it. She would need to carry in a bucket from the pump before she would be able to do the dishes after breakfast. Maybe she'd be able to catch Ben and ask him do it before he took off to the barn and his chores. Yesterday, she'd stopped at the pump and had given the long handle attached to the heavy iron spout a few pumps up and down. But no water came out. She wasn't sure how to make that happen; surely someone would show her. She sighed. There was so much to learn. Nothing was easy here. Work and know how seemed to be the key. Still, she wasn't going to let anything stop her from succeeding. She was a fighter, wasn't she?

Aries set the full pot back on the cold range. She dumped out yesterday's grounds, and paused, looking at the empty basket. How much? She measured in what she thought looked the amount of coffee grounds she'd just dumped out. She placed the basket back in the pot, and put the lid on. She'd watched Ted last night, and saw him pull the coffee pot to the back of the stove, when it had started to boil hard enough the lid bubbled up and down. He'd left it there on the cooler part of the stove letting it bubble and gurgle at a slower rate until the coffee was strong enough. She could do that. A sense of satisfaction filled her; she could master this small job.

She stepped back and gave the cold range a baleful look. The fire had to be started. She shivered in the cold and welcomed the thought of the heat the big range would soon generate. Gripping the handle of the specially shaped iron tool resting in the notch of one of the stove lids, she lifted. The lid was heavy and she was afraid she'd drop it as she gingerly sat it back down on the adjacent flat surface of the stove. Then she did the same with the other lid. She peered into the bowels of the stove through the openings where the lids had rested and saw only grey ash, and a few glowing coals, resting on the steel grates. *Now what? Wood. Of course.* Smiling to herself, proud of that small bit of knowledge, she went to the back of the stove where the wood box rested, and picked up two good sized logs of wood. Wedging these down through the two round holes, she piled them one on top of the other, then replaced the stove lids and stepped back, pleased with her efforts. Ted would be surprised. It would be nice to have his coffee ready for him when he came down the stairs and into a cozy warm kitchen instead of a cold, empty one, but it would be even nicer to see the look of surprise on Jarrett's face. She swallowed hard, not liking the realization it was Jarrett she wanted most to see, and to please.

The rooster crowed again. Aries gave into her building desire to step outside and greet the day. Opening the back door, she went out onto the small porch and leaned against the rail. The fresh smell of dew and grass, trees, and damp river carried to her on a morning breeze. She took a deep breath, and closed her eyes with pleasure. Peace, and a sense of belonging filled her. The two part whistle of a bird came from a fence post over by the large corral. The rich bodied melody thrilled her. The yellow breasted bird hopped up the rail, then raised its head and repeated the call. In her trunk was a small book of North American birds, cataloged by the late Mr. John James Audubon. As soon as it arrived, she would find out the name of this sweet-throated bird.

The minutes flew by as Aries absorbed the new smells and sounds of the Big Hole Valley awakening and greeting a new day. The sun was making a valiant effort, but it was only cresting the edge of the tall mountains, shrouded dark in the distance. She stood there until the cool of the morning became uncomfortable. *Tomorrow, I'll bring down a shawl, and I'll have my coffee out here. Just me, and the early morning.* Her feelings were mixed with anticipation of the cup of coffee perking by now on the warm stove, and the desire to stay outside. The waiting warmth of the cheery kitchen and the coffee won out. She pulled the door open and froze there, her hand gripping the knob.

Thick, black smoke poured out from every crack in the kitchen range. It seeped out from under and around the four lids on the top of the stove, from the edges along the sides, from the back, and even from where the ash pan rested in its groove under the grates. But it was the sound of cursing and shouts of anger, more than the smoke, that riveted Aries to her spot.

Jarrett rushed across the room, making his way through the smoke until he reached the side of the stove. Taking hold of the curled metal handle of the damper sticking out of the stovepipe, he gave it a quick turn until it was straight up and down.

"Dad," he roared, "what in the devil's the matter with you? You know better than to start a fire, and not open the damper." His angry words were punctuated by barks of coughing; as he brushed past her and threw open the back door. "Dad!" he yelled. "Where are you? The house is full of smoke, and he's nowhere around," he muttered angrily to himself. "Why does it seem I'm the only one on this ranch with any sense?" He scowled around the room, and saw Aries for the first time, standing to the side of the open door, her eyes wide in her face.

"What are you doing here?" he snapped, glad to have a focus for his anger. Glad to have a reason to ignore the quick burst of pleasure he'd felt seeing her standing there in his kitchen. "And don't you give me any crap about my language. Not one damn word. I suppose you've never heard cussing either? Your dad didn't cuss as well as not drink, I suppose," he said nastily. Jarrett's eyes narrowed, and he dared her to speak, to give him an excuse to vent more of his anger. His eyes were black and snapping; he was a stranger from the gentle man of last night, as he turned from her and grabbed up a dishtowel from the peg above the sink, and began fanning the air with it, twirling it above his head, driving the smoke out the open door. "Well, don't just stand there, help me," he barked.

She blinked her eyes, then came to her senses and grabbing up the other towel began mimicking the angry man.

"What the . . . ?" Ted peered into the room, taking in the smoke hanging heavy in the air, making its way slowly out the open kitchen door. He was bumped to the side by Ben, who stopped in his tracks and stood there watching his angry brother and the petite woman whirling dishtowels at the blackened air.

Then, from the side of Ben's legs, Timmy poked his head through to view the smokey show in the kitchen.

"Son, what happened? I appreciate the effort, but surely you have enough sense to . . ." Ted's comments were cut short by a coughing fit, and Jarrett's menacing look. Ted made his way over to the stove and, lifting the lids, peered inside. He muttered to himself. "Hunks of wood that size, no wonder."

"The size of wood has nothing to do with it," Jarrett said in a deadly cold voice. "You forgot to open the damper." Jarrett's eyes were a dark, stormy blue.

Ted slowly replaced the lids, and looked fully at his son. "Jarrett, I don't plan to stand here taking that tone of voice from one of my sons. Now, I didn't . . ." He stopped the words, chopping off the sentence as he noticed Aries' stricken face, her hands clutching the dishtowel to her mouth. Her eyes were wide as she looked from Ted to the stove and then back to Jarrett's tense body, only inches from her.

"I . . . I . . . I didn't," Ted fumbled, quickly looking for words, "I didn't realize I'd—"

"I did it." The voice rang, stopping Ted from finishing the sentence. Ben came forward and took the dishtowel out of Jarrett's tight grip. "Thank you, brother. It was my fault, not Dad's. I got so anxious for the coffee," he said, glancing toward the pot happily gurgling, sending the rich aroma of fresh brewed coffee to mix with the heavy smell of wood smoke, "I guess I forgot to open the damper. Sorry." He gave an apologetic grin, then walked to the cupboard, brushing past Aries and giving her a conspiratorial wink.

Jarrett's eyes narrowed. He brushed a thick curl from his forehead with the side of his arm. He turned and saw Aries, standing there, her face pale, her eyes too wide.

"You're both lying. Neither one of you . . ."

"No, Mr. McCabe, you're right. Neither one of them were to blame for the smoke in your kitchen. It was me." She took a few steps toward him, and in an unconscious gesture, curled her hands into fists, holding them tightly against her body. She tilted her chin forward, and her small nose tipped up as she looked the angry, formidable man in the face. "It was me that made the fire and didn't open the damper. I didn't even know there was such a thing. It would appear that you may be right in your brilliant deduction that you are the only one on this ranch with any sense. However, it would seem you've neglected to take into account there are two other men on this ranch who not only have an equal amount of sense, they have . . ." she sputtered looking for words, "they have kindness. The milk of human kindness to recognize and allow for error." She stood there, glaring at him, daring him to respond.

"Kindness? I have the right to wake up to some sort of peace and harmony in my own kitchen. Not this." He waved his hand at the disappearing smoke. "You're a menace, lady."

"And you're a bully," she said, her voice cutting through his. "A foul-talking bully. I will make mistakes, Mr. McCabe. But I will try; I will learn." Her words hung in the air, taunting him. The room was silent, broken only by sound of the cupboard door shutting as Ben gently closed it, and of Ted quietly clearing his throat. All eyes were on the two opponents, squared off in the middle of the room.

Jarrett's nostrils flared. A muscle by the side of his eye quivered. He swallowed hard, his jaw clenched as he choked back a response. He held himself taut for a few more moments, then slowly looked away from the spitfire facing him.

"I'll get my breakfast at the bunkhouse," he said tersely to Ted, his voice cold and clipped. Then he commanded, in the same icy voice, "Show her a few things will you?" Without looking at her again, he turned and, grabbing his hat, walked out of the room the door slamming behind him.

No one moved or spoke; then Ted reached to the top of the warming oven where the pot holders rested, and picking one up wrapped it around the handle of the coffee pot. He walked toward the table and stood there waiting with the pot in his hand.

Ben silently carried three cups over to the table and gently sat them down. Without a word, Ted poured the black liquid into the cups. He stopped pouring and leaned forward looking at one of the cups full of coffee. It lay thick and redolent in the heavy mug. His lips twitched and he slowly raised his eyebrows. Ben looked at his father, then stepped forward and looked at the cup. He sucked in the sides of his cheeks as he fought away a grin. Then both men looked at the silent woman still standing there, fists clenched.

Puzzled, she took a few tentative steps toward the table, and stopped. Her eyes filled with tears when she saw the poured cup of coffee.

"The coffee. It's . . . it's too." she stopped, her voice clogged with the tears, threatening to spill from her eyes.

"It's just the way I like it," Ted butted in. "Yep," he said, "Hot, black, and thick." The last word came out strangled as he choked back laughter. "Yes sir, black and thick."

The two men looked at each other, struggling with the effort not to laugh. Aries caught their looks, and pressed both her lips together as she stared at the waiting cups of brew. "Oh Ted, it's terrible isn't it?" She picked up her cup and slowly raised it to her mouth, then, stopping short, opted instead to take a quick smell of the black liquid. "Phew!!" She held the cup away from her nose, at arm's length. "Ugh! It's too strong!" She took a better look at the two men watching her, waiting for her response, fighting to keep from laughing, and all signs of tears left her eyes, replaced by a mischievous twinkle. "It's just right. Yep," she mimicked Ted's voice, "Hot, black, and thick. Jarrett doesn't know what he's missing, does he?" Smiles broke out as they raised their cups in silent salute. Then without drinking one drop of the black liquid, they set them back down on the table and broke into laughter.

## Chapter Twelve

Jarrett stayed clear of the house, and Aries didn't see him until supper that night, which was all right with her. Still, she caught herself looking for him each time the kitchen door opened, or she heard a step on the porch.

Ted had done as Jarrett had ordered and showed Aries a few things. She learned how to prime the pump with water before first pumping the handle up and down. It took both her hands to pull the long handle up and down, and she had to throw the weight of her body into the motion when the icy cold water gushed out the lip of the spout; the handle became even harder to pull down for yet another gush. Then, she lugged the heavy water bucket into the house. Both Ted and Ben had hauled in full buckets before leaving the house, telling her to call them if she needed more. But she hadn't. They had their own work, and they'd given her too much of their time already showing and explaining things to her.

Finally, she'd shooed them both out of the house, assuring them she'd be okay. It was good to be alone in this big, friendly house. She'd looked forward to it all morning. She knew just what she wanted to accomplish, and she didn't need anyone's help. She was going to start in the kitchen, by first washing down the walls, laundering the curtains, and then scrubbing the floor. If she hurried, she could finish before Ted came back to start supper. When he'd offered to grab lunch at the bunkhouse along with Ben and the absent Jarrett, she'd quickly agreed. Timmy followed Ben during the first part of the morning, but then when Ben left the immediate area, Timmy had wandered back to the house, not sure of himself enough to venture too far from Aries without the steadying presence of Ben. He was sitting at the big, round table copying letters Aries had put on a sheet of paper. His small tongue was clenched between his teeth and his face was wrinkled in fierce concentration. Aries smiled, watching him.

Filling a bucket with hot water from the reservoir on the side of the stove, Aries poured in the thick, glutinous soap Ted had gotten for her from a pail in the pantry, and putting her hand into the hot water, churned it into a froth as soap mixed with water. The fumes of the harsh soap made her eyes water, and her hands burn. "There," she muttered, "that ought to cut the grime on these walls." She shook her head at the once-white walls, yellowed with a mixture of smoke and grease, and evidence of years of neglect. Cleaning she knew how to do. Aries smiled as she remembered helping the housekeeper with the spring housecleaning. Still, she sighed, she'd been able to walk away whenever she was tired. Well, she wouldn't be walking away this time; there was no Polly to take over for her and finish the tiresome tasks, while Aries left to do rounds with her father. "Okay, Aries," she chided herself, "standing here fretting about it won't get the job done." She rolled up the sleeves of her dress, lifted the bucket of hot, soapy water, and placed it on the table. Pulling a chair to the nearest wall, she climbed up, reached into the bucket, wrung out the rag, and wiped it across the kitchen ceiling. Instantly a white swathe appeared. There would be no turning back now and she smiled, realizing full well she didn't want stop anyway. This was to be her home, and darned if it wasn't going to be clean.

She was amazed at how quickly the job went. She stopped only long enough to add wood to the range, just the way Ted had showed her, and to fix Timmy some lunch. As the day progressed, the sun, now full in the sky, warmed the kitchen, and Aries opened the windows and let fresh air into the room. Late in the afternoon, she dumped the last bucket of grey, grimy water out the back door, and went out to the clothesline to take down the curtains she'd washed earlier in the kitchen sink. Burying her face in them, she inhaled deeply the fresh scent of the clean mountain air. Now all they needed was ironing. She'd sat at Polly's feet often enough and watched the woman heat the iron on the stove, test it, then press it across the material, making the wrinkles vanish. Polly hadn't trusted Aries enough to correctly judge the temperature of the iron, and she certainly hadn't wanted to take the chance of scorching one of the doctor's white shirts. But Aries knew she could do this. And she did. She hunted in the pantry closet for an ironing board, and not finding one, improvised by padding the table with thick towels. She knew there had to be one somewhere. She'd ask Ben or Ted. Throughout the day, she'd come across remnants of a woman's touch and blessed Ted for not getting rid of Sarah's things. There were drawers still full of neatly folded tablecloths and linens. It was as if Sarah had stepped out of the house and Aries had stepped in.

Aries was able to ignore the dull ache in the lower part of her back. It was a tiredness fully compensated for by the feeling of satisfaction as she glanced around the room, so changed from earlier this morning.

She picked up the first heavy iron and putting her finger to her mouth, moistened it, then quickly touched the bottom of the iron. The drop of moisture sizzled and Aries recognized the same sound made by Polly's iron and knew the temperature was right. Still, she applied the tip of the iron to a corner of the curtain where if it were too hot and scorched, it wouldn't show. The curtains were resting in a basket where earlier she'd sprinkled them so they'd be damp and ready to iron. She was right. The iron was the perfect temperature. She pulled the second iron resting on the stove to the cooler part of the range, and proceeded to iron the curtains using first one iron until it cooled, and then the other. The curtains came to life in her hands, and when she finished and hung them back up, they looked proud and clean, without one wrinkle. Glancing out the sparkly clean window, she saw that dusk was beginning to fall. Ted would be coming to the house to start supper. Opening the back door, Aries called to Timmy and told him to come in and wash up so the men could have the sink when they arrived. She felt a pang of guilt when she saw her little brother leaning forlornly over the rails of a pen talking to the small calf inside. She hadn't paid much attention to him, leaving him to entertain himself, and realized that Timmy was doing here what he'd done back home. Staying out of the way and visible sight of adults, a little ghost of a person rarely spoken to or thought about by anyone else but her. She shook her head. Maybe Jarrett was right; Timmy needed jobs to do too. Perhaps tonight, she would ask him what Timmy could help with, that is, if Jarrett was at all approachable.

She pulled the perking coffee pot to the back of the stove and knew this pot of coffee would be a much better one than the pot of syrup she'd made that morning. Morning. It seemed like she'd been in this room all her life. Brushing her hair back from her face with a weary hand, she walked to the door and paused there, taking just one more look at a job well done. The kitchen shone with her effort. There wasn't a speck of dust anywhere; windows were clear, the table held a red checkered tablecloth, and a vase of flowers sat in the middle. Walls and ceilings were clean. A rag rug she'd found on a shelf in a closet, rested in front of the sink. Even the range had been attacked, and it too was dust free and ready for someone to cook a meal on its clean surface. Aries wished it could be her, but knew better than to push her luck. Soon. She left the room with a pan of hot water in her hands and slowly climbed the stairs to her room. She intended to take a quick cat bath, change her clothes, and be ready to help Ted with supper. She surprised herself with the thought that she was looking forward to seeing the men come home. It was the perfect ending to a perfect day. She didn't acknowledge the thought, though, that the man she looked the most forward to seeing, was the one who had left the house in anger with harsh words this morning.

Ted wasn't the first one to come home. It was Jarrett. He'd purposely stayed away from the house all day and had angrily jerked his thoughts back when they wandered to the woman who was the object of his wrath. He felt ashamed by his overreaction. It seemed that lately he was angry more often than he wasn't. He opened the kitchen door with trepidation and immediately stepped back. The room was as different as night and day from the one he'd left this morning. It was more than a room—it was the kitchen of old filled with love and a gentle touch. He closed the door softly behind him and stood there, drinking in the room and the memories that filled him with both hurt and happiness. He hung his hat on the peg, and stepped over to the range where the teakettle whistled softly. Pouring water into the basin in the sink, he rolled the sleeves of his shirt up his arms and proceeded to wash off the day's grime. Once finished, he glanced down at the front of his shirt. Might not hurt to change for supper. It was something they all used to do, but they were out of the habit these days. There had been no reason, the three of them didn't care what the other looked like. Come to think of it, they'd stopped caring about a lot of things. He certainly had. He went up the stairs and passed the closed door to Aries' room. The faint sound of a woman singing stopped him in his tracks and he stood, rooted outside her door. She was humming and singing a melody he had heard before. He couldn't quite catch the words, but her voice was sweet. Not like the voice she'd used that morning. His eyes crinkled, as smiling to himself, he clearly recalled her standing in the smokey kitchen, giving back to him as good as he gave to her. He shook his head at the recollection. She was a worthy opponent, he thought. She was probably the prettiest person to stand up to him in a long, long time. He went into his room and, as he unbuttoned his shirt, realized he was looking forward to supper and the evening tonight in a way that had nothing to do with simply ending another, hard day.

When Jarrett entered the room, Ted was standing at the range, stirring a pan of potatoes and onions. Ben was sitting at the kitchen table. His eyes went immediately to the woman bending over the kitchen table setting down a platter of steak. She'd changed her dress from this morning, to a bright gold and brown calico; she had tied back her hair with a ribbon that matched her silky, gold curls. Soft tendrils had pulled free and curled gently around her face. She was smiling at something Ben had said, and Jarrett felt a pang of envy at the easy, teasing way his brother had with her. She glanced up, and caught his eye on her. Still smiling, she carefully sat the platter down, then went back to the stove, picking up a bowl for the potatoes. Ted and Ben both glanced up, sensing his presence, and all talk stopped as they stared at the tall, dark man hovering inside the kitchen door.

"Darn, son, you clean up right nice," Ted said. "Didn't know we was changing for supper now," he said nodding at Jarrett's fresh shirt.

"Yeah," Ben chimed in enjoying his brother in a rare moment of loss. "You do clean up nice. What's the occasion?"

Jarrett started to growl a response when he was stopped.

"Hello, Jarrett," Aries said softly, "Please sit down. Supper's almost ready. And," she looked at the two grinning men, her voice lightly admonishing, "you two probably didn't have time to change before supper since you've been busy helping me. I'm sorry I monopolized your time, but I imagine tomorrow night will be different. I'm learning quickly, and I'm sure I'll be able to give you a few minutes to clean up." She smiled sweetly at them, then turned away as their faces fell and they cleared their throats and muttered, "Sure. Yeah, needed a little more time."

Jarrett's lips quirked as he walked around the table and pulled out Aries chair. It surely did feel good having her champion him. He didn't need it, of course, but still . . .

Aries sat down, and as Jarrett leaned forward, he caught the scent of her hair, a smell of flowers, a delicate scent of springtime. Lilacs. He stood behind her longer than necessary, then turned and sat back down at his seat.

Timmy was perched on his seat of catalogs, and, typically, had his eyes downcast. Jarrett's brow wrinkled. There was something about him that reminded Jarrett . . . of what? Then it came to him. He'd hired a cowhand a few years back, and the man had boasted how good he was with horses. Certainly, his horse was well-trained and responded quickly to his every command. There'd been some talk around the bunkhouse, but Jarrett had chalked it up to the other cowboy's suspicion of a new man, and maybe just a little jealousy of his abilities. Then, one morning he'd came out of the barn unexpectedly, and saw the cowhand in the corral with his horse. The horse shied when the man had started to mount it, and instantly he'd delivered a blow to the horse's ribs with the toe of his boot, causing the horse to whinny in pain; Jarrett heard the sound of the wind knocked out from the trembling animal. The animal then stood, docile and broken, his head down as the arrogant man mounted him. Jarrett remembered his red sear of anger as he crossed the yard and pulled the surprised man off the back of the horse. He'd flung him to the ground, and with the toe of his boot, delivered a swift kick to his ribs. Then he asked him how he liked having done to him what he'd just done to a helpless animal. Jarrett shook his head at the memory, and looked again at the little boy. Timmy had the same defeated look as that mare. He glanced over at Aries, and saw her smile tenderly at Timmy. She patted his shoulder and whispered a few words to him that brought a smile to his face. Aries was Timmy's champion, his rescuer, just as Jarrett had been the horse's that morning. It had to have been someone else in the boy's life, and he intended to find out who. Then he caught himself. *Why? Why should he care?* They meant nothing to him. Sure the house, well at least the kitchen, looked a damned sight better. And sure, the talk and atmosphere around the table seemed more relaxed and happier, but she was paid to work, just like any other hired hand. *Don't make too much of it*, he cautioned himself. *Keep out of it, don't get involved.* He helped himself to several pieces of steak, and concentrated on his meal.

"Uh, Mr. McCabe." There was no answer. "Mr. McCabe," Aries tried again. Jarrett glanced up reacting to the stillness of the others at the table, and saw their eyes on him.

"Mr. McCabe," she said again looking at him, "I was wondering. Earlier you had mentioned some chores that Timmy might do." At these words, the little boy looked at her in fear and astonishment.

"Yeah," he said slowly.

"Well, would you mind letting us know what they might be, and we'll see that they get done. Timmy has free time, perhaps too much free time, and he needs to help out the same as we all do, so I was wondering . . ." her voice stopped as she looked at the expression on Jarrett's face.

"Yes," he prompted enjoying her discomfort.

"I, that is, you said he had to work the same as . . ."

"Yes, and if I remember right, you set me straight on that issue, didn't you?" he prodded.

She took a deep breath, "Well, yes, I did. I might have been a little too quick to respond, perhaps I jumped to conclusions, Mr. McCabe. And while I still believe there needs to be a balance of work and play, I noticed today that Timmy seems at a loss." She met the piercing blue eyes of the man and realized he wasn't going to cut her any slack. His jaw was clenched, but she thought she could detect a hint of a smile playing around the corner of his mouth. He was enjoying this, enjoying her discomfort at having to admit she was partially wrong. He was arrogantly handsome sitting there, the long fingers of his hand curled around the knife, his fork poised over the steak. His broad shoulders curved forward and the dark chambray material pulled across the muscles of his back. He slowly laid his knife down, and looked over at Ben.

"Show Timmy how to care for the calf you got penned up, the one with scours. It needs some attention and we sure don't have time to give it. It'll probably die anyway, but maybe with him feeding it small amounts of milk throughout the day, it'll get stronger and make it." He looked back at Aries, and felt himself warmed by the smile on her face. Without realizing it, he smiled back at her, softening the harsh lines on his face, showing her another glimpse of the gentle man he hid so carefully. "Timmy," he addressed the little boy staring at him. "We got a bucket with a nipple rigged up on it. Think you can get that calf to drink?"

Timmy nodded slowly as if he couldn't believe his luck. He'd been hanging around the sickly calf all day, now he was going to be the one to feed and care for him.

"You see how his sides are sunk in?" Jarrett asked him gruffly. Timmy nodded. "Well, that's because he's got scours. His mama has too rich uh milk, and he's ate too much. Calves get that sometimes. Makes them sick, and they can die. Your job will be to see that he only eats a little at a time. He's a pig, and he'll want more. You can't be softhearted and give it to him no matter how much he begs. Understand?" He waited for Timmy's wide-eyed nod. "And I expect his pen to be kept clean. Scours is messy, you'll see what I mean. He'll mess on himself and sure as hel . . . heck," he corrected himself, "he'll make a mess of the pen. There's fresh straw, Ben'll show you. This is a big job, and I expect you to handle it."

"Yes sir," Timmy whispered. Then in the lull came his quiet voice, "Thank you, sir."

Jarrett looked sharply at the little boy, then turned quickly away, startled by the emotions pouring through him. He heard his dad cough, and looked up and caught Aries' eye. His body filled with a warmth reaching the cold, empty spots, and he looked away, not wanting her to see.

The next morning, Aries wasn't the first one up. When she went outside for her first breath of morning, she saw Timmy down by the calf's pen. She was filled with tears and gratitude for Jarrett's wisdom in selecting just the right job for Timmy. Aries didn't know how Jarrett knew the little boy needed something to care for, something to be responsible for, something that needed him as much as he needed it. She realized, then, that Jarrett was a complex man. "But," she said to herself as she went back inside to check on the fire she'd started in the kitchen range, "he's one worth getting to know, and I intend to do just that."

Breakfast was a much different affair than yesterday. Jarrett stayed for the entire meal; in fact, it seemed to Aries he was reluctant to leave the table, lingering for another cup of coffee.

"Mr. McCabe," she said, picking up the plates and moving toward the sink, "is there anything in the house I shouldn't bother?" He raised his head and frowned. "I mean, is there any room that's off limits, or supplies I shouldn't use? I know you've hired me as your housekeeper, but it would help if I know if there are boundaries."

"No." His response was quick and to the point. "The house is yours to care for as you see fit. As for supplies, I think you'll find the pantry and cellars fully stocked. Use whatever you want. If there's something you need, something else you want to cook with," he grinned at her, "that is, when you get that magic trunk and learn how to cook, just start a list and Ben or I will pick it up in Wise River." He got up from his seat and, taking down his hat, started out the door.

Aries followed him out onto the porch. "Mr. McCabe," she started, reaching out and touching the hard muscles of his upper arm. He stopped short. Her fingers, though light, seemed to burn through his shirt, searing his skin. He caught his breath at her touch. Turning around, he came face to face with her blue eyes looking directly at him and into him at once.

"Yes," he responded, low and hesitant. He held his arm stiff, not wanting Aries to release him, yet very much aware that his heart had sped up and his breathing labored.

She glanced toward the pen and the boy reaching up on tip

toes to open the gate to the calf within. Then, she looked back at Jarrett, only to find herself caught in the intensity of his look. She licked her lips, and his eyes followed the movement of her tongue across their soft fullness. "Thank you. For Timmy's job, for understanding." She lowered her hand, leaving his arm cold. Then she quickly stepped back inside the house.

He expelled the breath he'd been holding, and stood there staring at the closed door. Absently, he put his hand up to the arm she'd touched, and a flicker of pleasure crossed his face as he took the porch steps two at a time and walked across the yard to the barn.

Aries stopped midmorning from the task she'd set out for herself this day. She'd decided to systematically go through each room of the big house, cleaning it much the same way she'd done the kitchen, until the entire house sparkled. Today, though, there was something else she was going to do. She was going to bake a double batch of oatmeal raisin cookies. She'd checked yesterday, and everything she needed was on the shelves of the pantry. Ted had shown her how to keep the range at a constant temperature by feeding only a certain amount of wood into it. It was mid-morning, and a perfect time to start baking before the sun made the kitchen too warm.

Aries pulled on an apron she'd found folded up in one of the kitchen drawers; then, she raised up on her toes to pull down a crockery bowl, and went into the pantry to gather the rest of the ingredients. She knew the recipe by heart. Oatmeal raisin and peanut butter. Her mouth watered at the thoughts of sitting down at the table with a cup of coffee and several fat cookies for dunking. That's what she'd do just as soon as a pan came out of the oven.

Humming to herself, she put the correct amount of ingredients into the bowl and folded in the raisins. Then, taking the heavy cookie sheet, she smeared a thin coating of lard onto it. Stealing a bite of the cookie dough, she dropped it by table-spoons onto the sheet. Four across, and five down, twenty at a time. She filled the pan, and put it on the top rack of the hot oven, then busied herself with washing up the dishes.

She was flooded with happiness as she bent over the open oven door and took out the golden brown cookies she'd put in only minutes ago. The temperature was just right, they were perfect. She set them on a piece of thick butcher block to cool.

Minutes later, she again opened the oven door and bent over to take a quick peek, checking to see if that tray was ready. Intent on her task, she didn't hear the kitchen door open behind her. Jarrett stood there, eyes wide and dark as he absorbed the warmth of the kitchen filled with the spicy scent of fresh baked cookies, sunshine filtering through the clean windows, and Aries as she peered into the oven. An over-whelming desire filled him; he wanted to cross the room and wrap his arms around that small waist. He muttered to him-self. "What was the matter with him?" Frowning in an effort to banish the astonishing thought, he cleared his throat. The sound had its desired effect, and Aries jumped, the oven door dropping with a clattering bang.

"Easy," he crossed the room, and grabbing the pot holder from her hand, closed the door. "Didn't mean to startle you. I just came in to . . ." He cut the sentence short. His eyes widened as he took a deep breath of the enticing smell com-ing from the oven, "Tell me quick. Those aren't oatmeal raisin are they? Honest to goodness oatmeal raisin cookies?"

She smiled at the look on his face. "Mmm, hmm," she grinned at him. "I take it you like them, Mr. McCabe?"

"Oh yes," he said reverently. "I can't tell you the last time I had fresh baked cookies out of that oven." He stopped and a flash of hurt crossed his face. He knew exactly the last time.

After all these years, it still caught him unaware. Aries saw him pause, and surprisingly felt his pain.

"If you have time, Mr. McCabe, perhaps you'd like to join me in a cup of coffee and a couple of those cookies. They're still warm," she added tempting him, hoping against hope he'd join her. Not wanting to question why it was so important to her, she knew that having him beside her in this kitchen seemed right, and she didn't want him to leave.

He hesitated. A roguish grin pulled at his mouth, "Only a couple, Aries? Make it more like half a dozen, and you've got yourself a deal." His eyes twinkled as he lowered himself with a supple movement onto the chair he'd just pulled out. He looked up at her expectantly.

She chuckled, then said softly, "Deal." Moving quickly around the kitchen, that felt more like hers every minute, she set out coffee cups, filled them, then took the wide spatula and scooped several of the warm cookies onto a plate and set it in the middle of the table. The heat from the oven made her face flush and it glowed with a gentle beauty. She seemed unaware of the picture she made as she lowered herself to her chair, and took one of the cookies. Biting into it, she glanced up and found Jarrett watching her, his eyes a dark blueness the depth of a well. A small pulse beat in her throat, and the tension grew between them. Needing to stop whatever it was that was threatening to engulf him, Jarrett reached for one of the cookies. He took a big bite, and his eyes widened in surprise.

"Darn, woman! I thought you couldn't cook?" Not waiting for an answer, he finished off the cookie in one more bite, and reached for another. "These are delicious," he muttered around the chunks of cookie filling his mouth. Aries forgot hers as she watched the man across from her make cookie after cookie disappear, with no more than two bites each. Gone was the formidable, aloof man, and in his place was a stranger ruggedly good-looking and boyish in his pleasure. The sight made her heart stop. He caught her looking at him and smiled, pushing the near empty plate toward her.

"Here, forgot my manners there. Have another one."

"One, Mr. McCabe?" she laughed

"Well, maybe two, that is," and he looked worriedly at the oven, "if there's more where those came from."

"There are," she chuckled. "I made a double batch." She went over to the oven and took out the ready tray. She put them down to cool, and then picked up an empty tray and began to drop spoonfuls of dough on it.

"Here," he said, taking the spoon from her hands. "You eat, and I'll do this pan."

Her eyes met his, "Okay," she said, and gratefully lowered herself onto the chair, knowing that her legs felt too weak to support her. *This is crazy*, she thought, but pleasure filled her as she watched him alternate spoonfuls of the thick dough with licks of his fingers.

Finished with that pan, he sat back down across from her. The silence between them was easy and both felt comfortable sitting there enjoying the moment without the necessity to talk.

Once, in an automatic response, he leaned forward, and brushed a crumb from her mouth, his fingers light as they danced across her face. He pulled his hand back as though surprised at his action, and took a quick sip of coffee. He leaned back in his chair, and watched her take the last pan of cookies out of the oven. She sat back down, and brushed a golden whisp of hair back from her face.

"Aries," he said.

"Yes," she looked up at him.

"Tell me about Timmy."

"Timmy?" she said, her eyes shifting away from his.

"Yes. There's something wrong. He's spooked." Jarrett's words hung in the air. "He's like a horse that's never known a gentle hand. I've seen you with him; that hand's not yours."

Aries didn't answer right away, when she spoke, her voice seemed to come from afar. "My father was a hard man, Mr. McCabe. You might say unforgiving. He loved two things in his life, my mother and his medicine. I never really knew which one he loved most, but I do believe it was my mother. They were surprised when they found out she was carrying Timmy. They hadn't expected another child." She lowered her voice. "I don't believe they wanted another child. I was fitting in nicely to my father's plan of having someone follow in his footsteps. In many ways, I was the son he didn't have." She raised her eyes to meet his. "I loved my father, Mr. McCabe. I loved him dearly. When he died, I lost something precious. His death left a terrible emptiness. But while I loved him, I wasn't blind to his imperfections. My father had quite a temper. Failing Dr. Burnett was something you didn't want to do. Many a green medical student found that out." She stopped talking, and seemed to be gathering herself. Jarrett sat there, still and silent, offering her his strength.

"Timmy came breech." She waited, then offered as explanation, "He came feet first. It was a difficult birth not only because of his position in the birth canal, but because of my mother's age. My father, with all his medical knowledge couldn't save her. She died in his arms." Aries gave a deep sigh and Jarrett knew she was somewhere else, reliving the painful memory. He regretted asking, putting her through this.

"My father took one look at the baby that had taken his beloved wife's life and disliked him from that moment on. He could hardly bear to be in the same room with Timmy. I knew this, and made it my mission to keep Timmy out of my father's sight as much as possible. Father rarely acknowledged him, and as Timmy grew older, it seemed to irritate my father even more that he was alive and my mother was not. Ours was a big house, Mr. McCabe, but little boys have a way of getting underfoot." She swallowed hard and her voice dropped even lower. "Timmy was punished for the slightest infraction of the multitude of rules my father imposed on him. My father never raised a hand to him, he didn't have to. He did his punishing with his harsh voice, and his hateful, mean words. If I interfered too much, it only made matters worse and Timmy was berated even more. He broke Timmy's spirit by his continual fault-finding until Timmy finally learned to avoid him, and to cower. I can't begin to tell you the hours that little boy spent alone in his room, his only sanctuary from our father. That's why," and she raised her eyes to his, "I can't let anyone do that to him again. I miss my father—yes, I miss him badly, but I don't miss what he was capable of doing. I don't miss the man that let his loss change him into a rigid, angry man. He lost more than my mother that day; he lost his capacity to live and to love. He fed off of anger and a willingness to blame anyone, even a small boy for something only God could understand." She shook her head, and pulled her lip between her teeth. Then she got up and started cleaning up the clutter in the kitchen.

Jarrett slowly rose to his feet knowing the story could be his; he was only too aware of that. He moved to the door, pausing with his hand on the knob. He looked back, then closed it gently behind him. Standing at the top of the steps, he glanced around the yard. Then, with a purposeful stride, he walked toward the calf pen and the little boy standing there, hands in his pocket, staring quietly at the small calf. He watched Timmy turn around, and saw the look of fear cross his face as he realized Jarrett was coming closer.

"Timmy," Jarrett called.

"Yes sir?" the response was hushed, barely reaching Jarrett's ears.

"How would you like to ride with me out to check the creek? It was close to running over its banks the other day, and I want to make sure the channel I dug is doing its job."

"Ride, sir?" The little boy asked puzzled.

"Yep. With me. Buck's big and broad, plenty able to carry two of us. What do you say?"

A quick nod of his head was Jarrett's answer as he looked into a pair of eyes wide with disbelief at his good fortune. Jarrett felt a knot in his throat as he ruffled the sun warmed head of the small boy.

"Okay. Run back to the house and tell your sister where you're going. Oh, and Timmy," he called after the boy wasting no time running to the house, "tell her Jarrett said to send a few of those cookies along. No telling how long we'll be." Timmy flashed him a wide grin, and ran as fast as his small legs would carry him.

Jarrett walked to the barn and heard the kitchen screen door slam and Timmy call out, "Aries, Aries, Jarrett says I can go with him. On his horse. Cept we need cookies, Aries. Lots for both Jarrett and me. Hurry, Aries, hurry!"

## Chapter Thirteen

Over the next few days, Jarrett acquired a shadow. Wherever he was, around the barn, the corrals, or the house, a small boy walked by his side. Timmy's chair was somehow closer to Jarrett's. Jarrett, not Aries, was the one that dished up Timmy's food, cut his meat, and encouraged him to eat more. And when the catalogs were replaced by a cleverly made small chair that fit perfectly on the seat of the big one, it was Jarrett who placed it there with Timmy stating proudly that he and Jarrett had made it. And if most of Timmy's responses were prefaced by a quick look at Jarrett for direction, no one seemed to mind. In fact, there were many smiles and knowing looks passed over the heads of the boy and man.

And one night, at the supper table, when Timmy softly corrected Aries, saying that Timmy was a baby name, and that he wanted her to call him Tim, like Jarrett did, she only smiled and said she completely agreed, and that it would be Tim from now on, unless, of course, she forgot.

It was one of those late spring days when the sun was warm with mid-morning brightness, and the sounds of birds calling

143

to each other from their nests floated up from the trees along the river. Aries heard the sound of galloping horses. She wouldn't have paid any attention if she hadn't heard a strange voice call out.

"Hello. Anyone around?"

Aries opened the screen door and stood on the porch, letting her eyes adjust to the bright sunlight, as she peered at the two riders reining in, in front of the house.

"Morning, ma'am, Miss Aries." A tall, lean man spoke from the back of a long-legged fidgety horse.

"Aries," the woman next to him called out. "You're Aries. I barely can remember. I was so out of it—but I told Whip here I'd know you anywhere. I just knew I would."

"Whip?" Then Aries remembered. Was it only two weeks ago she'd arrived at Wise River? It seemed longer. This ranch was so much like home. "Whip and Callie," she called out, a smile on her face. She quickly walked across the porch and down the steps to the two people sitting side by side on two, nervously pawing horses.

She walked on out into the yard. "My gosh, it's . . . well, it's a surprise to see you here. I . . ."

She was stopped from saying anything else by the appearance of a scowling Jarrett followed by Timmy, coming from the corral behind the house. All three pairs of eyes turned to the imposing figure striding toward them, his body rigid, every muscle controlled. He hand reached down and touched the boy on the shoulder, slowing him, until he stood protectively behind the man. He moved lithely without saying a word and stood by Aries' side. Then, and only then, did he acknowledge the man in front of him.

"Whip." His voice was cold, unwelcoming.

Aries looked at him, puzzled by his stiff, unyielding manner.

"Jarrett," Whip replied, his long fingers brushing the brim of his hat, as he nodded his head, "This here's Callie."

Jarrett's eyes didn't leave the man. "Ma'am."

The silence grew and Aries seemed at a loss at how to break the tension growing in the summer day.

Whip cleared his throat. "We came to see Miss Aries." The explanation fell heavy into the air.

"Aries?" Jarrett's voice rang out in surprise. "Aries?" Then he shifted his eyes slightly from the man to take in the woman standing beside him. His brow wrinkled in puzzlement at seeing Aries smile in acknowledgment.

"How do you know . . . ?"

"That Timmy?" Whip asked as he leaned forward over his horse's neck. "How you doing, Timmy?"

"Fine, Mr. Whip. Jarrett and me been looking for a horse for me cause Jarrett says I'm big enough and he's . . ."

"Tim," the word fell and immediately the little boy stopped talking, quieted by the reproof in Jarrett's voice.

Whip didn't seemed surprised by Jarrett's cold welcome. Instead, he acted as though he expected nothing else. His eyes narrowed; then, he turned to the woman on the horse. She was silent, her eyes downcast, and some of the natural effusiveness she'd previously shown in greeting Aries was gone. She looked up at Whip, and he gave her a small smile of encouragement.

Watching them, Aries felt herself becoming angry at Jarrett's superior manner. She wasn't about to stand there and let him treat these two people as if they were less than he was. Of course, one was a gambler with a reputation, and one a . . . a dance hall girl, but that was no excuse for rudeness. She was about to speak when she caught a look pass between Whip and Jarrett. It was one of understanding. Not only understanding, but acceptance on both men's part. Whip respected Jarrett, and his reluctance to have a known gambler on his front doorstep. All things considered, Jarrett was handling the situation better than most men would have.

"What can we do for you, Whip? I know it's not social," Jarrett said.

"You're right. It's not. We're here to see the doc."

"Doc?" You're here to see the doc?" Jarrett repeated dumbfounded.

"That's right. Callie shoulda had those stitches taken out a few days ago. But," and he swallowed hard, "I tried. I hurt her some, and I . . . I just couldn't do it." He ran out of words.

"Me and Brett are on our way to Butte, and then maybe on to Billings, Mr. McCabe," Callie broke in. She reached out, and with a shy smile touched the arm of the tense man next to her, his gaze fixed on Jarrett's face. "He . . . he's taking me with him. He says its time we both move on, make a fresh start."

"You don't owe him no explanation, Callie," he said quietly to her. "What we do is our own business, no one else's." Then he looked back up at Jarrett. "We won't be bothering you long, Jarrett. Like I said, we're just here to see the doc. The stitches need to come out, and I'd appreciate it being looked at. Looks like it's healing all right to me, but I sure ain't no doctor."

"Neither are we," Jarrett's response was swift in coming, his brows furrowed with perplexion. *Was the man out of his mind?*

At those words, Whip's eyes shifted to Aries, standing there quietly, and immediately, he sized up the situation. She hadn't told Jarrett. Whip looked at her, then nodded an apology for what he had unknowingly thrust upon her. He drew the reins tighter in his hand, and started to turn his horse around.

"Wait." Aries called out. "Please, Mr. Whip. Of course I'll

look at Callie's arm. You're right, those stitches do need to come out. In fact, they should have a few days ago. I only hope they aren't imbedded. Callie," she smiled, "if you'll get down and sit here on the porch, I'll get my bag and we'll get this job done quickly. Mr. McCabe," she turned to him, a pair of steely blue eyes looking at her as if he was seeing a two-headed monster instead of the woman he'd barely come to know, "would you mind getting me a basin of hot water. If you'll set it down on the table there, I'd appreciate it." She gave the order in a self-confident manner. Gone was the Aries unsure of her role as his housekeeper, and in her stead was a confident, self-assured . . . doctor?

She nodded to the small table between the two rockers. Then she brushed by the shocked, unspeaking man and went quickly into the house.

The quiet was broken by the sound of her feet running up the stairs to her room. The three people stared at each other, not knowing what to say or to do. Whip couldn't help but take a vicarious pleasure in the gamete of emotions running across Jarrett's face as he turned from looking at the screen door closing behind Aries and back to the pair on the horses.

"Tim," Aries's voice rang out from the upstairs window, "get a white tablecloth from the credenza in the dining room and spread it over the table. "Hurry!" she called.

Whip swung down from his horse, then reached up, and with love and gentleness, took the watching woman by the waist and lifted her to the ground. He dropped the reins and both horses stood still where they were. Taking Callie's arm, he walked past Jarrett, and seated her in the rocker. Then he looked up.

"She'll be wanting the water, I expect."

Jarrett scowled and hesitated, as though he wasn't about to respond. He turned on his heel and followed Tim into the house. "Doctor?" he muttered under his breath. "What the heck?"

Whip turned to Callie, and an evil grin spread across his face. This had to be the first time someone had taken Jarrett by surprise. And a mere slip of a woman at that. Darn but this would be something to enjoy later on. *Not now. Now, the only important issue was getting those stitches out, and having the doc take a look at her wounds.*

"Whip?" Callie whispered.

"It's okay, honey. He may not like it, but looks like he's taken orders from her all right. I'll bet there'll be some lively conversation in this house tonight. Yep," he said, as he scraped a sulphur match down the leg of his pants, and lit a thin cheroot. He leaned insolently against the wood railing, his eyes on the screen door. "Real lively conversation."

Aries took the tablecloth from Timmy's hand and spread it over the table. Smiling reassuringly at Callie, she took instruments she would need out of her father's bag. When the screen door slammed, she looked up and motioned for Jarrett to place the basin on the table. One by one, Aries placed the instruments in the boiling water. She hadn't been able to look at him, fearing what she would see, and knowing there was bound to be a time of reckoning and explanation later. Jarrett turned his back on her, walked over to the opposite side of the porch, and leaned against the rail. He put some distance between the procedure, but remained close enough to let his presence be known. It was obvious to all, he was tensely watching over what was his, and that seemed to now include Aries and Timmy.

"This looks good, Callie. You've kept it real clean, and it's healing nicely," Aries said reassuringly as she unwrapped the bandage from the arm.

"It's Brett, doctor. He's the one been smearing on that

medicine you left and wrapping it up every day. He won't let me do nothing that might get it dirty either. He's," and her voice lowered in awe, "he's been taking real good care of me. Him and me, uh, well, he's taking me with him. I ain't gonna have to work as a dancer."

The rest of the sentence was muffled by a cough from Whip, as the man grinned, and looked over at Jarrett. Jarrett's only response was a flicker of muscle at the side of his eyes. His entire attention was riveted on Aries and her sure hands. She laid the bandage to the side, exposing a track of stitches. His face was closed, with a familiar remoteness, allowing no one access to the thoughts or questions whirling inside of him. He saw Aries as a stranger, probing the stitched arm. She was a very knowledgeable stranger.

Gingerly, Aries reached into the pan of hot water, and took out a pair of small scissors, the ends curved and sharp. "I'm just going to cut each thread, Callie, then we'll pull them out. Looks like a couple have grown into the skin. I'll try to be as gentle as possible." Callie glanced fearfully up, her eyes searching out the man leaned against the railing. Without a word, he ground the cheroot beneath his heel, and stepped over to the side of the girl. Gently he laid his hand on her shoulder.

"They many like that, Doc?"

"A few," came Aries terse reply. "We've done worse, Mr. Whip. I'm sure we can take these stitches out, don't you?" She smiled at the man as both remembered the day they cared for a bleeding and badly hurt Callie.

Jarrett saw the play between the two of them and a surprising jolt of jealousy grabbed him. He resented Aries and Whip sharing something he knew nothing about. He realized he resented her smile.

Whip nodded, then sucked in his breath as Aries deftly

placed the scissor tip under one of the threads and with a snip, cut the stitch in two. No one moved or spoke during the next half hour as Aries moved from one stitch to another, snipping then taking tweezers, pulling the thread out of the skin, leaving behind a puckered, but closed wound. Several times, while taking out the deeper, imbedded ones, Callie caught her breath, emitting a low moan. Whip tightened his grasp on her arm. Jarrett shifted uncomfortably. Tim wandered away from the scene; it was nothing new to him. He'd known nothing else during his life. Finally, Aries straightened up, and placed the scissors and tweezers for the last time in the basin of water.

"Done," she smiled the word at the two of them. "I'm going to mix up an antiseptic, and instruct you in applying it."

She took a mortar out of the bag, then proceeded to gently rub one ounce of tincture of calendula, and one ounce of pulverized boracic acid thoroughly into the mortar. When satisfied, she held it out to Whip. "Mr. Whip, could you strike one of your Lucifers and place the flame for a few minutes on the bottom of this mortar. We need to heat it gently."

He took the mortar from her, and gingerly held it over the lit match. Aries felt the bowl, and when the temperature was correct, she took it and again rubbed the mixture with a measured amount of pulverized goldenseal.

Jarrett stepped forward during this process, and stood only inches away from the table and the woman mixing the preparation. Here was a woman who couldn't cope with frying potatoes and was in awe of Ted's ability to mix up a pan of baking powder biscuits, but thought nothing of a preparation of this nature? A mixture of pride and awe came over him, and he promised himself he'd have a few answers before the day was over. Miss Aries Burnett had some explaining to do.

"This may be dusted directly into the wounded area. There

should be no affects other than," and she turned to Callie, "a scar, Callie. I would advise you not expose it to the direct sunlight, but other than that, you're as fine as you were before this happened." She turned back to the task of cleaning up, placing things back into the leather bag.

Whip bent down to Callie's ear, whispered something, then straightened up and walked across the porch to the horses. From a large reticule tied on the back of Callie's horse, he reached inside and scooped something out. With a furtive movement, he placed the bundle under his vest and slowly mounted the steps, stopping in front of Aries.

In one fluid movement, Jarrett stepped between him and the startled woman.

"It's okay, Jarrett," Whip growled "We . . ." Whip glanced around Jarrett at Callie.

"Brett and I have something for the doctor, Mr. McCabe. We owe her so much. I owe her my life," Callie gulped, and gathering her courage went on, "You see, she took care of me when no one . . . no one else would. It didn't matter to her who I was, or where I was. She fixed me up fine, and I'll never forget it. Will we, Brett?" She looked up at Whip and he nodded his head in agreement.

"Callie, you don't owe me anything. I'm a doctor. I only did what any doctor would do." Aries said.

"No, Miss Aries, that ain't quite true, and you know it. If you don't, Jarrett does." Whip said quietly. "You came into a saloon and gave help to Callie. I owe you for that. If you ever need me, for anything," and he narrowed his eyes at Jarrett, "anything, send word to me by Mae, and I'll come. That's a promise. But," and he pulled his hand from in under his vest, "for now, we'd like you to have this little guy." He held up a small ball of fur, its eyes squinted shut in the bright sun. A pink tip of tongue slipped out from between two tiny black lips, and then it squirmed and yawned in protest at being taken from its snug bed. Black and brown fur covered the small pup in a thick coat. There was a strip of white, making a soft collar around his small neck, and another white strip banded a wet, quivering nose. One of his front paws was brown, and the other was black. The tip of his tail also was black as though it had been dipped into an ink well. He opened his eyes, whimpered, and cocked both ears forward.

"Oooh," Aries breathed gently, she reached for the bundle in Whip's outstretched hands. "I've never had . . . my father wouldn't allow . . ." She stopped and raised the pup to her face. At that moment, the pup sealed his bond with Aries. His tiny, pink tongue flicked forward, and he bestowed a small, damp kiss on her cheek.

"Oh my gosh," she said in a low, barely audible voice. "I think he likes me. He's wonderful. Absolutely wonderful, Mr. Whip. I can't believe he's mine. Where did you get him, and what kind is he, and . . ." she laughed tripping over the questions, "does he have a name?"

"He's the winning pot for five of a kind, Doc. Five kings." Whip smiled. "As for kind, the man I won him off of said he was a collie, whatever that is. He said he was a cow dog, and that his momma was the best cow dog around. He was traveling through, and guessed he was surprised by a litter of pups. Twelve in all, and this one was the last of the bunch. Fella sold all the others. As for name, I figured that'd be up to you. He's yours to keep."

*To keep.* The words penetrated through the pleasure she felt holding the warm, squirming body. She raised her eyes to Jarrett. He stared at her with a look on his face she'd never seen before. She wet her lips, "Uh, Mr. McCabe. Would it be all right with you if I keep him? He could sleep in a box behind the kitchen range. There are plenty of scraps to feed him. I wouldn't let him get underfoot . . ." her voice dwindled off, the desire in it obvious to all.

He looked at the woman holding the pup tight in her hands and saw her vulnerability as she asked for something she wanted badly, something she'd been denied by her father. His jaw clenched as he turned away from eyes so blue they made him feel as if he were lost in an ocean. He walked slowly across the porch and down the steps. He needed to put distance between him and feelings he didn't know what to do with. "It's your dog, Aries," he said, his words muffled by his broad back as he walked to the barn, "it's yours."

She pulled the pup closer to her. "Thank you, Mr. Mc-Cabe," Aries said. Her words were soft, barely reaching the man, "I'll call him King. He's my winning hand too."

## Chapter Fourteen

Jarrett's mood had worsened over the day. Every since he'd walked away from Aries, he'd been haunted by her eyes. He wished he could go to her and be free enough to offer her comfort like Whip gave so easily to Callie. But he couldn't, wouldn't. He filled with the old anger and hurt. He was confused by feelings Aries brought alive in him, and he chided himself for being so weak that he'd allowed them to surface. Once again, he told himself he shouldn't have let her stay. He told himself things had been better before she'd appeared in his kitchen wet and mad. But the truth was, they hadn't been better. He knew that. He was angry because she'd lied to him about being a doctor. A doctor. The more he thought about it, the more vindicated he felt by his anger.

The men cut a wide swathe around him, and, by evening, several had received dressing downs they didn't deserve. Ted and Ben were aware of what had happened earlier. A ranch is like a small town; nothing goes unnoticed.

Jarrett pushed himself hard that day, not stopping for lunch, taking on the hardest, dirtiest jobs, and making short work of them as he tried to throw off the heavy tension gripping him. His muscles ached, and he went into supper feeling exhausted, both mentally and physically. He spoke to no one, and his steely silence encouraged the same from his father and brother. Even Timmy sensed there was something wrong, and sat quietly in his chair, watching.

The silence was palpable around the table that night. Aries had made the soup herself with only a little help from Ted. Although it looked good, she wished Ted had sampled it before filling the large tureen. Filled with anxiety about the taste, she was unaware of the tension in the room. She watched as the men filled their bowls with the hot soup, and it was only when she smiled a hesitant "thank you" at Jarrett for helping Tim, did she wonder at his withdrawn, mechanical actions.

Ted took a bite of the beef and vegetable broth, blinked both his eyes, and swallowed hard. He reached for a biscuit, and crumbled a chunk in his mouth. Aries frowned. *What was wrong?*

"Uh, hmm," Ted cleared his throat. "It's . . . well, it's . . ." He couldn't finish the sentence.

Jarrett raised his eyes, looking at his father, a puzzled line creasing his forehead as he put a spoonful of soup in his mouth.

"Son, I wouldn't." Ted tried to stop him, but it was too late.

Jarrett's eyes widened, then he swallowed hard, forcing down the liquid. He grabbed the cup of coffee sitting by the side of his bowl, and took a big gulp.

"Wha . . . ?" Her word was barely out before Jarrett exploded.

"What the hell kind of mess is this?" He knew he was over-reacting, but the day's tension finally surfaced. He turned to Aries, giving the offending bowl a shove, sending a splash of red liquid onto the snow-white tablecloth. "This has to be the worst bowl of soup—you can't call this mess soup. Brine. That's what it is, a bowl of brine." His expression hardened, and Aries pulled back into her chair. "Have you tasted it?" he sneered, his voice cold and disdainful; Aries sat, pale and stricken, her eyes wide. He felt a flash of regret, but he quickly stomped the feeling down. "Have you?" he snarled again. "Probably not, you've been much too busy playing doctor to pay attention to the one job you have, the reason you're here on this ranch. The only reason, I might add. Just what's so hard about fixing a decent meal? Huh?" He glared at her, daring her to respond. Aries was silent. "Answer me."

But she couldn't say anything. She forced her eyes away from the angry man to Ben and Ted sitting there, spellbound, shocked at the turn of events. Taking a deep breath, she blinked back the tears threatening to spill down her face. You will not let him see you cry—you will not, she silently commanded. Then, with the grace of a queen, she rose slowly from her chair and gripped the edge of the table for support.

"If you will excuse me please," her voice low and quivery. "I'm tired. I'll be in my room. Ted, if you would leave the dishes, I'll see they get done." Pushing her chair back in under the table, she left the room, leaving behind a shocked silence.

Jarrett expelled his breath, then turned to meet the cold, angry faces of his brother and father.

"You're too hard on her, son," Ted said, between gritted teeth.

"Hard? I'm not being hard enough. Salt, the soup's full of salt." The words were spoken in defense. His voice was low as if he lacked the effort to respond. He moved as though to stand up, "I'm going to the bunk house. There has to be something better than this mess to eat."

"No you're not." Ted's voice cut through the air. "Sit

down," he ordered. "Ben, you take Tim to the bunkhouse for supper."

Ben jumped to his feet, and lifted Timmy from his chair. Neither one wasted any time leaving the room. Ted turned back to his scowling son who was coiled and ready to spring.

"Now you listen, son," he said, his voice low, his eyes piercing. "I've watched you all day going around like a bear with a sore tooth. I don't interfere with your running this ranch, and I've tried to be understanding. But darned if there's any understanding of what you just done. That young lady's worked hard for you every since she's came. And the only acknowledgment you've given her is to remind her she's here as your housekeeper, and even that position is on trial. Two months," he snorted, "what the heck! Look around you, son, this house is cleaner than its been in . . . all right, I'm going to say it— since your wife died. That's the real problem, isn't it? You're so full of hurt and anger over first your mother's death, then you wife's, you lash out at anyone in your path. I've watched it eat at you. I've watched you change, become hard, cold, but today, this—" he waved his hand at the supper table covered with bowls of uneaten soup, "this was uncalled for. She tried. Now what's to find fault with? Sure, it's not fit, and you're right, it's too salty, way too salty. But, Jarrett, your mother was a terrible cook when I first married her." Jarrett's head flew up. "Oh yeah," his father chuckled, "I've ate some pretty awful meals. But she learned, and" his voice lowered, "I loved her for trying."

"But I let both of them die." The words were softly spoken and each one was laced with pain as it fell from Jarrett's lips.

"No one let them die, Jarrett. No one is at fault. Childbirth just took both of them. We don't know why things like that happen." He took a deep breath. "There wasn't a darned thing you could do son in either case. If I could live it over again,

I'd never taken that trip to Wise River. I'd never have left you here, a boy to face what you had to face." He swallowed hard. "I'd never of gotten her withchild again. Not if it meant losing her."

Neither man spoke, both reliving the nightmares that had changed their lives.

"You got a chance, Jarrett. But if you're not careful, it'll pass you by. These last two weeks have shown me something's been missing from this house. A woman. I'll grant you, she's a bit more than we bargained for. I didn't expect to get no doctor. But, she's quick, I'll give her that. Show her once, and she's got it. She's bound to make mistakes, and we're gonna have a few more meals like tonight. Makes a darned fine batch of cookies, though. I seen you sneaking in here every day just about the time they come out of the oven." He smiled, "Don't deny it," he said to Jarrett's sound of protest. "Funny how you manage to find a reason to stop in this kitchen for a cup of coffee and a plateful of them cookies. And, if I was a bettin' man, I'd wager cookies wasn't the only lure snagging you. She's sure pretty, and it's you she wants to please."

"I'm her boss. Staying here depends on her pleasing me."

"Be that as it may, I don't see you stuffing them cookies in your pocket and leaving. I've seen you more relaxed, and smiling more when you come back out that door than I have in years. Ain't nothing to be ashamed of. But your actions tonight are."

"She lied to me. She never told me she was a doctor. A doctor. No one has a doctor for a housekeeper."

"You do," his dad grinned.

"Yeah." Against his will, a smile broke out across Jarrett's face.

"She didn't lie you know. She just didn't tell you. Neither

did Ben or I. You should have heard Ben tell about what happened in Wise River that day. Lord, we knew you'd have a
conniption fit if you heard how she waltzed into a saloon, and
big as if you please, fresh off a train from Philadelphia, sewed
up a dance hall girl's sliced arm. Ben said she was something
else." He got up from the table and, taking the coffee pot from
the stove, filled his cup and gestured toward Jarrett.

Jarrett shook his head. He sat there, the silence easy between the two men. Easier than it had been in a long time.
Slowly, he rose from the table, and stood there a moment,
meeting the older man's eyes. Giving a slight nod, he reached
out and put his hand on his father's shoulder and gave it a
squeeze, then turned and walked out into the gathering night.

Night had long since fallen, and still Jarrett couldn't bring
himself to come into the house. He did his best thinking while
working, and tonight all his energy was focused on the barn.
He was bent over, nailing a broken slat in a barn stall, when he
became aware of someone standing behind him. He straightened up, uncoiling his lean body in a fluid and precise movement. He didn't have to turn around to know who was there.
The sweet scent of lilac floated in the air and mixed with the
familiar smell of fresh straw and horses. It shook him to realize how her mere presence affected him.

"Mr. McCabe." Her voice was low and carried softly on the
air. Mr. McCabe, I need to talk to you."

He turned and faced her, and immediately his heart did
something crazy and painful when he saw her pale face, and
knew she'd been crying. Self-loathing filled him, and he
moved to her, then stopped as he saw her step back. She was
leery of him. *Well, who wouldn't be?* "What is it, Aries?"

She took a deep breath, "I'll be leaving, Mr. McCabe. I've
caused you enough concern. I misrepresented myself to you.
No, not to you directly, to Ben, but," and she rushed on, her

words coming out jumbled, "but ultimately to you. You've been gracious enough to offer me a trial period, but," she continued, her eyes filling with tears she quickly brushed away, "tonight has shown both of us it's no use. I'm not a housekeeper, Mr. McCabe." His eyes focused on her trembling lips, and a need to press his mouth against them, stop their trembling, filled him. He had to steel himself against the action, and force himself to concentrate on what she was saying.

"I think I could be, but I'm not sure. It was wrong of me. No, please let me continue," she said, stopping him from interrupting, "to not tell you about my being a doctor. I am one. I'm not credentialed, but other than that, I'm a doctor. I love it, Mr. McCabe, and it pained me greatly to give it up. Still," and she looked around the barn, "I've come to love it here. In two weeks, this place has taken hold of my heart." There was a sound of wonder in her voice. "And," she took a deep breath, "I thank you for that. I also thank you for your kindness to Timmy. I'll never forget it. Neither will he. You've been the first male in his short life to treat him with kindness. You're a good man, and I regret that I've upset your life. If you would be so kind as to allow Ben to take Timmy and me to Wise River tomorrow, we'll be out of your hair. I regret that I must accept a ticket back to Philadelphia from you, but I assure you I'll pay you back. I'll be working for my aunt, and I'll send you every extra cent until I clear the balance. I only hope," and she raised her pale face to his, her eyes moist with unshed tears, "that I haven't caused you too much embarrassment by my actions in the saloon." She turned away from him, and moved toward the door.

"Aries," her name came out in a groan, as his hand reached out and grabbed her arm. She stiffened at his touch, rigid and unyielding in his grasp. She'd apologized. She had asked a man who threw angry words of reproof at her only hours ago, for help so she could leave. He knew how badly this hurt her pride, but she'd done it with grace and managed, in the process, to retain her dignity. She was something, and he was about to lose her. A panic filled him, and he knew he couldn't let that happen.

"Aries," he said, his voice low, "its not you that owes an apology. It's me. I don't think I have the words to tell you what I feel like right now, but the way I acted tonight, at the dinner table, was inexcusable." She stood with her face turned. Jarrett needed badly to see her eyes, to see if she was listening to him, to see if she was accepting his apology. He reached out, and with a gentle hand, cupped the side of her face, and turned it to him. "Please forgive me," he whispered. "Don't leave." His eyes looked deep into hers and said what his lips couldn't. The pain, the longing, was evident in his face. The fingers of his hand slowly traced her high cheekbones, then moved down her delicate jaw, feather soft in their touch, yet searing her skin with a delicious flame. Then gently, ever so gently, he lowered his mouth to hers and his lips brushed a velvet soft kiss across her trembling mouth. He backed away from her, leaving her lightheaded and aching for more of his touch.

She'd come here, prepared to face his wrath, never dreaming she'd face his sweet mouth. She raised her hand to her lips, and whispered, "I won't." Then, she fled the barn before he could respond, before her legs gave into the weakness she felt, before she allowed herself the joy of reaching out to him, touching him, wanting him.

## Chapter Fifteen

Aries had the coffee ready early the next morning. She'd spent a night tossing and turning, reliving the moment in the barn. Toward morning, she convinced herself she'd read more into the kiss than was meant. It was a part of an apology, that was all, and nothing more. Still, the memory of it lingered on her lips. Tired of the bed, she rose earlier than normal, and spent more time fixing her hair and getting ready for the day. She longed for her trunk and the extra dresses packed there. Sighing, she'd put back on the one suitable work dress, and consoled herself by tying her hair back with a fresh ribbon that matched the blue of her eyes. She went silently down the stairs to the empty kitchen.

A little later, she heard footsteps on the stairs, and her heart increased its tempo. But when she turned it was Ted, and not the man she wanted to see.

"Good morning, Ted," she said, surprised at how normal her voice sounded.

"Aries," he smiled. "You sure look pretty this morning. You sure the sun doesn't come up just for you?" He teased another smile from her, and felt a sense of relief fill him. Somehow, someway, last night had been taken care of. He wished he knew how.

She took down the heavy, cast-iron skillet, and began to lay strips of bacon she'd cut from a slab earlier that morning into the pan. She then slid the pan to the middle of the hot range top and the sizzle and aroma of bacon frying began to fill the air.

"You've come a long way in a few days, Aries," Ted said, nodding at the range with the belly full of wood snapping and crackling in the early morning, and filling the room with a welcoming hominess.

"Not far enough, Ted. But I will." The words fell soft into the room, but the man was reassured by the strength behind them.

Before anything else could be said, Timmy and Ben came into the room. Pulling out chairs, the two men started discussing the distribution of the day's work. Still, there was no sign of Jarrett. If Ben and Ted noticed his absence, they kept it to themselves.

Aries managed to fry the eggs, breaking only a few of the yolks, and doing what Ted referred to as crocheting lace around the edges. He showed her where to place the frying pan on the stove so the eggs wouldn't cook as fast, and how to gauge when they were ready to be turned over. She smiled to herself, pleased with her efforts, she was learning, and improving.

Ted saw her glances at the door and knew it was Jarrett she was looking for. He pursed his lips, then took a swig of coffee. He'd been right. It was Jarrett she was aiming to please.

The men left as soon as they had eaten, taking Timmy with them. They headed toward the barn and the morning chores. Aries stood at the window, watching them leave, feeling the house settle around her and a morning peace fill the rooms. Holding a cup of coffee, its steam rising toward the window, she brushed back her hair. She was filled with joy. "This is my house, my home." The words slipped from her lips. She stopped, freezing the cup halfway to her mouth. Then, she smiled. It was her house, she felt it, felt the welcome of each room as it responded to her touch cleaning and freshening them, breathing life back into them.

She frowned when she saw Timmy come back out of the barn and walk toward the corral and his calf. His skinny arms were wrapped tightly around a stack of straw that blocked out his face. It wasn't his face she noticed, though; it was the way he was walking, straddle legged and stiff, as though he didn't want to bend his legs or move them. She watched him set the straw down, then reach up and open the latch to the pen. The spotted calf ran to him, knowing that the sight of the small boy meant comfort and the possibility of milk. Deciding he was probably imitating the cowhand's rolling gait, she shrugged and was about to move away from the window when she saw Jarrett step out of the barn and walk to the corral. He stopped in front of Timmy, and then reached out and helped him swing the gate open. Jarrett stood and watched Timmy scatter fresh straw; then, he walked over, bent down and said something that brought excited nods from Timmy. Aries could see his smile; she saw him raise his hand to grasp hold of Jarrett's outstretched one. The two of them walked back into the darkness of the barn, Timmy moving with the same stiff legged gait. Turning away from the window, she glanced around at the kitchen with its breakfast clutter, and, with a sense of excitement and pleasure, began the day's work.

"Aries." The sound of her name was followed by the sight of Jarrett. She felt herself stiffen, and knew that she'd been working with half of her attention, waiting and watching for him.

She looked at the door leading into the living room, and called out, "I'm over here."

Jarrett followed the sound of her voice into the room, then stopped just inside the door. Every piece of furniture had been moved and pushed into the center of the room. The heavy drapes had been pulled back from the window, and the room had a fresh scent about it. He carefully walked around the jumble of furniture and stood tall, and imposing, in front of the leather sofa.

"I'm behind here, Jarrett."

He frowned, then leaned over the back of the sofa, and looked down on the backside of Aries.

"Yes?" she questioned softly.

He cleared his throat, "I'm going into Wise River this morning and I'm taking Tim with me. I, uh, I just wanted to see if that's okay with you. We'll be back tonight, but it'll be late. I'll bring your trunk back if it's in."

Aries reached her hand up and daubed her forehead, pushing back an errant strand of blond hair. Her eyes smiled, and he felt warmed by them. "Oh, Jarrett, I'd love to have my trunk. I've been waiting for it to come. Thank you. Of course Timmy can go; he'll love it. Where is he?" She gracefully rose to her feet. "I'll have to make sure he's clean and neat, dressed . . ."

"He's upstairs," Jarrett's hand closed over her arm stopping her movement, "let him do it himself."

"Aries," a small voice interrupted them.

Both of them turned toward the door. Timmy proudly walked into the room, around the sofa, and stood beside Jarrett in Aries full view.

Jarrett heard her suck in air.

"Timmy, your pants. What—What did you do to them? Do you realize how much they cost?"

"Jarrett foxed them for me, Aries. Jarrett says I can ride better with them like this.

Jarrett rubbed his hand over his mouth muttering something indistinguishable under his breath.

"Mmmm," Aries smiled sweetly at him, her blue eyes sparking, "is that right, Mr. McCabe? Perhaps you can explain what this foxing is and why you took it upon yourself to ruin a new pair of Levi's. Hmmm?" She put her hand on Timmy's shoulder.

"Aries, don't be mad at Mr. McCabe. I'm a big boy now and I need pants I can ride in." It was the first time he'd ever defied her. The first time he'd taken someone's side against her's. The pride she felt in him was diminished by the hurt of realizing there was someone important to him now other than herself. He was standing as close to Jarrett's leg as he could.

The silence hung heavy between them as Aries looked into the deep-blue eyes of the man watching her. His mouth softened, and he gently took her by the arm and sat her in the closest chair.

Her eyes were filled with unshed tears. "I didn't realize," she started, then forced herself to go on, pulling her thoughts together, unsettled more than she realized by the close proximity of the man. "I guess I'm having a hard time realizing he's growing up. He has always needed me." she finished lamely, hurt in her voice.

"He always will, Aries." Jarrett's voice was gentle, caressing her as if he'd touched her. "Just in different ways."

She nodded halfheartedly, then raised her eyes to his and forced a smile. "What's foxing, Jarrett? Is that right? Foxing?" She said the word as if it were strange and embarrassing to her tongue.

"Yeah," he smiled. "It's an old cowboy trick to prevent galling and it helps you grip the saddle better. You sew some soft deerskin into the legs," he paused fumbling over his words, looking everywhere but at the woman so close to him he could smell her sweet scent.

"Yes?" she asked.

"Well, you sew it in the legs." He ran his tongue over his lips. "Anyway, that's what I did. They'll wear just as long, and be a darned sight more comfortable."

"I see," she said. "Interesting. Yes. Very interesting, Mr. McCabe. Thank you."

Anxious to change the subject, he asked, "Is there anything you need from town? If you get together a list, I'll bring it back. Don't skimp, Aries. I want you to have what you need to keep house and to cook with."

She stood up and brushed her hands down the front of her dress, smoothing away the wrinkles. "I'll get started on that list, but at the moment, I do know of one thing we're short of, Mr. McCabe." There was a mischievous sparkle in her eyes.

"Yes?" he asked, finding it hard to take his eyes from her face and her trim figure, yet puzzled by her apparent hurry to slip out the door.

"Salt," she said, her face creasing into smiles as her voice filled with laughter. "Salt, Mr. McCabe. I, uh, I used it all in the soup last night." Before he could respond, she was out of the room leaving him standing there grinning at the empty doorway and the woman who once again managed to have the last word.

## Chapter Sixteen

The ride into town went quickly, and Jarrett was surprised by how much he enjoyed the little boy sitting close beside him on the wagon seat. Throughout the ride, Jarrett smiled at Timmy's many questions and observations seen through a child's eye. Several times, when he bent closer to him, the little boy smell of sun-warmed hair filled his nostrils.

"You need a hat, Tim," Jarrett said as he lifted him down after looping the reins around the hitching post in front of the Wise River General Store.

"I do?" Excitement filled Tim's face and spilled over into his voice.

"Yep."

Hand in hand, the two of them walked into the store, and emerged some time later, Timmy wearing a tall, wide-brimmed hat, sucking on a peppermint stick, and Jarrett carrying the first of several loads of supplies.

When the last bag was carried out to the wagon, and Jarrett was unwrapping the reins from the hitching post, a loud voice boomed from behind.

"See you got a helper, Jarrett. Where's the pretty doctor that goes with the package?" Mae's big body came into view.

"Mae," Jarrett tipped his hat, "she's at home. You know Tim, I see."

"Sure do. How are you Mr. Tim?"

Timmy grinned up at the big woman, "How do you do, Mrs. Mae? Jarrett and me came into town to get us some supplies and Aries' trunk. 'Cept, I got me a hat." He reached up and in an effort to emulate the man he admired, he tipped his hat at her.

"Lord, I'll say you do. Won't be a lick of sun hit your face. No siree, not a lick. That's a dandy hat, Timmy."

Smiling broadly at the praise, Timmy went on, "Jarrett says a man has to have a hat out here for lotsa reasons. It's real handy to scoop up water to get you a drink outta the creek, and you can pull it down over your face for shade when you take a nap under a tree. Ain't that right, Jarrett?"

Mae eyed Jarrett, and enjoyed the look of discomfort on the man's face. It was a new side to the usually taciturn man. She pushed closer, watching his long fingers as they pulled the reins through a loose knot. Then, she saw something else that made her smile. Jarrett glanced over at the boy, and a look of caring whispered across his countenance, changing it from the coldness she was used to seeing, into a warmth that made her catch her breath. In just a few short weeks, Timmy had managed to penetrate Jarrett's shell. "I wonder if his sister has too," she mused, and then she was determined to ask enough questions until she had her answer.

"How's the lady doc, Jarrett? The town's still buzzing about her. We find it real comforting to have a doctor that close to the town, don't you?"

"It's not that close, Mae," he said defensively.

"Shoot, on a good horse it'd be no time. Darn sight better

than what we have now. You willing to share her with the town, Jarrett? Folks are waiting for her to get settled in afore they start coming for her help."

"It's her business what she does. I'm not her hus . . ." he faltered over the word, not liking the direction of the conversation. Darn Mae and her big mouth. He tried to move closer to the wagon only to find Mae had closed the gap between them, filling it. Her hair was piled on top of her head, the trademark white feather skewed into the tight curls.

"Husband?" She bellowed out the word, and Jarrett looked around, hoping no one was listening. "Is that right? You're not her husband yet are ye?" She narrowed her eyes screwing her jowls up higher on her face. "You ain't married her yet, huh? Thought that was the line of reasoning again bringing her here. Least ways that's what Ben told us. Said she came from Philadelphia just to marry up with you. Now how come that hasn't happened, she not to your liken?"

"Of course she's to my liking," he snapped, then stopped, realizing the woman had baited him into making that response. A flicker of irritation crossed his face at his stupidity in being manipulated by such a skillful gossiper. "It's nobody's business what I like or don't like, Mae. And it's sure nobody's business who I marry. Now if you'll excuse me," he said pointedly fixing her with a cold look, "I'll be on my way. I've still got a couple of stops, and we want to be home before it's too late."

"Don't get high and mighty with me, Jarrett. I'm just asking what every person in town is thinking but afeared to ask. You got a pretty, young woman living out there on a ranch with nothing but men on it. You got to admit, it's enough to set a few tongues a wagging."

"Yeah, Mae," and he brushed past her and lithely vaulted up on the wagon seat, grabbing up the reins, "I imagine there's those here in this town that don't have anything else to do but wag their tongues. Aries is a fine woman, and I'd advise against anyone saying anything to the contrary. Understand?"

Mae gave a short nod of her big head. Oh yes, she understood. She understood a lot more than Jarrett thought she did. She had the answer to her question, the one she hadn't asked. Yes indeed, it was answered in full. She moved on down the sidewalk, humming softly to herself. Nothing made a person feel so good as to be proven right.

Scowling, and filled with disgust at the woman's nosy questions and her sly hints, Jarrett snapped the reins and headed the buggy toward the train depot. Timmy stayed in the wagon while he went inside. A few minutes later, he emerged, carrying one side of a heavy trunk. Together he and the station master heaved the trunk into the back of the wagon. Then, with a sense of profound relief Jarrett headed the wagon out of the town. He clucked his tongue at the horse, and, snapping the reins, let the animal know he was in a hurry. He had a ways to go before he would get to the ranch he loved and the woman who had dominated his thoughts all day.

Stars filled the wide sky when Jarrett pulled the wagon to a stop in front of the big house. He carried a sleeping Timmy up the steps and kicked open the front door. Once he got him in bed, he'd unload the wagon. Smiling to himself, he realized he was looking forward to telling Aries the much anticipated trunk was sitting outside in back of the wagon. *I suppose we'll be sampling some of those recipes*, he thought. "It ought to be interesting," he said to the quiet room as he laid the tired little boy in the bed he shared with his sister.

He stood for a few minutes in her room, smelling the scent of lilacs and seeing evidence of the woman throughout. He felt like a trespasser, yet he didn't want to leave and stood there, soaking up her presence until he realized what he was doing. Disgusted, he looked at the sleeping boy in the double bed. Timmy needs a room of his own, he thought, knowing that he was making yet another commitment to keeping Aries a part of his life. He closed the door softly behind him and stood on the landing. They'd come far these past few weeks. There was little doubt in his mind that Aries would make good on the two-month trial period. In fact, there was no doubt at all. He wasn't about to have it any other way. He'd tell Aries to clean out the small room at the end of the hall, and fix Timmy up in there. He'd be closer to Jarrett than to Aries, but that was okay.

He was thinking about this when he pushed open the door to an empty kitchen. It was then that the full silence of the house struck him. By this time of night, everyone would have finished supper and would either be in the kitchen or in the living room. He glanced around the room, cast in shadows with only moonlight coming in the window. Jarrett keenly felt Aries' absence. The room was more than empty. It was lost without her. There wasn't one item in the homey room that didn't bear her imprint, including the man standing there in the doorway. The house was too quiet and too empty. Where was she?

He walked through the other rooms seeing glimpses of her everywhere. A rug placed in front of a waxed table. A vase of flowers. Chairs grouped together just so, his desk cleared of all clutter, his pen, ink, and journals waiting for him. He looked around the room, remembering how things had been before she'd come. It wasn't hard to remember. The empty coldness was too raw, too recent. It wasn't hard to remember how empty they'd all been, not just the rooms. The men had been lacking and waiting, including himself, he admitted, for her? He shook his head, not yet ready to answer his own question. He let the screen door slam shut with a bang behind him as he took the steps two at a time and strode over to the wagon and the waiting supplies. He'd have to have Ben help him with the trunk.

He was setting the last of the supplies down in the pantry when he heard the kitchen door open and shut. An involuntary rush of pleasure filled him.

"Aries," he called out. "Your trunk's here."

There was no answer, then a voice, not the one he was listening for, said, "She's not here, son."

He straightened up and slowly walked out of the pantry into the kitchen and Ted's somber face.

"Where is she?" His voice was strained, hoarse.

"She left right after you and Timmy pulled . . ."

He didn't get to finish the sentence.

"Left?" He wheeled on his dad, pinning him with a dark look. "How—why?" he sputtered, then got control of himself and with a cold voice reminiscent of the Jarrett of old, said between clenched teeth, "Where is she?"

"The Delaneys."

"Delaneys? What's she doing there? How'd she get way over there, and why? Well, don't just stand there, poking at the fire, what's going on?"

"Son, sit down." Ted's back was to the angry man, and the smile of satisfaction that dared to creep across his face came and went without being seen.

He put two cups of coffee on the table and slid one over to the chair directly in front of his son. Raising his eyebrows to the coffee, he took the chimney off the lamp in the middle of the table and began lighting it while he talked.

"You'd only been gone long enough to be out of sight, when Delaney came in from the opposite direction driving his team like a mad man. You know he's got eight kids?"

Jarrett's scowl was the only response to the information,

letting Ted know his patience was about to run out. "Get on with it," he muttered.

"Seems as if the whole passel of them is sick. Especially the last one. Aries listened to what he was telling her, and when he finished, she said one word: measles. She started putting things in that black bag, and before I knew what was happening, she was gone. From the way she acted, it sounds bad." He looked up at Jarrett, his, coffee untouched. He knew he shouldn't be, but he was taking pleasure in his son's evident disappointment at Aries not being in the house, waiting for his return. Maybe there was hope after all.

"Measles," Jarrett muttered. "She say anything else?" The words came out with difficulty, hope laced around each one.

"Yeah," Ted smiled. "She fired off a few instructions for you."

The harshness of Jarrett's face relaxed, and the corners of his mouth twitched, "Me? What?"

"Said to ask if you'd see that, that scratch out back she's calling a garden gets watered, and if you'd keep an eye on King, not that he's going to waddle far without someone picking him up," Ted said disgustedly.

"That all?" He tried to keep the disappointment out of his voice, not wanting Ted to hear his need.

"No." Ted fished into his pocket and pulled out a folded piece of paper. "She asked me to give you this. I didn't read it," he offered quietly as he handed the paper over to his son.

The only sound in the kitchen came from the range as a piece of wood popped and the teakettle filled the silence with a thin whistle of steam.

Jarrett quickly read the note, then read it again. He shook his head, and still not meeting his father's eyes slid the note across the table to him.

Ted slowly unfolded it, and read.

*Jarrett,*

*Sorry I won't be home when you get back. This is serious. Measles can be life threatening, especially in the young, and it sounds as if the baby is bad. I don't know how long I'll be gone, but the family will have to be in quarantine until there are no further outbreaks. Jarrett, I have to ask something of you, and I have no right to do so. I'm all Timmy has. If something happens to me, please do not send him back to my aunt. Would you allow him to stay on at the Big Hole Valley Ranch? It's become home to him. And would you continue to take a hand in his upbringing? He admires you so much, and he couldn't have a better person to look up to. I never worry when he's with you. I had the measles when I was younger, so I don't think there is that much of a risk. Still I worry, not knowing exactly what awaits me at the Delaney's. I wish I had more of my father's medicine, and more of his knowledge. I hope my leaving during the two-month trial period won't jeopardize my position as your housekeeper. I'll make up for it when I return, so please extend the time.*

*Aries*

*p.s. There's a plate of cookies hidden in the breadbox. They're for you. If you don't sit down and eat them all at once tomorrow with your morning coffee, they might last until I return.*

The muscles on Jarrett's face were taut. The only sign of emotion was the quiver at the corner of his eyes as he looked everywhere but at the man silently reading the shared note.

Neither man said anything; the note lay on the table between them like a wide, uncrossable river.

Finally Ted cleared his throat and said into the still, "She means that much." It wasn't a question, but rather a statement of the obvious.

Jarrett took a gulp of the cold coffee, not tasting it, then slowly lowered the cup and met his dad's too knowing eyes.

"Worried about the two months." The words came out slowly. Jarrett rubbed his face, his long fingers brushing across his jaw in a slow, tired motion.

"Yeah," Ted answered. "She left you cookies," he smiled, trying for lightness.

"That, and the most precious thing she has: Timmy," Jarrett answered. "I don't know a thing about measles." His voice was harsh with resentment over his inability to meet the unknown challenge.

"You had 'em."

"I did?"

Ted smiled, "You was sickern a dog. Your mother made you stay in a dark room and wouldn't let you use your eyes for fear the measles would settle in them like they're known to sometimes do."

Jarrett looked over at his father with new respect and a smile pulled at the stern corners of his mouth.

"You were a might hard to convince. Laying in bed didn't come easy to you." He laughed. "Lord but you had a million reasons why you just had to get up. Course the fact that you were a mass of red bumps, itching like crazy didn't seem to faze you. You knew you'd be better if you could just get outside." The man's voice lowered, and love crept into it, "When the fever was high, you begged your ma and I to let you go down to the swimming hole. All night you pleaded, telling us you wouldn't swing from the rope." His eyes met Jarrett's. "Yeah, you let it out that you had you a rope swing hidden in the top of that cottonwood. Guess you forgot to mind what your mother said about never taking chances if we let you swim there."

"I never knew she knew." His words were soft with longing.

"No, we didn't have the heart to tell you, or to do anything about it. Your ma worried every time you headed for that swimming hole. She was sure you'd bust open your head, or . . ." and he grinned, "break an arm?" The words were delivered as a question edged with laughter.

Jarrett's head raised, "You knew?"

"Heck yes. Poor old Dolly took the blame, but your ma and I knew she wasn't capable of bucking you off. Course the fact that your hair was a might wet didn't help your story much. You were green around the gills, and we figured the pain you'd went through drying off and dressing yourself, then havin' to come ask for help was punishment enough for the fib. By the time you made it back to the house, your arm dangling at your side, we figured you'd been through enough." He waited, then said, "I saw the man you would become that day."

"A man who would lie to his mother and father?"

"Nope. The boy did that. The man took his punishment without a whimper. You clenched your jaw, just like you do now, and didn't utter a word when I pulled that arm straight and splinted it. Your ma told me she could feel you tremble the whole time she bound it up tight, but not a word came from your lips. You didn't take me up on the offer to do your chores that night, or any night." Ted's eyes were misty, and he fixed them on the coffee cup in front of him. "Nope, you pulled into yourself and spurned any offers of help." He leaned back in his chair, looking full at his son.

"It's a fine trait, son, just don't carry it too far. We all need someone sometime, and that's not a sign of weakness."

"No." The word was heavy. "But sometimes that need can bring with it a pain that's too hard to bear. A different kind of pain that lodges inside of you like a cold lump, and never leaves."

"We're talking about Aries, now, aren't we?"

Jarrett forced a thin smile from his closed lips. "Yeah."

"Aries, your wife, and your ma . . ." Ted let the sentence hang in the air.

"Yeah," Jarrett repeated. After several long minutes, he went on. "If you love, you lay yourself wide open to that pain. If you even care, you still run that risk. Just like this. Measles. We could lose her. If it ain't the measles, it could be any other thing she sets out to heal and care for. She'll never be able to turn her back on someone's need, will she?" The question was asked, but no answer was expected. "Why take the risk? Why put yourself through the loss of someone you love. Someone that filled your days with laughter and light and love."

Ted knew he wasn't just talking about Aries now.

Jarrett shook his head and shifted his body in the chair, then stood.

"Jarrett," his father's voice stopped him.

"Don't say anything, Dad. I've heard it all. If you haven't said it, I have. Every night since she's come, I've argued with myself. Argued not to reach out and strangle her a few times." He gave a mirthless laugh. "Argued not to give a darn. Argued that she was only hired help, on trial at the best." A sardonic grin flashed across his face, "She's a lousy cook." He threw it out, challenging a reply.

"That she is."

"Doesn't know squat about anything to do with ranching."

"Nope."

"Makes a mean batch of cookies," he offered.

"That she does."

"Aw, who am I kidding?" He looked at Ted, challenging him to show any sign of contempt for the weakness his words revealed. It wasn't there.

"She listens. Listens with those deep-blue eyes of hers, and doesn't say a word—just listens, hearing what I can't say."

Ted watched his son wrenching out the words, aching for him as he dug at the pain inside of him.

"I'll have Ben and one of the hands carry in her trunk." He rubbed the back of his neck. "No problem for you to take over tomorrow, is there?"

"Nope."

"Fine. I'll . . . ," he stopped, then shrugged his wide shoulders, looking fully at the man who had also heard what he was unable to say, "I'll be riding on over to Delaney's. See if there's anything she needs out of that darned trunk." The next words floated softly back over his shoulders as he stepped out the back door. "See if those eyes are still as blue, see if the star is still shining."

## Chapter Seventeen

An ache filled Aries, and she knew she would never forget this, her first case fought alone. And fought she had. Fought the pneumonia. Still, she had lost. It started with a slight cough, the mother said. It had rapidly progressed to a fever and swollen glands in his neck. By the time they'd come for Aries, it was too late. He was too young. She poured a strong infusion of yarrow down him, past his tongue covered with white fur. Even with the fever raging, leaving his skin dry and hot, she'd insisted they keep him warm, knowing that his temperature would only escalate until the eruptions appeared. But, her greatest fear was realized. The chilling he'd somehow experienced had closed the pores of the skin, and the measles were driven inward. She wanted to change from the yarrow root to a more practiced infusion of pulverized white root, called pleurisy root, and pulverized ginger. This, sweetened with honey and given by tablespoonfuls every hour, would cause slight perspiration, rendering the skin pliant and as open as possible, allowing the poisonous material endeavoring to get out through the surface, the skin a means to escape. Then eruption would occur. She shook her head, blinking back tears of frustration and exhaustion. She didn't have any pleurisy root. Oh, she had plenty. In a trunk. Waiting at a railroad station. *Why hadn't I thought to bring it with me. Why?* The question rolled through her tired mind with a persisting shriek. The answer was always the same, and while it was justified, it brought little comfort. Aries hadn't anticipated needing it. And there had been only so much room in her medical bag. She'd never imagined being thrust into a situation like this. She raised her head and looked around the cluttered room. Signs of sickness were everywhere. Sickness and death. The Delaneys had lost their baby early that morning. The minute she saw him, she knew he was lost. But, dear lord, she'd fought. And when she allowed her medical mind to overrule her heartsick one, she was able to justify that she'd done everything medically possible. They'd waited too long to come for her. No, that wasn't quite true. Had they been in Philadelphia, blocks away from a physician, instead of on an isolated farm miles from help, the outcome probably would have been the same. Measles, compounded with pneumonia in one so young, was serious and often turned the simple childhood disease fatal. She pushed her tired body up from the table and, arching her back, tried to roll away the ache from her shoulders. She allowed herself a small smile of satisfaction. The other four children, also down with the highly infectious disease, were resting peacefully.

The sounds of hammering carried faintly into the room from the barn where the young father was putting together a rough coffin.

She glanced over at the rocking chair in the corner of the big room. Marge Delaney's head had fallen back and her eyes had finally closed. The room was dark, blankets had been hung over the windows, blocking out any light that would irritate sensitive eyes.

According to Marge, the children sickened over varying lengths of time. Aries knew that once the poison erupted and a rounded, slightly-raised raspberry dot appeared, healing would begin. Usually on the third day of eruption the dots grew rough and scaley; and on the fifth day of eruption, most commonly the ninth day of the attack, it would disappear, leaving behind a slightly yellowish spot. The fever would abate as desquamation, or losing the scales, occurred, and then the major obstacle would be keeping her patients quiet and contained. Children were fighters, and usually their strong bodies fought off this childhood disease. Usually. Her father had so often said, "Nature is often the best guide to treatment, Aries." Yes, but nature was often a harsh, unforgiving guide.

Aries wandered over to the window and a feeling of suffocation overwhelmed her. She needed fresh air. The air inside the house was sick, full of fever and heartache. Quickly she moved to the door and, stepping outside, gently closed it behind her. Aries stood, squinting in the midmorning sun. She raised her face and gulped the sweet Montana air. It was nectar.

She wandered down the path, stumbling on the rutted outline of a road. It was the road she'd traveled in a wagon, bouncing her from side to side just yesterday? She felt she'd been trapped inside the small farm house for weeks. She stopped in under a tree and stood there, her hand resting on the rough bark. She looked back at the farm this courageous couple tried so desperately to carve out. It was nothing like the Big Hole Valley Ranch. No, she thought, it wasn't at all like home. Home. Just saying the word sent newfound energy through her. "Home," she said aloud to the tree. "It is my home, and I need it so badly now." She closed her eyes, seeing behind them the kitchen she loved, with its ever present pot of coffee. Seeing a man, a man with shoulders big enough to shelter someone, arms strong enough to wrap around and pull into the safety of his chest.

"Jarrett," she whispered, the name softly escaping into the mountain air. *When had this happened? When had this . . . love? No*, she shook her head, *no*. She couldn't love him. But she did. The knowledge had laid buried in her heart, but now, now the need for him forced it to the surface, forced it bubbling into the open, demanding she face it. How? When? She knew the answer. From the moment she'd first seen him, sitting tall on his horse, shadowed by the arms of the big cottonwood, arrogantly barking orders and chastising Timmy for not being watchful.

A harsh breath escaped her. This love was too much for Aries to deal with. It was too much to acknowledge. Too much to allow to happen. Leaning even more into the tree, she slid down its rough bark and sat hunched, her knees pulled up to her chest; she allowed her head to drop wearily to her folded arms. She would only sit there a moment. Just a moment. And she would not allow herself to think any more. There was no sense dwelling over what could never be. She was the housekeeper on the Big Hole Valley Ranch. Nothing more. And that was tenuous. She blinked her eyes, fighting closing them, and allowed the heaviness to overtake her heart. There had been so much to accept lately in her life. This was just another challenge, another hurt to push down into a deep recess. Her eyes won the battle and closed, her lashes casting feathery shadows against the pallor of her cheeks, and her chest rose slowly as sleep she'd been denied claimed her. Sweet sleep would heal and block the hurt that came with the simple word: *love*.

He saw the form huddled against the base of the tree long before he could identify it. But even before his eyes told him who it was, he knew. The crazy racing inside his chest told him. Aries. Aries sitting there, small and vulnerable. He smiled. She'd hate being seen like this, vulnerable and defenseless, the fight gone out of her. He pulled his horse up short, a few feet from her, and sat there looking down on her, her hair falling around her face, shrouding it with waves of sunlight. Most of it had escaped from the knot she'd pulled at the base of her neck, the same knot she contained it in when she was cleaning or cooking. And the smile on his face grew, as he acknowledged how endearing her lack of cooking ability had become to him. It was hard to believe he'd berated her for the soup just a few short nights ago. *You, Jarrett McCabe,* he thought, *can be a real jerk.* He accepted the realization, but instead of allowing the coldness to fill him, he kept the warmth, letting it seep through him.

His first impulse was to quickly dismount and grab her up into his arms, to fold her body against his and take her back home with him where she belonged. But he didn't give into this impulse. The iceberg inside of him may be melting, but it wasn't completely thawed.

His horse shifted restlessly under him, and the woman's eyes shot open. Wide yet clouded with sleep, Aries stared at him without comprehension while her back stiffened against the tree.

"Seems like I'm forever finding you under a tree. Only difference is," he drawled laconically, "this time you have your clothes on."

A glad cry escaped her. "Jarrett." His name fell like music. "Jarrett," she repeated. "I can't believe . . . what are you doing here?"

He didn't answer. He wasn't about to share his real reason. He started to swing his leg over the saddle, knowing he shouldn't dismount and place himself so close to her, not now, not while his need for her was so strong in him.

"Stop!!" Her voice rang out loud. She jumped to her feet

and started backing away from him. "Don't come any closer, Jarrett. I could be infectious."

He settled back into the saddle, his movements slow, a frown hardening his face.

"What do you mean?" he asked quietly.

"Measles." She shook her head tiredly. "Four of the children have them. "We lost the baby this morning."

He drew in his breath, his face closed and without realizing it, he shifted his body, pressing himself into the back of the saddle, moving away from her. His body revealed his thoughts: death. Here it was again in this hard, uncompromising land where it seemed that the weak and innocent were often victims for the dark voyeur.

He heard the hammering and glanced toward the old barn.

Aries followed his look. "Mr. Delaney and his three older boys are building the coffin." She hated to tell him, hated to see the hurt in his eyes, hated to see the remote coldness settle on his face.

"You've got a lot of business here," he said harshly. He hadn't turned back to face her. He was looking at the barn. "A hell of a lot of good it did, you putting yourself at risk."

She drew in her breath at his cruelty.

He turned to her. Her hand was over her mouth, and her eyes were pools of anguish. He cursed himself for his lashing out, hurting her, allowing his anger at death to spill out in this manner. He clenched his jaw as coldness filled him. It was more comfortable than the earlier emotions he'd allowed to surface. Yes, much more comfortable. And safer.

"Get your things together," he ordered. "I'm taking you home."

She raised her face to meet his, tilting her chin up. Gone was the anguish from her eyes; now they held a determination equal to his.

"No," she said with hard finality. "No, Jarrett. Regardless of what you may think, I do have business being here. I'm a doctor, and whether you accept it or believe it doesn't matter. I did everything possible to save that baby. My being here, my knowledge, couldn't stop what was inevitable, but I did my best. I tried, and that family in there knows that. I cannot save everyone. No one can." She let the quiet between them grow, then said in a softer, gentler tone, "He was too far advanced, Jarrett. Too little, and too sick. But there are four others in there," and she motioned toward the small house, "and those I will save. Those I will help. Just like I will help others. Anyone, Jarrett, anyone that comes to my door seeking a physician. I will try to help." She straightened her shoulders, gaining strength from her words. She had healed herself just like she'd seen her father do countless times after losing a patient. She allowed a smile of satisfaction to play across her lips and she pushed away from the tree. She was a doctor now; she'd had her baptism.

"Thank you for coming, Jarrett." Her voice was more formal now, not allowing her love for this stern and often angry man to surface and show. "But I don't want you exposed. Measles are highly contagious."

"I've had them," he said shortly.

"Good. Timmy hasn't."

Jarrett swallowed hard, fighting down his need for this woman who had more courage than he had. Aries could face death, straighten her shoulders, and walk away from it, without it entering her, killing her with its finality.

"Your trunk's here. What do you need."

She looked at him for several moments knowing that he was telling her, in his own way, that he accepted what she had just said. Jarrett was offering his help. She loved him more in that moment than she dreamed possible, because she knew the sacrifice he was making.

She smiled up at him, and it was as if the sun broke through. "The key is in the dish that holds my hair pins, on the dresser in my room. You'll find several containers of herbs. Please bring me some of the pleurisy root and ginger. It's labeled. A small amount will do." Her voice lowered and filled with sadness. "I probably won't need it, but I'll never be without it again."

He saw in that moment what the death had cost her and he berated himself for his callous words earlier. "I'm sorry, Aries."

"I know." She rested her eyes on his face, made even more handsome now by her acknowledged love. "I know."

"Anything else?" he asked gruffly, fighting the urge to get off his horse and hold her, to offer her the comfort he longed to give.

"Yes. A clean dress." She chuckled in embarrassment at the request made of the lean cowboy. "I'll be here several more days until I'm sure all danger is past, and I know I'm not contagious. I know Timmy needs to have these childhood infections, but I don't prescribe to the theory of exposure. I believe nature will do that on its own without help from me. Besides, I'd like to see him stronger. And, thanks to you, Jarrett, the ranch and the chance you're giving me, he's getting stronger each day. He'll grow to be a fighter," she paused, "just like the man he so admires."

He shifted in the saddle, embarrassed by her words. He knew there were some things he'd stopped fighting years ago. But maybe, with this woman's help and belief in him, he'd find the desire to fight again. He knew this thought would stay with him and, later, when alone, he'd struggle with it again.

"How's Timmy?" Her words broke into his thoughts. "I'd forgotten all about his trip to town."

"He's got a hat so big his ears had better grow a few more inches to hold it up," Jarrett chuckled. "Didn't have one small enough for him, but he was so darned determined to walk out of that store with a hat on his head." He shook his head, remembering. "Kept telling me over and over, 'This one fits real fine, Jarrett. It's only a little big.'"

Aries laughed, missing her little brother, but enjoying the fact that he'd manipulated this man in a way few were able to. "And?" she waited for his answer.

A grin spread across his face, "And we stuffed paper inside the crown, and left with it. Like I said, his ears better start growing. Anyway, there won't be a drop of sun hit his face, not likely, with that brim hiding him." He waited a minute, then said, "He's got his sister's determination. He knew what he wanted, and he wasn't going to leave that store without that hat on his head."

She laughed. "Oh, Jarrett, I'm so sorry. I've never seen him that way. He's usually so meek and accepting. I know it's not a behavior to be encouraged, but it's so good, so normal. I thought the fight had been taken from him."

Jarrett smiled at her. "Well, it hasn't. Like he told Mae, 'You gotta have a hat to drink out of, and to pull over your face for shade when you're taking a nap'."

"He didn't!" Aries asked, struggling to hold back her laughter.

"Yeah, he did. Told her I'd told him that."

"Did you?" She couldn't stop it, and laughter bubbled out of her as she enjoyed his discomfort.

"Yeah. Just didn't think the little cuss would tell everyone he saw. Especially that gossip, Mae." He paused, "She was still singing your praises. Let me know that the town's just waiting for you to get settled in before they start coming for the doctor. Looks like you'll be busy, Aries."

She heard the unspoken question in his words, and knew that, like Timmy, this man needed reassurance. "Yes, but not too busy. I won't ever be too busy for my job, Jarrett. I'll always have time to bake those cookies, and now with my trunk and recipes here I'll be able to make different ones. I imagine you're tired of oatmeal raisin aren't you?" She asked the question, knowing his answer.

"Not hardly!" Then as an afterthought, he asked, "What other kind can you make?"

"You'll have to wait and see," she teased. "And I'll have Mrs. Ellis's recipes," she said happily. "Oh, Jarrett, I can hardly wait to get into that trunk. I can't wait to get home." The words came out before she could stop them.

He looked at her, his eyes so deep and blue they were like ebony, as he sat there, tall in his saddle, his back straight, the reins laced through his long, capable fingers, his hat tilted back, a wave of dark hair falling over his forehead.

"Me either," he said softly, then turned his horse away from the beautiful woman. "Me either," he repeated as he gently dug his heels into the horse's flanks.

She watched him leave her. The horse, responding to the slight touch, made the distance between them quickly grow until he was swallowed up by the hilly road, lost to her sight. And still, she stood there. Then giving a sigh, Aries started toward the house; she again became the doctor instead of the woman, watching the man she loved ride out of sight.

## Chapter Eighteen

Jarrett's plan was to ride back over to the Delaney Ranch the next day, but the Big Hole Valley Ranch had a mind of its own, and, like a jealous mistress, supplied several good reasons why that was impossible. It was late afternoon on the third day when he was able to catch his breath enough to push open the door to her room. He stood, seeing first the unmade bed, and second, Timmy's clothes on the floor, mixed in with his tin soldiers scattered every which way. He shook his head. He was being too lax with the boy. They might be a household of men, but each one had to pull his own weight. Just as soon as he got what he needed from her trunk, he'd have Tim straightening up. Yeah, and while he was at it, he'd get a couple of the guys ... He stopped himself. No. He'd move Timmy himself. Today. A smile flickered across his face. He'd have a surprise of his own waiting for her when she returned.

He crossed over to the dresser and fished the key out of the glass dish. It was mingled in with her hairpins, just like she said it would be. He didn't know why she bothered trying to capture and tame that mass of golden curls into a tight bun. It only escaped making her look—"Too appealing," he muttered to himself. Not liking the way his mind was running, he put the key into the small brass lock and opened the lid.

No wonder it had been so heavy. There wasn't an ounce of room left. Every available space was filled with medical books and medical paraphernalia. Bottles of pills and dried herbs were wrapped in articles of clothing. She'd used her dresses as protection for the precious medicines. Gingerly, he reached in, feeling as though he was an intruder. The Aries who had packed this trunk came from a life he could only imagine. It was a life far removed from the one he lived.

Jarrett gently unfolded a dark blue satin dress and immediately pulled away. Subtle waves of lilac, trapped within the folds, filled the room. The material stuck to his work roughened hands, telling him in yet another way, what different worlds he and the woman who had worn the gown came from. Laying the gown down, he closed the trunk lid and rose to his feet. He had no business here in her room, seeing, touching this part of her. He again cursed Ben and his father for bringing her into his life. The differences between then were as wide as a gulch cut by the Wise River. He swore into the empty room.

Then, resolutely, Jarrett opened the lid again. He'd do what she asked. He'd bring her the medicines she needed and the dress. He hadn't asked for her to come. He hadn't asked for her to turn her back on Philadelphia and all it could offer. But she was here, here in this room. Here in his life.

Jarrett lifted item after item out of the trunk. He set aside anything that looked like it belonged to Timmy. He also unwrapped Aries clothing, separating it from the medical equipment. Anything to do with medicine went to one side. She'd have to find a place for all of it, but where? There was enough here to stock a doctor's office. Then Jarrett realized how out of place these things looked in the ranch house. He was seeing her father's office. At least the part Aries could pack. And, judging from the small piles of personal belongings, she'd given her father's things first priority. Aries had packed little for herself. But the dresses Jarrett unfolded were unlike any he'd ever seen. To say they were exquisite was an understatement. The yards of satin and lace were beautiful, and, impractical. He hurt for the woman who had worn them in a life she had to turn her back on.

He found the herbs she'd requested and set them aside. He started to close the lid, when he saw the stack of handwritten papers tied with a narrow ribbon, and he knew in a moment what they were. Her notes. Her precious recipes. The corner of his mouth pulled into a grin, and his eyes softened. There was a folded paper with her name across it on the top, and, knowing that he had no right, he gently untied the pack, and opened the letter.

*My Dearest Aries,* it began.

*Or should I say, My Dearest Mrs. Ben McCabe?* A crease deepened on his forehead, and his eyes narrowed reading the words. Mrs. Ben McCabe. What the . . . ? Then he realized that Mrs. Ellis didn't know that Ben wasn't the one Aries had been sent for. She had no way of knowing, and, of course, thought that by now Aries and Ben would have been married. He wasn't prepared for the jolt seeing those words gave him. His Aries married to someone else. There was a knot in his gut, and he started to close the letter when the next sentence caught his eye.

*I hope your rancher is everything you imagined and hoped he would be.*

He quickly folded the letter, not allowing himself to read further.

"Later," he told himself. Later, Jarrett would pull those words out and worry them in his mind. There was no, "your rancher" and, he was sure nothing, nothing at all was what

Aries had imagined and hoped it would be. Well, it wasn't his fault. He hadn't been the one making the empty promises.

Finding no comfort in his rationalization, he started to replace the letter on the stack. But he was stopped by the bold handwriting on the next paper: TO PRESERVE A HUSBAND. A herd of wild horses could not have held him back. Clenching his jaw, he opened the single page. As he read, the hard lines around his mouth slowly began to dissolve, disappearing entirely into a wide grin.

*Aries,*

*This was a recipe my mother gave me. I share it with you.*

*HOW TO PRESERVE A HUSBAND*

*"Be careful of your selection. It is wise not to choose one too young. Be cautious that you take only such varieties as have been raised in a good moral atmosphere. When once decided upon and selected, let that part remain forever settled and give your entire time and thought to preparation for domestic use. Some women insist on keeping them in a pickle while others are constantly keeping them in hot water. However, it has been found that even poor varieties may be made sweet, tender, and good by garnishing with patience, well sweetened with smiles and flavored with kisses to taste. Wrap them well in a mantle of charity and understanding—keep warm with a steady flow of domestic devotion, and serve well with peaches and cream. When thus prepared, they will keep for years. Yours will be a home to envy as shared love twinkles and shines throughout.*

He rose to his feet with the "recipe" in his hands. Slowly he folded it into a small square, unbuttoned his shirt pocket, and gently slipped it in, where it lay heavy against his chest. He had no logical reason for this action. In fact, it was contrary to anything he'd ever done. He just knew he wanted, no needed, to have it. The message would be delivered only to him; because it was as if the woman, Mrs. Ellis, saw across the miles and had sent him the recipe. He felt an affinity for a woman he'd never met; somehow this Mrs. Ellis, who had been such a guide for Aries, would understand and condone his taking of this directive. Even if Jarrett didn't.

Jarrett took a dress out of the wardrobe and grabbing up the herbs she'd requested he left the room. It was too full of the presence of the woman who created this chaos inside of him.

She caught herself watching and listening for him. No matter how busy her hands were her mind seemed to have a will of its own. The other children had settled into the normalcy of their illness, having fully erupted with the strawberry-red dots. Her medical knowledge wasn't needed now as much as her hands, and those she willingly lent to the task of helping the weary mother bathe and soothe the itching, restless bodies. It was easy to let her mind wander, and Jarrett seemed to be the favored direction. Unknowingly, a smile would play about her lips when she thought of him, remembering each moment, starting with their stormy first meeting, and ending with her watching him ride away.

She had thought he'd return the next day and had spent that day listening for the sound of his horse. She would stop what she was doing and go to the door only to be met with the normal ranch sounds and the sight of an empty road.

"Aries," Marge's voice cut into her thoughts.

"Yes?" Aries said, smiling at the woman. A friendship had been forged by the illness and sharing of loss. Aries admired this woman who was able to take whatever this unsettled land threw at her and yet remain steadfast and filled with love for her husband and children. The loss of the baby, a toddler of two, and the hardships she faced daily hadn't broken her. She still had a smile and a soft word of encouragement for everyone. The only sign of the pain she suffered was a dim fleck of hurt in her eyes when she looked toward the small knoll behind the house, where her infant son lay.

"Let's grab us a moment and take a cup of coffee, and a piece of toast outside on the porch. I'm going to be losing the pleasure of your company any day now, and I want to take every advantage of the time we have. I've made oven toast, and I've still got some of my chokecherry jelly you like so much."

Aries straightened up from the child she'd just tucked back into bed. Her back ached, and she more than welcomed the offer to sit in the rocker on the porch, and visit with her new friend. She gave a tug to the skirt of the too-big dress. It was an old one of Marge's, and it would have been too big even before Aries had lost weight. The dress hung on her, held only in place by a band of string. The first few days, there hadn't been time to eat; now it seemed she was too tired to even want food.

"Chokecherry?" she laughed. "Now you've said the magic word." She followed her out into the sunlight and gratefully sat down in one of the rockers.

Marge pulled her rocker closer to the small table between them and picked up a piece of the lightly browned toast. She took a bite of the toast, then said around a mouthful of crumbs, "I swear, Aries, your bread is ever as good as mine. You've got a real knack for baking. Took right to making bread. Hard to believe you'd never made a loaf of bread before in your life. My," she continued, her voice wistful, "I can't remember when I wasn't baking bread. Why I can recollect standing on a stool so's I'd be high enough to knead the dough." She smeared some of the jelly on the toast and took another healthy bite. The sickness was over, and here she was with another woman to share her day. She heaved a sigh of contentment. Amidst all the heartache and sorrow, there had been one bright light. The good Lord had seen fit to put in her path another woman. And, if that don't beat all, a doctor at that.

She looked Aries over, sitting there so proper-like in the roughly made rocker, taking small, ladylike bites of the bread, and sips of the strong coffee. Even in the worn, homemade dress hanging from her slight frame, it was obvious she was every inch a lady, raised for a life much different than the one she was living now. Marge wanted to know more about her, but knew she'd never ask. There was a code in this beautiful land that was strongly imbued in each and every person. You didn't pry. You didn't judge a person by what they'd been. You judged them by what they were right now. And, in Marge's mind, Aries couldn't come much higher in her esteem. Doctor Aries Burnett.

"My goodness. It's still hard for me to believe you're a doctor. A woman being a real doctor." She clucked her tongue and smiled over at Aries.

Aries accepted the friendly wonder of the woman. She'd faced it before, phrased in a lot unkinder words.

"The bread is good, isn't it?" she asked, the amazement evident in her voice. "I can't believe it, Marge. I can bake bread. Honest to goodness loaves of bread. Marge," and without realizing it, her voice took on a softer tone, "can you imagine the surprise and delight Jarrett, uh, I mean all the McCabe's will have when I serve a loaf of bread for supper? Bread instead of Ted's ever present biscuits," she chuckled. "I know they haven't had it for years." She leaned back in her chair, sipping the coffee, unaware of the woman's scrutiny.

"Matters to you what he thinks, doesn't it?"

"Hmm? What do you mean? Of course, it matters to me. It matters to me what they all think. That's my job—cooking and keeping house. I need to know how to do so much and," she gave a laugh, "you know how few skills I have in that area. Your house still has a slight odor of burned bread permeating it."

"Hmmpf," the woman snorted, "wasn't your fault the oven was too hot. How was you to know I'd just stuck a stick of firewood in?" She rocked for a few minutes, then glanced at Aries, who stared down the empty road with a look of longing etched on her delicate face.

"He'll be here," the woman said, breaking into the still that settled around them.

"Who?" Aries asked, as she turned her attention back to Marge, a flush creeping up over her cheeks.

"Land sakes, Aries. That big cowboy you been looking for. Jarrett, that's who. Now don't get all rattled. I got eyes, don't I? Doesn't take much smarts to notice you been wearing out that road with looking. Course," and her voice lowered con-spiratorially, "if I had me a man like that, I'd look for him too. You done all right by yourself, Aries. Now, you understand, just cause I ain't insensible to the way he sits a horse, and the size of his chest, not to mention them eyes of his, don't mean I don't love my Malcomb. No siree, it don't," and she gave a laugh. "Why, it just means I ain't blind or dumb is what it means." She was still chuckling as she took another big bite of the toast. "Nope, just appreciative of what nature done took and did with that one."

Aries eyes widened at Marge's comments and, looking away from the all-knowing woman, she fumbled an explana-tion. "He's, he's not my man, Marge. Jarrett is nobody's man, and certainly not mine. He's my boss." Her voice dropped so low with these last words, Marge had to lean forward to hear them. "Just my boss. He's been good enough to give Timmy and me a home, and to give me two months to prove myself. But," and she brightened, "I've upped my chances now, Marge. My trunk is here with Mrs. Ellis' recipes and best of all I can make bread. Big, brown loaves of bread." Her eyes sparkled as she looked over at Marge. "I can't thank you enough, Marge. You've taught me so much."

"Shoot," the woman interrupted, "don't you be thanking me, Aries. It's you I'm beholding to. All of us are. I just wish I had some way of paying you. I know you being a doctor, you need payin'."

"Marge Delaney, you just stop. You've paid me in full. As I just said, you've shown me so much, and I don't mean the bread baking. You've shown me how to be strong. How to face adversity and not lose the pleasure in the life still around you, and the love for those left behind. I admire you, Marge. I only hope I can be as strong as you. I'm sorry it took something like this to bring us together as friends, but I'm so glad I know you now. It helps to have someone, doesn't it?"

"Surely does." Marge rocked as she spoke. "Now, Aries, it ain't none of my business, but that ain't never stopped me." She laughed. "I think you got that young man figured out wrong. Now," she said, seeing Aries shake her head, "you just give it time. He's had a rough go of it, and you were kinda sprung on him," she chuckled, recalling the story Aries had told her of how she came to be in Wise River, Montana. "But he's too smart to let you go; he just don't know it yet." She lowered her cup and nodded. "Peers to me, you'll be able to judge how he's feelin' for yourself. Ain't that a puff of dust down that road a spell?"

Aries whipped her head around and a smile broke out across her face. "Yes," she said softly, seeing the outline of a rider come into view. "Yes it is, Marge. And I know who's making it. Jarrett." Her tongue nervously flicked across her lips, "Of course," she said soberly, not wanting to let Marge see the aching need inside of her, "he said he'd bring me a clean dress and the medicine I asked for. I had no doubt he'd keep his word." She raised up out of her chair and walked to the end of the porch stopping to lean against the support post. The fatigue had vanished, filling her with a queasy anticipation as the rider came closer to the house. She smoothed her hands over her hair wishing she could dart back inside the house and pull a comb through it. She couldn't. She didn't want to face Marge's too knowing eyes, and she didn't want to not be here, holding onto the post, watching Jarrett slowly ride into the yard.

Jarrett's eyes quickly came to rest on Aries standing so quiet and still on the porch, her arms wrapped around the post, her honey-blond hair golden in the morning sun. He watched her with an intensity that blocked out everything and everyone but the two of them. She felt herself tremble, unable to speak or move, under the power of their unreadable blackness. Then, he shifted in his saddle, freeing her from his gaze.

"Morning, ma'am," he said, tipping his hat to the woman sitting still and watching, her rocker quieted by his arrival.

"Jarrett," Marge answered, her voice quiet with respect.

Then, in a dismissive turn of his head, he allowed a hint of a smile to play across his firm lips as he focused back on the woman he'd covered so many miles to see, and his hand settled back around the horn of the saddle, the reins threaded taut between his fingers.

"Aries," he said her name into the air, giving it a proprietary ring. "Sorry it took me so long to get back with what you asked for. I started to come yesterday, but Black decided to choose that moment to start acting like she was going to foal."

"Did she?" Aries asked the question with excitement lacing her voice. She knew how much Jarrett thought of the mare, and knew he'd been anxious about this colt.

"Nope," he smiled, "looks like she changed her mind. I sat with her most of the night, and along toward morning, she wandered over to the hay and started eating like she didn't have anything else on her mind." He chuckled. "Guess she decided to have that colt another day. When I left, she was snoozing in the sun. I figured I could make it over here and back before anything happened."

While he talked, he lithely swung down from the saddle. Looping the reins over the saddle horn, he walked to the back of the horse, running his palm along the horse's flank, then resting it on the powerful rump. He untied a large canvas roll from behind the saddle. While his fingers nimbly undid the rawhide, he turned back to the two women watching him.

"Marge," he said, "I'm sorry for your loss. I hope you'll accept this," and he nodded at the canvas, "as a small measure of condolence from one neighbor to another." He paused, then lifted the heavy parcel from the back of the horse. The muscles in his back bunched and rippled under the heavy weight. He shifted it awkwardly in his arms and started toward the porch. "I won't get too near either of you," he said, shooting Aries a glance, remembering her warnings about being contagious. "I'll just lay it on the porch, and you can do with it what needs done." He made his way up the porch steps, and slowly bent over, dropping the heavy bundle, and, with the toe of his boot, slid it back out of the sun. Stepping back, he distanced himself from the two women.

"What is it, Jarrett?" Aries asked looking at the large, ungainly package.

"It's a hind quarter of beef. Thought it might come in handy." His words were clipped, self-conscious. "I, uh, we," and he emphasized the word, "regret the loss of your little one. Please give your husband our condolences." He stepped back off the porch, and with an easy grace, slowly walked over to his horse.

"Why, Jarrett. I don't know how we can accept this," Marge said, moving to the canvas roll. "But we will." She looked up at the man as he lowered his head in embarrassment. "You didn't need to do that, Jarrett, but I ain't fool enough to turn down such a generous gift. Some good beef broth will put the strength back into those young uns real quick. We're trying to get ours to a better size before we go butchering them, and, well, right now, venison's about the onliest meat we have. This will go down real easy. Real easy, and I thank you."

"It was no problem," he said over his shoulder, the words muffled by his back as his fingers untied the lacing on the saddlebags. Reaching inside, he took out a small package, and a folded dress.

"Aries, I hope this is what you needed. Looks like you fixed yourself up with a dress though. Little big, isn't it?"

"Some," she laughed, taking the things out of his hands.

Just as she turned away, he grasped her wrist in a lightening-quick movement, stopping her close to him. "You've lost weight," he said accusingly. "Why?"

"She liked to near worked herself to death, that's why." Marge interrupted.

He pulled Aries closer to him and held her there in the darkening gaze of his eyes. "How much longer?" The words came out like a razor slashing through any subtleties. The words and his actions showed Aries that Jarrett's patience was about to run out.

She wet her lips but made no effort to pull away from his grasp. His fingers burned through to her skin, and she held her arm still, hoping he'd forget they were curled tightly around her slim wrist. It was the second time he'd touched her, and although it was only her wrist, waves of pleasure snaked up her arm to her heart. His touch was firm, yet gentle, like the man.

"Well, I . . ."

She didn't finish the sentence. Marge broke in, her words driving a wedge between them, and Jarrett slowly let her wrist slip from his fingers.

"Much as I hate to say it, Aries. You could take leave right now. It ain't as though I'm not appreciating all you're doing, and Lord knows I surely enjoy your company, but all's that left of those measles is four itchy young uns, and it don't take no doctor to take care of that."

"Is that right?" Jarrett asked.

"Yes, I suppose it is. I don't think there's any danger of exposure now. I doubt that I could carry the infection back to Timmy."

"Okay," Jarrett said, nodding toward the house, his manner and words decisive. Aries' face was pale, and there were dark circles under her eyes. She looked as if she could fall over any moment, and the ugly dress only emphasized her slimness. She was exhausted, and he blamed her for thinking so little of her own well-being. He clenched his jaw at the protective anger filling him, and it was all he could do not to pick her up, and hold her in his arms, shielding her from the abuse she willingly gave herself up to. "Get your things." His words were clipped, leaving no doubt he expected to be obeyed.

Aries looked up at Jarrett, and her body swayed toward him. She longed to give herself up to the safety of his arms. Then, she caught herself. "I'll have Mr. Delaney bring me back tomorrow, Jarrett. I need to check on a couple of things before I leave."

"What?" His voice was cold, and she knew she'd better have a good answer.

"Now, Aries, we're gonna be just fine."

Then, Marge's voice was drowned out by a deeper one coming from around the side of the house.

"We done took up enough of your time, Aries," Delaney said, stepping into view. "Morning McCabe. 'Preciate your riding over to bring her things. We're beholden." He walked up the steps and stood with his hand on his wife's shoulder.

Jarrett looked at the two of them and envy filled him. He glanced around the meager ranch, and knew they had to fight for everything they managed to squeeze out of the land, but they had something he didn't have. Something that, up until lately, he hadn't thought he'd been missing: the love shared between a man and a woman.

The way Malcomb's hand rested on the woman's slight shoulders spoke volumes. The way she smiled up into his face, left no doubt this man of hers was the focal point of her life. They seemed to grow strong from being in one another's presence.

"I'll hitch up the wagon and take the doctor back to your ranch."

"That won't be necessary," Jarrett said, his voice leaving no room for argument, "Buck can carry two. Aries, get your things," he said, and added with emphasis, "now. I want to get back before dark, and we can do that, if you'll hurry." And then, before he could stop himself, he gently brushed his thumb against her cheek. "Go on now. For once, don't argue, Aries." His words were gentle, but not as gentle as his touch.

She turned away from him, and followed Marge into the house, coming back out a few minutes later, the familiar black bag in her hand. The Delaney's followed her over to the big horse, blowing and shifting his weight from one foot to another, anxious to be on his way.

Jarrett took the bag from her hand and tied it on the horse.

He turned back to her and before she knew what had happened, put his big hands around her waist and lifted her into the saddle. Then putting the toe of his boot into the stirrups, he lightly swung his leg over the back of the horse and eased his body in behind hers. He reached around her and, taking the reins in his hands, turned the horse's head to the side.

Malcomb cleared his throat. "I don't have no way of paying you now, Doc, but I will."

"Mr. Delaney, you don't owe me anything. And if you did, Marge has already paid it in full by something she taught me," Aries said, giving the woman a secretive look.

"I'm going to miss having you around, Doctor Aries Burnett," Marge said, her voice thick with tears. "You got me through this, and if I had my way, I'd keep you here just to sit there on that porch and visit with me."

"We're not all that far, Marge," Aries tried to offer the words in meager comfort. "You send for me, and I'll come. Always," she promised.

"Well, now," and Marge's face broke into smiles, "might be taking you up on that sooner than you think. In fact, I just might be sending Malcomb for you in, say, about seven months. Think I'll have me a real doctor for this un." She looked up into Malcomb's surprised face, and gave a laugh. "Didn't tell you, but guess we'll have us another un, and by golly, Malcomb this one better be me a girl."

The man grinned down at her and put his arm around her shoulder, pulling her closer to his side.

"Guess I'll be coming after you, Doc. Marge gets her mind made up, and a team of mules wouldn't drag her from whatever she fixes on." There was pride in his voice.

"I'll be there. Don't you wait too long to send for me," Aries admonished. "I suspect you'll have this baby with no effort at all, but that doesn't mean I don't want to be there when it happens."

Jarrett closed his arms around her, shifting his weight in the saddle as he pulled the reins against the side of the horse. Then, lightly pressing with his knees, moved the big horse away, and effortlessly walked it out of the yard and down the road.

Aries held herself stiff in front of him, not daring to relax, as she pushed against the saddle horn, leaving as much space between her and the man behind her as possible. The heat of his body threatened to engulf her, and she didn't know how she'd manage to hold herself the few inches she'd placed between them for the hours it would take to get home. She was only too aware of his nearness, and drew her arms even tighter against her sides as the sleeves of his shirt brushed against them.

They'd gone a short distance, neither one of them acknowledging the other, when Jarrett pulled back on the reins.

"You're exhausted, Aries, and we've got a ways to go. If you fall asleep, I won't let you fall," and making a clucking sound with his tongue, nudged Buck forward.

She wanted to fight him, and tried to make her body rigid and hard, not allowing herself to rest against the man behind her. He felt her resistance as he shielded her with his arms, protecting her with his body.

Involuntarily, a sigh escaped her, and she allowed herself to relax. She closed her eyes, drinking in his scent and strength.

"I'll only rest like this for a few minutes, Jarrett," she said softly. "You shouldn't have to hold me, I know I'm . . ."

"Shhh," he whispered in her ear, his lips gentle against her hair. "Let someone else take care of you, Doctor Burnett, just for a few minutes. Just a few minutes."

And holding her close to him, wrapped in his arms, he took

them home to the Big Hole Valley Ranch. Lulled by the rocking gait of the big horse, Aries' heavy eyes closed in sleep. Jarrett breathed in the sweetness of the woman resting so trustingly in his arms. And, gently, so as not to awaken her, he secretly placed his lips against her hair, stealing from her in sleep what he dared not allow himself to do when she was awake.

## Chapter Nineteen

It was good to be home. And feeling a twinge of guilt at the thought, Aries hoped no one else would come riding down that road, needing her so badly they took her away from the ranch, and the man, who was late coming in for dinner.

"I'm hungry, Aries, ain't we gonna eat ever?"

She smiled over at Timmy, sitting at the table, his face freshly scrubbed, fidgeting in his special chair.

"I told you not to climb up there yet, Tim. And no, in answer to your question, we're not going to eat until Jarrett comes into the house. Just like I told Ben and Ted. Now, why don't you get down, and run out to the barn and tell Jarrett that dinner's ready?"

"Aww, I already done it once, Aries. He just tole me to go on and he'd be up to the house in a minute. It's been a minute, hasn't it, Aries?"

She chuckled. "It's been several, Tim. But," and she smiled toward the warming oven, "we're not eating without him."

At that moment, the kitchen door opened and Jarrett's tall body filled the frame. He paused in the threshold of the room,

207

then gently closed the door behind him. The kitchen was warm and welcoming, filled with the smell of supper and something else he couldn't quite identify. Something delicious. He breathed deeply and a smile curved about his lips. It wasn't supper and the mystifying odor that captured his attention. It was the woman who seemed to hold the heart of the ranch in her hands. She stood over the stove, a dishtowel in her hands, her face flushed, but her eyes glowing, as she smiled a welcome at him. He felt his heart catch, and he wanted to pull her against him. Swallowing hard, he walked over to the sink and started washing up.

"Ben, Ted," Timmy yelled, "he's here. Jarrett's here, so's we can eat now."

"Timmy!" Aries admonished.

"Well, he is here, Aries. You said we all had to wait until he got here even if it was ten o'clock tonight. Ain't that right, Aries?"

Jarrett stopped drying his face with the towel and grinned over at her. "That right, Aries? Ten o'clock, huh?"

She turned her face away from his grin, aching to put her hand over Timmy's mouth. "Timmy talks too much."

"He does?" The words were spoken in her ear. Jarrett had moved across the room, and was standing close behind her. He was so close, she could feel his warm breath as he whispered the words. She felt his hand as he reached out and gently brushed the curly strands of hair that had escaped and played around her neck. "You smell good," he said softly. He held himself, knowing it would take all his self-restraint not to pull her into his arms. The fact that Timmy was sitting across the table from them, and his dad and brother were in the next room, was all that stopped him.

"Other than you, what's that good smell?"

"It's a surprise." Suddenly, what had seemed such a good

idea earlier in the day, now filled her with reluctance. She turned and looked up into his twinkling eyes. She started to say something, then stopped, not able to form the words, held captive by the depth of his eyes, and the softness of his mouth.

"What's a surprise?" Ben asked, coming into the room.

Jarrett pulled back, and Aries quickly turned to the stove; she began dishing up the food. Jarrett walked around the table and stood behind her chair.

"Well . . . I," she stammered, trying to answer Ben's question, yet unable to say the words.

"Sit down, Ben," Ted ordered, coming into the room, and sizing up the situation. "Aries will tell you when she's good and ready." He glanced over at Jarrett, standing behind her chair, and smiled. He took his seat and lowered his head. A feeling of peace and happiness entered Ted. He felt the waves of love in the room, and knew they came from the girl, lifting something out of the warming oven. He knew they were directed toward his son, waiting to seat Aries at his table.

Aries turned around; there was a collective gasp as she set down a board holding two perfectly formed, brown loaves of bread.

"My gosh," Ted breathed.

"Real bread," Ben said in awe. "Real honest to goodness bread."

She walked over to her chair, her eyes seeking Jarrett. His was the only response she wanted. His was the only approval she sought.

A look, followed by a private smile, passed between them; his eyes softened. He gently pulled out the chair, then pushed her closer to the table. He paused, then lay his hand on her shoulder.

Both Ben's and Ted's faces mirrored surprise that had nothing to do with the bread. They took in their brother's hand, and quickly became interested in the dishes in front of them.

"That's what Marge taught you, huh?" he said quietly to her.

She nodded.

"You never cease to amaze me, Doctor Burnett." He cupped the side of her face. Then, with great reluctance, he dropped his hand, and took his place at the table.

He picked up the bread knife, and reached for the board, when he heard Ben's muffled snickers.

"What?" he asked, looking over at both Ted and his dad. A sheepish grin played at the edges of his mouth, and a faint flush crept up his neck. "You'd think you two never seen homemade bread before."

"Ain't the bread, although that in itself's a wonder," Ted said appreciatively. "Nope, it's seeing the fall of the king." He looked over at Aries, and saw the love shining from her eyes. "Yep, right hard fall." Ted smiled at the perplexed look on his son's face.

"You gonna keep that bread all to yourself?" Ben interrupted, "or are you just gonna sit there with that knife in your hands grinning at Aries?"

Jarrett laughed, and slowly cut the first piece of warm bread. He gave Ben a smug look, brought the bread to his own mouth and took a huge bite. He closed his eyes, and making sound of sheer ecstacy, slowly chewed, and swallowed. When he finished the slice, he teasingly licked the few remaining crumbs from his fingers.

The table erupted in laughter. This was the Jarrett they'd all but forgotten existed. He smiled over at Aries, then, with a show of deliberate precision, he cut several slices of bread, offering it first to the woman who had surprised them, and finally passing the remainder to a muttering Ben.

## Chapter Twenty

Aries got her wish. No one came looking for a doctor, and nothing unusual interrupted her day. She had time to complete Timmy's move from her bedroom to one down the hall. He loved it, and so did she. She had time to empty her trunk, and make neat piles of the medical equipment and medicines she'd brought. Jarrett had been right. They took up the majority of space in her room, but she didn't mind. Her room felt like her father's office; Aries woke to a feeling of home. *But*, she thought, looking around the congested room, *I'm not as lonely for home as I was.* In fact, there were times when she wondered how she'd ever lived such a shallow life. No, shallowness was too harsh a word; her medicine had given her life purpose in Philadelphia. Emptiness, then. Yes, emptiness described it.

She walked out of the house, and hurried to the barn where she knew Jarrett was. Aries closed her eyes and took a deep breath of fresh air mixed with the earthy smells of animals, green grass, and honeysuckle coming from the bush at the side of the porch. The fingers of pleasure reached deep within her. The music of chickens clucking, and the bawl of Timmy's

211

calf rested easy on her ears. Her heart increased its cadence as she neared the barn and the man capable of bringing joy or sadness with a glance of his dusty blue eyes. She knew it was wrong to let someone have such control over her. But, wrong or right, he did.

She stepped into the darkened recess of the barn and stood a few minutes, letting her eyes adjust. She walked past the area where Ben turned the cow in to be milked each day. The half-sided walls of the pen were headed by a wooden gate. She knew the name of this gate, and was pleased by her knowing. It was a stanchion. The cow would willingly walk up to the stanchion, poke her head through and start eating the mixture of oats resting there on the floor. Then, Ben would pull a wooden handle, and the opening would tighten, leaving only enough room for the cow's neck. She couldn't pull out of the opening, and had to stand there while she was milked. As long as there were plenty of oats, the cow didn't seem to mind. If the oats ran out, she became restless and moved from side to side. Then Ben would start singing. He claimed the sound of his voice calmed the cow, but Aries couldn't see how.

She chuckled to herself. Ben had one song, and sang it loudly and without tune, all seven verses of it. It was about a cowboy who left his mother to ride herd on a roundup.

The chorus was mournful, made even more so by Ben's nasal melancholy wrenching of the words, "And he'll not see his mother when the work's all done this fall." Of course, the verses told in great detail why he wouldn't see his mother. The cows stampeded, the young cowboy couldn't turn them, and his horse fell beneath the hooves, and . . . Billy wouldn't see his mother when the work was done that fall.

It didn't end that easy, no; the last verse was a real tear jerker. Billy lay dying, and gave away his few possessions, telling the other cowboys he wouldn't need them where he was headed. He asked them to think of him kindly, as they remember them all, because he wouldn't see his mother when the work was done this fall.

At this point of the milking, Ben's voice could be heard all over the barnyard. Aries wasn't sure if the cow was lulled because of the singing, as Ben thought, or if she just held still, knowing that when the last verse was painfully shouted out, Ben would shut up, rise from the small stool, pick up the bucket of frothy milk, and open the stanchion, and release her from captivity, his audience for another torturous rendition of Ben's song.

Aries smiled, remembering how she'd tried milking. Ben had assured her it was easy. He'd had her sit on the three legged stool, lean her head into the flank of the cow, and grasp the swollen teat in her hand.

"Squeeze off the top, then gently play your fingers down the side of the teat," Ben had told her, over and over. She did manage to get a thin, weak stream of milk out after much squeezing and pulling. It was at that moment, though, that the cow, swatted Aries with her tail, nearly knocking her off the stool. The tips of the tail were encrusted with hardened manure, and that, coupled with the strength of the swat left a red mark across Aries face. She'd cried out, and scared the cow, who promptly picked up a hind leg and placed it in the bucket of warm milk. Jarrett heard the commotion, and flew around the corner into the stall, and, grabbing Aries from off the barn floor, proceeded to give Ben a dressing down that made the other cowboys duck their heads and find plenty to do elsewhere.

It hadn't bothered Ben a bit; he spent the next few days coming up behind her and giving out a pitiful "Mooo," laughing about her having manure on her face and spilled milk on her butt.

"What's so funny?" Jarrett's voice came from behind her, startling her. "You're miles away and grinning like a fox."

"Oh, just remembering my one and only attempt at being a milkmaid."

Jarrett laughed. "Cow's never been the same. She sees you, and I swear she starts shaking."

She laughed with him, her eyes shining like blue sapphires in the darkened barn.

Together, they walked over to the corral, and paused to look at the ebony mare standing there. They leaned against the poles of the corral. Jarrett put a booted toe up on the lowest rail, and leaned forward, his long arms hanging over the top rail, as he gazed at the mare. He shook his head, puzzlement on his face.

"Darned if I've ever seen the like. Last time she foaled, she wore a path around the pen with her continual pacing. Now, she looks like she doesn't have a care in the world. Like she's biding her time until the colt is ready to come, and then she'll make short work of the process." He paused, "I sure hope so, because last time, I was sure we'd lose her. She couldn't seem to settle into the labor. She's high strung but . . ."

"But you wouldn't have her any other way, Jarrett."

"No," he grinned down at her. His eyes darkened and he moved one arm from across the rail, and took a wisp of her hair, gently tucking it back behind her ear. "No, guess you could say I'm attracted to spirited things."

She stood, stilled by his touch.

"I hope you also like meddlers."

A frown creased his brow. "What do you mean?"

"I mean, well, I've been meaning to tell you, but with the Delaneys and my being gone, then after I've been back, I've been so busy . . ." She dwindled off.

His voice was low, and there was a smile on his lips, "Say it. Just spill it out, Aries, I'm not that bad. I won't beat you. What'd you do?" he asked, letting his hand play with the errant curl.

She didn't know if the touch of his fingers in her hair, or what she was trying to tell him was the reason for the strange feeling in the pit of her stomach. She worried the top of her lip, her teeth pulling at it.

Jarrett shifted his position. She was so darned cute when she worried her lip like that. He'd come to recognize the action as precluding something that was difficult for her to confront.

He let go of her hair, and moved his hand back up to the rail. His eyes clouded over, and he took a deep breath. Ever since that night she'd made the bread, he'd had to make himself walk a wide path around her. She was the last thing he thought of before he went to sleep at night, if he could sleep, and the first thing he thought of in the morning. His life had become invaded by images of Aries smiling, Aries kneading bread, Aries proudly serving a meal she'd cooked all by herself, Aries lancing a boil on the cook's neck, Aries hugging Timmy— Aries, Aries, Aries. He resented the time she spent with anyone else but him, and had to hang onto his temper when he saw the glances the other hands gave her when they thought he wasn't looking. Why wouldn't they look? She was like golden sunshine, and she'd managed to captivate everyone on the ranch. Him included. He was the biggest fool of all, and worst of all, he seemed powerless to change his feelings, even if he'd wanted to, which he wasn't sure at all he did.

"Jarrett," she repeated, "it's the vinegar." Her voice penetrated his wanderings.

"What?" He pulled himself back to what she was trying to tell him.

"Jarrett, don't be mad at me please. I know it won't hurt her."

He let go of the rail, and put his hands on her shoulders. That was a mistake, touching her, and he cleared his throat, searching for the words lodged somewhere beneath the beating of his heart.

"Aries, start all over again. At the beginning. I don't know what you're trying to tell me. I'm not mad, honey." The endearment slipped out, unnoticed by either of them.

"I gave Black vinegar."

"Vinegar?" his eyebrows rose. "Vinegar?" he asked again, his voice incredulous. "Why?"

"Because," and the words spilled out of her, "it's a calming agent for birthing." She hurried into the explanation, not able to look at his face. "It's been known to be effective in animals giving birth. You just put some on their oats a few weeks before they are due and it calms them and helps the birthing go easier. I don't know for sure, but my father often said plain old vinegar has more power than we give it credit. I read about its effectiveness with animals, and I knew how you were worried about Black, and . . . Jarrett, I just went ahead and did it." Her eyes stayed on the last button on his shirt; it was easier to look there than in his eyes. She felt his hands, strong and firm.

At first, there wasn't a sound in the barn. "I'll be," he said softly under his breath. He took the tip of his finger and gently raised her face until the blue of her eyes met his. His eyes were soft and shining as they looked deeply into hers, and the sides of them crinkled with laughter. His generous mouth was shaped into a delightful grin. "What am I going to do with you, Doctor Burnett?" The question was spoken in a caressing whisper, his mouth so close to hers she could feel his warm breath. His thumb outlined her lips, then with infinite care he raised them to meet the downward pressure of his, as with butterfly wings, they fluttered and touched hers in a hesitant kiss.

Her eyes went wide with disbelief.

Then he grasped her arms with both hands and gently pushed her away from him. He tried to take a deep breath, and whispered her name, "Aries," he said, "you make it hard to remember why I've been fighting against you."

Suddenly the rumble of a wagon and the sound of a voice calling out, ripped through the fog surrounding them.

"Someone's out there," he said quietly. Then bending down, he kissed the tip of her nose. With a scowl deepening on his face, he left her standing there and slowly walked to the door of the barn.

She leaned back against the rails of the corral, telling herself it was possible to breathe if she did it in short gasps. She was pushing aside the fears and questions his kiss had brought when she heard her name called from outside the barn.

"Aries," Jarrett called. "Aries." His voice penetrated her lassitude. She pushed away from the pole, and moved toward the open door

She walked out into the sunlight, and stopped. "Yes?" Her voice was hesitant then became more forceful as she walked toward the sound of his voice. "Yes, what is it?" She tilted her head, then saw Jarrett standing beside a buggy. The horse in the buggy traces heaved; its head was down between its legs. Flecks of foam lay on its chestnut body. It had been driven hard.

A tall, painfully thin man stood by the horse, the buggy whip still in his hand. He was saying something to Jarrett, and, at the sound of her voice, turned sharply. In a jerky motion, he jammed the whip back into its holder, and started toward her. Jarrett's hand reached out and in a quick movement rested on the thin arm encased in a black suit that hung from the man's gaunt frame. Jarrett's grip was light, yet restraining. The man paused, then stopped in his tracks.

She walked to the two of them, trepidation in every step. Her physician's instincts told her there was something wrong-something that involved her.

"What is it, Jarrett?" she asked, ignoring the man beside him.

"Aries." Jarrett's voice was strong and clear. "This is Reverend Wilson, from Wise River."

"Reverend," Aries said.

"Ma'am," he replied, taking off his hat and worrying it in his thin hands. He shifted from one foot to another, then found his courage. "Are you a doctor, ma'am? A bona fide doctor of medicine?" He held his hat still, and he seemed not to breathe, waiting for her answer.

"I am," Aries said. "I am a physician, Reverend Wilson, trained by one of the finest. However, I am not board certified. That is, I have not been allowed to take my exams." She stood there, regal as a queen, daring him to utter one word of disparagement.

"I'm sorry to be asking these questions, ma'am, but it's important I know. Could you pass those exams if you had the opportunity?" His eyes seemed over-bright and his hands shook as they fumbled with his hat.

She leveled her gaze and answered clearly, "I could."

He breathed a sigh of relief, and his body seemed to sag. Jarrett shot out his arm, and gripping the man's shoulders, steadying him.

"I think you'd better come up to the house, Reverend, and sit down."

"No," the man said, quickly righting himself. "I . . . I can't. I don't dare waste any more time." He turned his attention back to Aries. His face was haggard, and he looked as if he hadn't slept for some time. "Doctor . . ."

"Burnett," she supplied.

"Ahh, yes, Doctor Burnett, I have a most unusual, well, perhaps the word is urgent request to make of you." His words rushed out. "Two days ago, our son took ill. He was sick to his stomach; as the day wore on, he was cramping something fierce. Mother and I thought he'd been at the crab apples in the back yard, and she gave him a dose of laxative." He licked his lips. "That only seemed to make things worse. And early on this morning, he started cramping again. He lay curled up in his bed, his knees drawn up to his chest."

"Did you try to lower his legs?"

"Why yes." the man answered, "we did."

"And?"

"He screamed out with pain, just at our touch. He said it eased him some to have them curled up under his stomach."

"Was the pain localized?" Her questions were sharp and precise.

"I don't know what . . ."

"Was the pain centered in one specific area, Reverend?" she rephrased the question.

"Yes." He shuffled his feet and looked away from her.

"Where?" Aries tried to keep the impatience out of her voice.

The man swallowed hard, but didn't answer.

"Reverend Wilson. You didn't ride all the way out here, in some haste, to not tell me what your son's problem was, now did you?"

"It was in his . . ." The words were low and delivered to Aries shoes as the man choked on the ending.

"His groin area, Reverend Wilson? Precisely on his right side?"

"Why yes, ma'am," and his eyes raised in surprise.

"Your son needs to see a doctor, Reverend Wilson."

"Well, ma'am, that's where the problem begins. Mother did send for Doctor Tavish. And thanks be to God, the man was sober. He came right to the house, took one look at Davy, and said he diagnosed him as having an inflammation of the vermi . . . the vermi-something."

"Vermiform appendix," she supplied softly. Then she whispered the word, "Appendicitis."

"What?" the man asked.

"Appendicitis," Aries repeated. "What else did Doctor Tavish say?

"Well," he began slowly. Aries wanted to shake the words out of him. "He made a hot poultice and placed it on his side. Then he gave him several doses of medicine. He said we was to sustain the boy's strength by broths, and to keep him quiet in bed. He said that if his bowels didn't move soon, he would start injections of . . ."

"He's a fool." Aries voice exploded into the air, silencing the reverend and bringing a quirk to Jarrett's mouth.

"Reverend Wilson, your son's condition won't improve by hot poultices and broths. And giving him enemas can kill him." She clamped her mouth shut, willing herself to proceed with patience and consideration when she saw the reverend's face blanch under the onslaught of her words. In a gentler tone she went on. "Reverend Wilson, when the vermiform appendix becomes inflamed, the medical term is appendicitis. The symptoms of this are a sharp pain in the region just above the right groin. The pain becomes intense upon pressure or movement, which is why your son is finding some relief by drawing his legs up to relieve all tension of the muscles in the affected area. While there are cases where people experience these attacks only to have them lessen and leave, then occasionally be repeated, there are other times they only intensify as time passes. It sounds to me as if your son's condition is worsening. Is it?"

"Yes. I think it is."

"But?"

"But, you see, Dr. Tavish doesn't. He says it takes time for nature to take its course. He says . . ."

"What do you say, Reverend Wilson?" Her hands were on

her hips, and her eyes shot shards of blue steel at the man. Every inch of her was the doctor, and the woman who had been kissed just a few moments ago was gone.

Jarrett stood back, watching the metamorphoses, knowing that he found delight and pride in both women, the doctor, and the soft, kissable woman.

"I say something has to be done or . . . or," and his voice lowered pitifully, "I'll lose my son. His mother and I waited ten years for him. We thought we'd never have a child, then Davy came along. He's been the light of our life, and I thank God for him every day."

In a gentler voice Aries asked, "And your wife, Reverend Wilson, what does she say?" The question had to be asked, but the answer was known.

"Well, she, that is . . . she thinks we should place our trust in the Lord, and in Doctor Tavish. She was against me coming here to ask you." His voice dwindled off, then regained strength. "She doesn't want anyone else but Doc Tavish looking at our boy, especially . . ." and he bit off the sentence with regret.

"Especially a woman, Reverend? Isn't that what she said?" Aries heaved a sigh of disgust and acceptance. It was the same wherever she went, Philadelphia or Montana.

"Then why'd you drive hell-bent for leather all the way out here?" There was a snarl in Jarrett's voice as his words cut through to the heart of the issue.

"Because, I'll try anything before I let my son die. And he's getting sicker and weaker as the day wears on. He's hurting worse today than yesterday, and I can't stand by and see him suffer. Not without trying. Don't you see?" he asked plaintively. "I have to try everything." He lowered his head. "Please ma'am, uh, Doctor Burnett, please would you come look at him?" His eyes pled with her, as he stood looking from Aries to Jarrett, waiting for a response.

"Reverend Wilson," she said gently, "I can't."

Jarrett's looked over at her, surprise etched on his face.

"It's an ethical decision. You have a physician looking after your son. It would be unprofessional, and an insult to Doctor Tavish for me to push my way into his . . ."

"Don't say no, Doctor Burnett," the man interrupted, his words a cry of anguish. "Please don't say no. My boy's life has to be worth more than a worry of whether you are being unprofessional. I'm asking you. Ain't that enough?" He let the words fall.

Aries closed her eyes, and ran her teeth over her lips worrying them while giving her head a slight shake. Opening them, she faced Jarrett, looking to him for guidance, seeking his strength.

"Get your bag, Aries." He said in a voice soft with understanding. Then, he added what she needed to hear, "I'll hitch up the wagon; we'll leave as soon as you're ready." He didn't say more, he didn't have to.

She whispered a soft, "Thank you," to him, and turning away, ran toward the house, cataloging in her mind everything she'd need. She knew she faced the possibility that she would be too late, that the boy's appendix had ruptured, and he would be dead by the time she arrived. She also knew she faced opposition from the mother and from Doctor Tavish. Then, another knowledge filled her—the strongest of all. She would have Jarrett there, by her side, lending her his strength. He would be her buttress, and would sustain her while she fought whatever challenges waited there.

Her feet were light as she threw open the door to her room, and gathered what she feared she would need, to do what she had to do, to save this little boy's life.

## Chapter Twenty-one

The sun was just starting its drop behind the hills when they drove into town. Even with the urgency, Jarrett had insisted they stop several times and let the horses blow. Still they made good time, but was it good enough? That thought hung heavy between them, blocking out any desire for talk.

Aries sat on her side of the wagon, coming in contact only with Jarrett's arms when the jostling of the road threw her against him. She had a far-away look on her face, and several times when he glanced at her, he could see her lips moving. He knew, without being told, she was reviewing the medical procedure needed for appendicitis. Going over and over what she'd been taught.

They pulled up in front of a small, whitewashed house, and before Jarrett could lift Aries from the wagon, the Reverend was running up the walk, and jerking open the front door.

Aries held back, standing in the shelter of Jarrett's arms. He clenched his jaw, his eyes darkening. Then, he took the heavy bag out of her hands, and, placing his other firmly at the small of her back, he guided her up the walk and through the open door.

They stood in a small hall, hearing raised voices from the back of the house. A door slammed shut, and in a few minutes, the Reverend appeared.

Aries looked at his face, then visibly relaxed as she read the answer to her question.

"He's alive." Reverend Wilson's voice was hushed and wonder filled the words.

He glanced at Jarrett. Not a hint of emotion was revealed on the rancher's face, or in his cold stare. He stood close to the woman, and there was a distinct aura of protectiveness about him. The thin man shifted on his feet. He was glad Jarrett was here, beside the woman wanted here by only one person— himself.

"Doctor Burnett," he began. His words were cut short by the sound of feet coming swiftly up the hall. A short, heavy set woman burst in, and pulled at the sleeve of the minister's coat, as she ignored Aries and Jarrett. Her eyes were wide with unshed tears, and her hair had pulled free of two tightly-wound braids on top of her head.

"Ed, please Ed, don't do this."

The man looked down into her eyes, then firmly placed one hand on top of her fingers still imbedded in his sleeve. "Mother, I'd like for you to meet Doctor," and he emphasized the word, "Aries Burnett from Philadelphia."

The woman stood still as if reeling from a blow, then drawing herself up to her full five feet, turned to Aries, and, with glacial tones said, "I'm please to meet you Miss Burnett."

Aries felt Jarrett stiffen beside her. "It's Doctor Burnett, ma'am, and you must be Mrs. Wilson. I regret that we have to meet for the first time under these circumstances." Aries voice was firm, and she held her head high as she made the correction, yet acknowledged the introduction.

A hint of a smile creased Jarrett's lips, and a light flickered in the blue-black recess of his eyes as he looked down at the slender woman at his side.

"Now, if you'll show me to the patient, I'll be able to offer my opinion that much faster, as I believe time is of the essence."

The woman pulled back, as if struck by Aries words, and a sound of protest escaped her lips.

"Of course," her husband said. He took a firm grip of his wife's elbow and led the way down the hall.

The room was made even smaller by the presence of five adults. The focus of each set of eyes was the bed in the center of the room in which the too-still form of a child lay huddled under a sweltering pile of quilts. A whiskered, middle-aged man in a rumpled suit sat, guarding the side of the bed. A string tie and collared shirt emphasized a grizzled Adam's apple, and gave the impression of a man who, at one time, placed some value on his appearance.

Aries stopped short, just inside the door. Jarrett stood behind her, in the hall.

The malevolent look of the physician made her suck in her breath, and lean back as if struck by a blow.

"There is already a physician in the house, Madame. I am Doctor Winston Tavish. I believe I was, uh, under the weather during your last, or should I say, first visit to our illustrious town, and did not have the pleasure of making your acquaintance." He touched each word with sarcasm, his tongue lingering on the word *pleasure*.

"You were drunk, Doctor."

He gasped involuntarily, and his eyes narrowed. This wasn't going to be as easy as he thought. The woman standing in the doorway, slight though she may be, wasn't going to be easy to intimidate.

"Is that another of your brilliant diagnoses, Miss Burnett? Similar to the one you're going to subject this good family to regarding this simple illness?"

Jarrett put his hand on Aries shoulder and gently, with a determined force, pushed her into the room, following closely behind her.

The doctor's eyes widened when he saw Jarrett standing there, his hand balled into a fist where it rested on the woman's shoulder, a look on his face and in his eyes that chilled the room.

"She told you once, don't forget it again. Her name is Doctor Burnett." Jarrett's words were hard as flint.

The doctor shifted nervously. "McCabe." The name came out in hoarse catches. "I . . . I didn't realize you were there. Good to see you," he said falsely.

Jarrett didn't acknowledge the greeting, such as it was. He let the silence grow in the room, never taking his eyes off the man who had made the mistake of treating Aries in an unacceptable manner. He felt a warmth enter him, and he liked this new feeling. He knew in that moment that Aries Burnett was his. As much as he could allow her to be, and as much as Aries, her shoulders squared, ready to take on the world, would allow herself to belong to him.

"Doctor Tavish." Aries voice cut into the silence. "I realize this is an awkward situation, and I appreciate your willingness to allow another physician to offer an opinion on your case. My father often said it was a fool who was so wrapped up in his own ego, that he placed it in front of the well-being of a patient. I can see you are no fool."

Jarrett looked down at the floor, trying to stop a grin at Aries skillful turn of words.

"Yes, well, haruump," Dr. Tavish said, clearing his throat. He moved to the side, nearer to the wall, and allowed Aries the freedom to approach the small boy lying, unaware of the importance of the decision that had just been made—a decision that would be of magnitude in his life. "I certainly agree with your father. Was he, by chance, the esteemed James Burnett?"

"He was."

"I never had the privilege of meeting him, but I am aware of his qualifications. I am to assume you trained under him?"

"I did." Aries answered each question respectfully, volunteering nothing more.

"Then, by all means, proceed, ma'am." Dr. Tavish looked quickly, and in apprehension, at Jarrett. Seeing his scowl, he quickly amended his words. "Uh, Doctor," he corrected weakly.

Aries moved to the side of the bed and removed the layer of quilts, only to stop at the sound of protest from the boy's mother whose hands were white with gripping the brass footboard. Aries straightened her back, and looked at Reverend and Mrs. Wilson.

The minister's hands dug into the woman's shoulders, and he gave a curt nod of his head. "Yes, Doctor Burnett, please proceed," he said in a reedy voice. "We'd be much obliged."

Aries drew back the quilts, and sucked in her breath at the small form lying on his side, knees drawn up, his thin legs sticking out from under a flannel night shirt.

"Davy," she said quietly to the child. "Davy, I'm Doctor Burnett, and I need to examine you. I know Doctor Tavish has already done so, but I must ask you to endure yet another probing. I'll be as gentle as I can."

The boy opened his eyes, brown orbs in a too-white face. "Will it hurt?" He whispered, and the breath touching her face was heavy with fever and pain.

"Yes," she said.

He lay there, his breath coming in short, shallow gasps. "Okay."

Aries knelt beside the bed, and gently raised the night shirt. Trying to block his small body with hers, she exposed his guarded abdomen, and then gently laid her fingers across his right groin, probing the tenseness and swelling. The boy groaned at her touch, gentle though it was. Aries heard the mother sob, and slowly she got to her knees, and drew back a single quilt to cover him. Then she turned to the doctor watching her every movement.

"What is your opinion, Doctor Tavish?" she asked respectfully.

"Inflammation of the vermiform appendix." The words were delivered somewhat pompously.

"I agree. And your plan of treatment?"

"Bed rest, continue with the hot poultices of mullein-leaf, and if evacuation of the bowels doesn't occur soon, an infusion of peppermint, at least a quart."

"And that will kill him." The words flew out into the air, each one a firebrand igniting the ear of all present.

"Ed," the woman's voice was shrill, "I demand you make her leave. At once. I've taken all of this, this charade I intend to."

"Hush, Mother, please," the man implored. "Please." The word was a supplication to his wife and to his God.

"No, let her continue. I find it," Dr. Tavish began, darting another glance at Jarrett, then quickly amending his choice of words, "I find it . . . enlightening. And what would be your plan of treatment, Doctor," he used the title heavily, "Burnett?"

"Surgery. Immediately."

"Absolutely not," the doctor roared. "Absolutely not!"

Aries turned to the father and looked fully into his anguished face. "Reverend Wilson, your son will die without the immediate removal of the inflamed appendix. I have seen them left too long, with the treatment Doctor Tavish has just prescribed. The appendix, in those cases, became increasingly inflamed until they burst, leaking poisons into the abdominal cavity. The patient always died. I don't even know if the surgery will save him. I'm concerned too much time has elapsed, but I do know for sure that if you allow enema's or additional treatment of that nature to transpire, you will contributing to the death of your son. I know that for a fact." She lowered her voice, but not its strength and conviction.

"There will be no surgery. Not while I have anything to say on the matter," Doctor Tavish interrupted, his voice loud and demanding. "I know that surgical operation for the removal of the appendix is often called for, but I believe, in almost all cases, needlessly. Young lady, doctor or no, the removal of the vermiform appendix is a fad. Nothing more! It is often performed by a surgeon who can persuade others to submit to his desires. That will not be the case now. No it will not be!"

Reverend Wilson folded his wife's sobbing body into his meager chest and held a comforting arm to her back, patting her as if she were a child.

With tears pooling in his eyes, he asked, "Can you do this surgical operation, Doctor Burnett?"

"I have never done one before," she admitted quietly, "but I have seen it performed numerous times, and have assisted my father during the procedure. I have no doubt of my ability to perform the operation. However, I must caution you, your son may be too far advanced in the inflammation to recover, even with my best efforts."

"You see," Doctor Tavish broke in, "she's giving herself an out. She's admitting this . . . this fad is not the success she claims it to be. It is not needed nor called for."

"I am not making allowances for any lack of my abilities, Doctor Tavish. I am merely stating the truth. Davy's appendix may be near rupturing, and if that is the case, neither your nor my plan of treatment will make the difference. However, if I am to have any chance at success, the operation must take place immediately. And," she fixed a piercing look at the doctor, "I'll need your assistance, Doctor Tavish. I'll need your facilities, and your assistance in administering the ether." She turned back to the father. "The decision is yours, Reverend." With that, she stepped back from the bed, and moved in closer to Jarrett, letting her body touch his, drawing courage from his power and presence.

"Reverend," Doctor Tavish began.

"Please, Doctor, this is a decision between my wife and our God." He let his sad eyes roam the room, taking them all in. "Could I ask all of you to step out? There's a small parlor just down the hall, if you would wait there. I'd . . . I'd like to be alone with my wife and son at this time. I assure you, Doctor Burnett, we will be mindful of the need for quick action." Then, not waiting for their reply, he and his wife moved to their son's side.

## Chapter Twenty-two

Aries stood at the lace-covered window, peering out, seeing nothing, her back to the two men standing so silently on opposite sides. There had been no conversation, and the only sound was the movement of the doctor's hand as it brushed across the heavy stubble on his jaw. Aries leaned her head against the pane of glass, and closing her eyes, slowly and methodically walked herself through the operation she'd just said she could perform. She could see, as clearly as if she were in the room, her father cutting through the abdominal wall, and explaining his every step to the students around the table. Under her father's guidance, she had been allowed to perform the majority of the operation, but never alone. Never without his harsh voice guiding and prompting her. Aries raised her head and stiffened her back. The same voice that had guided her in a surgical room in Philadelphia lived within her. He would guide her now, just as he had since she'd come to Montana and had acted as a physician. The physician he knew she could and would be. With those thoughts strengthening her, she turned and met the Reverend and his wife as they walked into the room. She pulled herself up to her full height, and waves of confidence emanated from her as she readied herself for the decision.

The man wasted no time. "Doctor Burnett, my wife and I have prayed for guidance in this." His voice caught. "And we want you to perform the surgical operation." A tear wandered down his cheek, and he sniffed into the sleeve of his coat as he quickly wiped it away.

Aries looked over at the doctor, standing there in stiff silence.

He took a deep breath of air, and with a glare of acceptance said, "I'll be willing to assist you in the operation. Of course you may have the use of my office." The words were haltingly given, but the result was the same.

All eyes turned to Aries.

"We'll need to move him there. I want to get started immediately. Doctor Tavish, I've my father's instruments, but I'll need . . ." and she rattled off the list she'd rehearsed in her mind.

The doctor nodded, then left the room, shutting the door forcefully behind him.

Jarrett walked over to her, and handed her the bag he'd been holding. "I'll get the boy."

She followed him into the room, and watched as he bent over the small frame and with extreme gentleness, scooped the small body into his arms. Holding him tight against his chest, Jarrett walked from the room and out of the house.

He was followed by a silent entourage. The only words spoken came from the Reverend as they reached the door to the doctor's house. "I'll get it." He held the door open for his son, lying so unresponsive in another man's arms.

Jarrett went through an empty room obviously used as a waiting room, and into where the doctor stood, a forbidding look on his face. He started to place the boy on the high, wooden table, but Aries stopped him. "Don't lay him down just yet, Jarrett." Silently, without question, he obeyed her.

"Doctor Tavish," she addressed the man standing beside the table. "Do you have any carbolic acid?"

"I do."

"Then would you please wash the table thoroughly with it?" She gave the request, and not waiting to see if it was obeyed, set her bag on a nearby table.

"You want me to wash the table with carbolic acid?" he asked incredulously? "Do you know how offensive a solution that is? It has a most disagreeable odor, ma'am."

"I realize that, Doctor, but it is also a very good disinfectant." She turned back to face the man, "I subscribe to Doctor Lister's practices, and we will disinfect all that comes in contact with the patient. Including ourselves, Doctor Tavish." She stood there, no expression on her face as she waited for his reply.

Jarrett's voice cut in, "Do as she says. And if you delay this one more minute with your questions and attitude, I'll put this little boy down, and you and I will go outside. I hope I'm making myself clear."

The doctor swallowed hard, but taking one look at Jarrett's face, moved quickly to do as Aries asked.

Aries smiled a thanks. The smile was sweet, and moved across the room to his heart. There could have been no one else present but the two of them.

"Now," Aries said, turning to the mother and father standing helplessly. "Could I ask you to please step outside of this room, and close the door? We must keep this area disinfected, and you will be much more comfortable waiting in Doctor Tavish's living room. We may be hours," she said softly. "But I will keep you as informed as possible." She looked over at

Jarrett who was just straightening up from lying the boy on the freshly washed table. The offensive chemical odor of carbolic acid permeated, lending a dimension of fear and awe to the strange room of medicines and instruments.

Jarrett watched the couple reluctantly leave the room, letting strangers take control of the most precious thing in their lives. Then, he said in a voice that left no room for discussion. "I'm staying."

Aries gave him a nod, then walked over to the pan of water boiling on the small stove, dropped in the instruments she would need. She silently handed Dr. Tavish a clean apron.

"Are you ready, Doctor?" she asked him glancing over the equipment he'd laid on the small table next to the boy's still form.

"I am." His reply was gruff, though no longer resistant. He accepted that the operation was going to go on with or without his help. And, calling on the physician imbued deep within him, he knew it would be with his full assistance.

Aries unwrapped the boy. "Davy," she said, "Doctor Tavish and I are going to make the pain go away." There was no response. "But we need your help. Can you do that?" Weakly his eyes fluttered open, followed by a weak nod of his small head. "Good. Now Doctor Tavish is going to put something over your nose. There will be a strong smell, and you might not like it, or the way it will make your head feel. But, and Davy, this is very important, you must not fight us. Do not try to remove the mask even though the smell is offensive. Can I count on you?" She watched closely and was rewarded with another nod.

She stepped back and looked at Jarrett "We may need your help," she mouthed silently.

Jarrett smiled with what he hoped was more confidence than he felt. The room, the smell of the disinfectant, the instruments now laying on a clean cloth, the scalpel lying to one side, even the woman he realized he didn't really know, seemed to belong here, and he felt the intruder.

Aries finished washing her hands, then motioned for Doctor Tavish to do the same. He followed her direction without hesitation. "Please open the window, Jarrett. We'll need ventilation when the ether is administered."

He moved across the room, and let in the evening breeze, and the sounds of the town as it settled into the evening, impervious to the fight being staged in this room. He settled back against the wall, and swallowed the excess of saliva collected in the back of his throat.

Doctor Tavish moved closer to the boy. As he began the preparation, the words of a known surgeon ran through his mind. It was something to the effect that the patient made unconscious by chloroform hangs over his own grave until he regains his consciousness. The same could easily be said for ether, and he knew full well how dangerous it could be in the hands of anyone less than an expert. While he wasn't an expert, he knew he was a good physician. Lest ways, he had been until . . . and he let the thought dangle. He folded a towel in the shape of a funnel and inverted it over the boy's small mouth and nostrils. He would drop the ether onto the inside of the funnel, folding up the side, allowing as little as possible of the ether vapor to escape. He waited, poised above the makeshift funnel. He gave a short nod, and dropped the first drop. Immediately the vapor spilled out into the room. The boy stirred, and his hand raised slightly.

"Davy," Aries voice penetrated through the towel covering his face, "this is the part I was talking about. It will be easier if you would take deep breaths of the special medicine Doctor Tavish is dropping on the towel. This medicine, although it has a strong odor, will help you to go to sleep, and, Davy, it will take away the pain in your side."

The form was still, then the sounds of deep gulping breaths came from under the funnel as the child welcomed anything that would relieve him of the pain.

Aries watched closely; Dr. Tavish watched too. They saw the moment his hand unfurled. They saw his chest rise and fall as the ether vapors overtook him.

She looked over at Jarrett and smiled unaware of the picture she made, bent over the naked body, the sharp scalpel in her hand. "Jarrett," she said, "perhaps you now would be of more help lending comfort to the parents. He's asleep. There will be no chance of his fighting the ether now."

"She's right, McCabe," the doctor's voice followed hers. Then, in a kinder tone, he added words that he knew Jarrett had to hear. "Doctor Burnett and I will be just fine. You'll be on the other side of the door should we need you, but I don't believe anything will occur that the . . . the doctor and I cannot handle."

Jarrett straightened away from the wall. A wooziness washed over him, and it took more effort than he wanted to admit, to be steady. He knew he'd make it through the operation. He was sure he would. Yet, seeing the knife in her hand, and knowing that it would cut through the little boy's skin, was more than he wanted to face unless she needed him.

"It's fine, Jarrett." she said again reassuring him, giving him permission to leave, letting him know that she understood, and would be okay.

"I'll be right outside the door. Call me if you need me." he said the words to Aries, but his eyes were hard on the other man's face. Then, without a backward glance, he opened the door and left the room.

Aries felt empty without him the moment the door closed. She looked down at the still child. And, forgetting everything but her reason for being here, she put her finger on the top of the knife, and applied pressure, making a thin, sure cut into the small, rigid abdomen.

Doctor Tavish raised his eyes to her, and there was undeniable respect in them, as he leaned forward to see and to learn from this woman who not only had more knowledge than he, but courage as well. He watched as her fingers flew, surely and decisively. He filled with gratitude for her presence, in this room, performing this operation, fighting to save the life of this little boy.

## Chapter Twenty-three

Time dragged. Several times, Jarrett rested his hand on the knob of the closed door, then slowly withdrew it. The parents sat on two of the straight-back chairs. They tightly grasped hands and watched the door, as if by standing guard, they could influence their boy's chances of living. They seemed impervious to Jarrett's presence; he leaned into the wall while he let his mind run free with all that had happened that day.

The only sound in the room was the tick of a mantle clock as it counted out the minutes, then the hour.

Jarrett gave up his post by the door and lowered his supple frame into one of the remaining chairs, his long legs stretched out in front of him.

Mrs. Wilson's head lay wearily against her husband's shoulder. He murmured words of comfort to her. Then the door opened, letting the noxious odor into the room. All three rose to their feet, fear and dread etched in their faces.

Aries entered the room, and stood quietly just outside the door. Her apron was covered with blood, but her hands were clean as she held them protectively in front of her. Wasting no time, she spoke.

"He's going to be okay."

With those few simple words, Mrs. Wilson gave out a cry, and would have crumbled to the floor if it hadn't been for the support of her husband's arms.

"Mother," he whispered, "Mother, our boy's okay." He gulped out the words, holding the woman close to his side.

"Your son's a fighter," Aries said to the two of them. "We were in time—barely. He's still heavily sedated, but you may come into the room and see him for just a second. Don't touch anything," she admonished, "Not even your son." Her smile softened the words, and she went back inside.

Mr. Wilson looked at Jarrett, his homely countenance transformed by profound joy. And with tears streaming down both of their faces, his arms supporting the woman, together they followed Aries through the door, into the room where their son lay.

Jarrett could hear Aries talking to the parents. Then the sound of voices stopped, and Aries and Doctor Tavish came out into the waiting room, not wanting to intrude on the parents' happiness.

Aries walked over to Jarrett. She looked pale in the waning light, and Jarrett knew the last few hours had taken their toll. "Are you okay?" he asked, looking down into her face. He shifted his body closer to hers, protectively.

"She should be," Doctor Tavish answered for her. "She saved that boy's life. Mighty fine piece of cutting, Doctor." He smiled and looked at Aries with admiration and respect.

"We did, Doctor Tavish. We saved his life. I couldn't have done it without you."

"Bull! Excuse me, Doctor Burnett, but that's just plain bull

and you know it. I believe you would and could do most anything you set your mind to. And that couple in there had best
be thanking you instead of their God that their boy is alive.
We both know he'd be dead by now if they'd listened to me.
No, don't try and spare me," he cut off her sound of protest, "I
don't mind admitting when I'm wrong." He lowered his voice.
"I've been pig-headed all my life, but today I almost lost the
life of a child. I'm not a bad doctor, Aries. There was a time, I
was reputed one of the best. And I will be again. I'm going to
take some time off. With you here in these parts, I can do just
that. I'm going to get myself together—eat right, do some
reading, resting and," his voice faltered, "and get off the
sauce. Then, I'll be ready to be the kind of physician I once
was, the kind these folks deserve." He fixed his eyes on hers,
bleary and red from the ether he so carefully administered.
"There's room for both of us here, Doctor Burnett. I can learn
from you, and I hope you might learn something from me. We
made a good team in there." His voice dwindled off as he
looked at her, waiting for her reply.

"I'd be proud to be associated with you, Doctor Tavish.
While I may have more recent knowledge, you have experience that is irreplaceable. I love my profession, but I have
other obligations. Jarrett's been generous enough to provide a
home for my little brother and me in turn for housekeeping.
I'm finding out," she said, blushing, "that I enjoy that more
than I thought possible." She kept her eyes on the physician,
not daring to look at Jarrett. "Sharing the needs of the people
living around Wise River would be perfect for my situation,
that is, if Jarrett agrees to . . ." and she let the words trail off.
Then, fearing a response, she said hurriedly, "We'd best rejoin
the family in there, don't you think, Doctor? Davy will be
coming to soon and we both know he will soon be one sick little boy, not to mention the pain he'll experience as the ether

wears off. I fear we have a long night ahead of us." She smiled wearily at Jarrett. "I'm sorry you've had such a long wait, Jarrett. I'll be fine if you'd like to return to the ranch. Later, after Davy is recovered from the effects of the anesthesia, I'll get a room at the hotel. I'll get someone to bring me back to the ranch as soon as I can. Davy will recover quickly under Doctor Tavish's care." She waited expectantly for his response, not wanting him to see how desperately she wanted his answer to be different from what she had just offered.

"Aries, I don't intend to leave you here. Dad and Ben will manage just fine without me. While I was hitching up the wagon, I talked to both of them. My only worry was Black, and thanks to a certain physician's remedy," his eyes smiled into hers, "that's even less a concern. You do what you need to do here. I'll leave now and get us both rooms at the hotel, and tomorrow, if everything's okay, we'll go home together." He looked deep into her eyes, his every word and movement confident. "I won't be long."

She could only nod her grateful thanks. She wouldn't have to face the time here alone. Jarrett wouldn't leave without her. It was a new and wondrous feeling.

Ignoring Doctor Tavish, Jarrett touched the side of her face, and in a gesture familiar to both of them, tucked the forever errant whisp of hair behind her ear. He smiled, and laid his hand against the satin smoothness of her cheek, leaving it there for too brief of a moment, feeling her lean into his cupped palm. Then, with a nod to the other physician, he left the house, quietly closing the door behind him.

It was after midnight when Doctor Tavish and the Wilsons persuaded Aries to leave with the patiently waiting Jarrett. Davy had been nauseous and had vomited, crying out with pain with every wretch of his sore stomach. As the effects of the ether wore off, Jarrett once again scooped him up in his arms and laid him to rest between the crisp sheets on the bed in the physician's spare room. With one final look at the incision, Aries allowed Jarrett to lead her from the small house and across the street to the hotel, leaving the boy in the hands of the two people who loved him and the remaining physician.

She stumbled once with weariness, and Jarrett put his arm around her, offering his body for support.

"I'd pick you up and carry you, Doctor Burnett, but I don't think that would do much for your professional image." He whispered the words into the flowery scent of her hair, now edged with ether's heavier aroma. He smiled to himself, accepting that uniqueness as yet another part of her; she was becoming so precious to him.

They stopped at the front desk where the sleepy owner handed her and Jarrett the keys to their rooms. He'd dropped his arm from around her shoulder as they entered the building, and with all propriety distanced himself from her. "Thank you," she said quietly to the man as she took the key.

"Uh," he fumbled for words, then said, "there'll be no charge for that room, Doctor Burnett."

She raised her tired eyes, sensing Jarrett's disapproval at the man's words.

"I . . ." she started to protest only to have the stammering man stop her.

"We're beholding to you for what you done for Davy Wilson. Heard all about it. Heard you done an operation on him that saved his life." The man lowered his head and mumbled, "Peers like the least I could do would be to not charge you for the room. I'd like to do that."

"Thank you," she said, her voice filled with emotion, "that's very kind of you, and most appreciated."

The man bobbed his head, a pleased look on his face.

Jarrett's light touch was one of guidance, nothing more, as they went up the stairs and down the dimly lit hall.

Taking the key from her and opening the door, he stepped into the room. Before he let her enter, he took a cursory look around the empty room, then stood aside.

It was a typical hotel room. The brass bed, with its faded wedding ring quilt, took up most of the room. There was a tall table, holding a ceramic wash basin, and two towels folded neatly at the side. A high boy dresser, with a curved mirror, completed the furniture. It was simply furnished, but clean.

He placed the key in her hand and said quietly, "I'm next door. You get some sleep. I'll be close, if you need me."

He started to move away, when her hand reached out and her fingertips grazed his arm.

"I need you." Her words were a whisper, and for a moment, he thought he'd imagined them.

His throat felt constricted, his body tense. Her words set off a chain reaction of emotions inside of him.

"Aries," the word sent a shard of air into the room.

Her eyes were huge in her face, the dark circles under them pronounced. Her bottom lip worried by her teeth.

He started to reach for her then jerked his hand back. His eyes closed briefly as though searching through his reserves for a strength that was absent.

When he spoke, his voice was tight. "Aries, honey," his lips brushed against the top of her head then, with a Herculean effort, he stepped back and his hands fell limply to his side as he turned and walked out the open door.

## Chapter Twenty-four

Aries was pulled from sleep by a pounding on the door. She felt a rush of disorientation. As she lay there in the nether world between sleep and waking, a roaring wind of memories swept over her, tossing her emotions about like a matchstick in the wake of a flash flood.

"Doctor Burnett. Doctor Burnett," Doctor Tavish's familiar voice penetrated the door, and pushed apart the cobwebs in her mind.

"Doctor Burnett." Her name came with greater persistence, and she heard urgency and agitation in the pitch.

"Yes," she called back. She struggled to free herself from the soft cotton quilt. "Yes, I'm . . . " and she quickly groped for the pieces of clothing placed on the chair. "I'm getting dressed."

Suddenly, fear filled her. *Had something happened? Had Davy taken a turn for the worse?* She jerked her slip over her head, and hurrying to the door, called through it, dreading the answer. "Doctor Tavish? What is it? Is it Davy?"

"No." Dr. Tavish's tone was emphatic. "He's resting comfortably." There was a pause, then he rushed on. "It's something else. I just got word that Laura Simm is in labor. Has been for two days, it seems. That fool girl wouldn't let them send for me, and now it sounds like she's in a bad way." He grumbled with an irascible undertone that did little to hide his concern. "Well, anyhow, I thought as since you're already here, you might be willing to ride out to their place with me and lend a hand. It's on the way to the Big Hole Ranch, and Jarrett could pick you up there." The invitation dropped into the waiting silence.

By this time, she'd thrown her dress over her head and was buttoning the last button. She raised her hair, and started to twist it into a bun. With trembling fingers, she pinned it tight against the nape of her neck.

Taking one last quick look around the room, she picked up her bag, and opened the door. She stepped through the slight opening and closed the door behind her.

"I need to tell Jarrett. His room is next door. He must be . . ."

"He's not there," the doctor said flatly. "The clerk said he left the hotel early this morning and hasn't returned. I left a message with him. He'll tell Jarrett where we are. He'll know where to come get you," he said reassuringly. "He practically lived at the Simm's place growing up. After they got married, Tommy moved Laura in with his ma. He's run that ranch ever since his dad died." The words came tumbling out, as though he sensed the need to get them said and out of the way. He hurried on with his explanation, "The three of them went to school together. As a matter of fact, Tommy and Jarrett were best friends. Didn't see one without the other, and then when Tommy discovered Laura, they just took her along with them on their escapades. She's a tough one, too tough." Worry creased his face. "Something's wrong for her to be laboring this long. Granted it's their first one. Still . . ." and his voice trailed off.

Then he picked up his train of thought and got to the reason for his standing outside her hotel room door. "I thought that as how you've got more recent training, maybe know some trick I don't, you'd . . ."

"I'd be glad to assist, Doctor Tavish."

The words were no sooner out of her mouth than the doctor's hand was on her arm, propelling her down the stairs and past the desk.

"I'll watch for Jarrett, Doctor. Don't you worry none," the clerk called after them, bobbing his head with importance as they went out the door.

Aries felt as though she'd stepped back in time, and was again sitting beside her father on the hard seat of the black buggy, hurrying through the streets of Philadelphia, not knowing what they'd find waiting for them at the end of their journey.

But this time it wasn't streets she was racing through; she and Dr. Tavish rushed down a dusty, rutted road. The small town they left behind was, by no stretch of the imagination, a city. Still, there was the same need for haste. And, the man sitting beside her was a physician. There was, however, another change. Aries wasn't a daughter, reciting in her head procedures, anticipating the medical emergency ahead, hoping she wouldn't let her father down, and feel the wrath of his displeasure. No, she was a physician in her own right, knowledgeable and respected for that.

She glanced at the surroundings as they sped past; they followed the Wise River, and were indeed headed back in the direction of the Big Hole Valley Ranch, the home of the man she loved. Aries filled with warmth, and she closed her eyes as memories assuaged her. She owed him so much, so much.

Because of him, she was becoming part of this rugged land, filled with beauty and hardships. Because of him, she was given the chance to follow her calling. Because of him, she knew love.

An aching need threatened to overwhelm Aries, and she longed for Jarrett, his calming strength, guiding her with steadfast dependability.

Dr. Tavish was impervious to anything but the horse pulling the buggy, and the reason for the urgency. He made no attempt at conversation. Aries was glad, as she needed time to compose herself, and to marshal her thoughts back to those of physician.

A slight pressure on the reins turned the galloping horse onto another road, branching off to the left, filled in with patches of grass and weeds.

The rig rattled down a small incline, and with dust flying behind them, hurled into the front yard of a stone, two-story house. The doctor jerked back on the reins, sawing the bit into the tender mouth of the horse, forcing it to a trembling stop. A large, yellow dog came running and barking, and over the sounds of the horse blowing and the buggy creaking came the thin screams of a woman.

Aries grabbed her bag, and jumped out of the buggy, not waiting for the doctor to round the back and help her out. The door of the house slammed open, and a young man rushed to them, his eyes wild in a too-white face, a grey stubble of beard showing.

Ignoring Aries, he headed straight for the man beside her. "Doctor Tavish. She's . . . she's . . ." he gasped the words as another scream rent the air.

The two men turned as one, and moved up the steps to the house; following close in their wake, Aries entered behind them. She paused inside of a small foyer and was greeted by the warm smell of gingerbread and spices. She followed through rooms that seemed light and airy, and she knew that if the conditions were different, she'd find a homey welcome awaiting her here. She sensed happiness in the walls, and hoped fervently that nothing would happen today to mar that.

The young man led the way up some stairs and to a room at the back of a hall. The hardwood floors were waxed to a honey brown, and the clean smell of bee's wax mingled with the gingerbread created a delightful ambrosia.

The young man paused for a moment, his hand on the doorknob; taking a deep breath, he braced his shoulders before opening the door.

Inside was a large, spindle bed, with the bloated body of a woman in it. She was restlessly tossing her head back and forth. Her breath came in short gasps; her fiery, red hair lay damp and matted on the pillow.

An older woman stood at bedside patting the girl's face with a damp cloth, and murmuring softly to her.

Doctor Tavish dropped his bag by the door and crossed to the girl's side. The woman stopped her ministering, and gave him a look of welcome and profound relief. "Thank God," she softly. "Thank God." Then she saw Aries, and her face mirrored a question.

"This is Doctor Aries Burnett." He made the short, terse introduction to the room. "She's from Philadelphia," he said, as if that were all the explanation needed. He picked up the limp hand resting on top of the quilt and said, "Laurie, honey, looks like you need some help bringing that young un into the world." He shook his head, "Just like his daddy, now isn't he, contrary to the end." She smiled weakly at him, biting an already blood crusted lip. Then she looked over at Aries.

"You're the woman living at the Big Hole, aren't you?" Her whispered voice was reedy, each word punctuated with effort.

"Jarrett . . ." She didn't finish the sentence as another pain grabbed her, and the mound that was her belly, constricted with contractions rippling across it.

She tensed herself, readying for the onslaught of pain she knew would follow. Her fingers curled into hard fists.

"No," the command was quick and harsh. Then in a gentler, yet firm voice, Aries said, as she moved past the husband and took a spot directly beside the woman's head, "Breathe into it. Don't hold your breath. Breathe. Pant like a dog." There was no doubt that the orders were expected to be followed quickly and without question. Slipping easily into the role, Aries took charge of the situation. "Do it until the contraction stops. It will help you relax," she said more kindly. She put her hand on the young woman's stomach, and stared into the pain-ravaged face. Hesitantly, then with greater force, the sound of breathing could be heard as eyes met eyes, and a look of trust crossed Laura's face.

"That's it . . . that's it." Aries smiled at her, then said, "Keep going, keep going, ride with it. It's almost over. There! You can rest for a moment." She glanced up at the husband and mother-in-law.

"How long have contractions been this intense?"

"She's been at this since early yesterday. She hid it from us until last night, didn't want to call attention to herself." Her husband's words were filled with love, pride, and fear, and he reached out and lightly laid his hand on the outline of her foot.

Aries straightened up and met Doctor Tavish's look. She gave a slight nod.

"We need to exam her," he said without preamble. "Tommy, why don't you wait downstairs. We left word for Jarrett to come soon as he returns to the hotel, and then you and he can get caught up on all the news." The doctor delivered the words, knowing they were empty and placating. "Mrs. Simms," then he smiled relieving the sternness of his face, "both Mrs. Simms," he amended softly, we'll take a look-see, and between this fine doctor and myself, we'll get this son—or daughter—into this world. That sound okay to all of you?" The question wasn't an option, and he backed up his words with action as he moved to the door and held it open. "Tommy, I could sure use a cup of coffee. And, Anne," he addressed the older Mrs. Simms, "I roused this young lady out of bed after being up most of the night performing a life-saving operation for the Wilson boy, and brought her here without a drop of breakfast. Come to think of it," and he focused his attention on Aries, "I don't remember you having anything to eat yesterday afternoon, or night, as far as that goes."

Anne smiled at Aries, her brown eyes lively and understanding. "I'll have something ready before long. Come on, Tommy. I think our Laura's in good hands." She looked up at her son, and put a workworn hand on his arm, "It'll be okay. God knows you and I need her. He sent us not one, but two doctors. Now, the least we can do is feed them." She pushed him from the room, his step heavy, his eyes filled with reluctance. He stood for a moment in the doorway, looking to his wife for understanding and guidance.

"I'll be okay, Tommy," she said weakly. "Leave," she gasped as another contraction started the upward spiral of pain, "now. And don't come back, darling, until I can present you with . . ." she gave a sharp cry, and feeling the pressure of Aries hand on her shoulder, reminding her, she started to breathe, short and fast.

Aries and Doctor Tavish stood close together on the landing outside the closed bedroom door. Laurie was resting after another long, fruitless contraction. Between the two of them, they had examined her without causing too much discomfort, and the results of that examination brought knowing, hard looks between them.

"Breech presentation," Aries said quietly. I've seen it before." She did not add that, more times than not, the mother died trying to give birth to the child whose head was not in the proper position in the birthing canal. In fact, the child's buttocks were presenting first. With no head to assist in the opening of the canal, the labor became intense, and expulsion could not occur.

Doctor Tavish nodded his head. There was no need to say what they both knew. He rubbed his hand in tired frustration across his jaw, the stubble making a rasping sound.

"It's things like this that drive a man to drink," and he looked at her, daring her to disagree. Not getting a reaction, he moved toward the stairs. "We got a long night ahead of us, Aries. Let's go get us some coffee. He muttered under his breath, "How am I gonna tell Tommy? She's been the center of his life since she wore that red hair in pigtails."

"I'll go back in with her, while you get a cup. Then you can spell me. You know the family better than I do. You should be the one to talk to them, and I don't want to leave her alone. I'm afraid another contraction will come."

As if on cue from her words, the air was rent with a scream, and together the two of them hit the door with their hands, knocking it open, as they both rushed to her bedside. This time, Aries coaching did no good. The pain enveloped her and blocked out any sound or awareness; her body felt torn in two as her baby struggled to be born.

The crescendo built, as if the pain sensed the finality of the diagnosis and now had free reign to encompass the woman. Her cries grew, filling the house and yard with anguish.

Aries never left her side over the next few hours. There

were times when she straightened her back from bending over the bed, her hand tightly clasping Laurie's hand, every bone in her body cried out in protest. The condition was no better; in fact, it had grown in magnitude as the house held its breath in eerie stillness between each contraction and the weakening cries.

Bending over her, seeing the dark circles of pain under Laurie's eyes, Aries tightened her lips, and as resolve filled her, made a decision. She laid the girl's hand alongside of her body, and with a firm step, left the room.

She quickly descended the stairs and found her way into the kitchen, led there by voices.

Dr. Tavish had left the room a short time earlier, torn between the woman suffering upstairs, and the young man hurting downstairs. He had tried to get Aries to come with him, but, again, she chose to stay with the patient. It was as if by staying, she could somehow will the child to turn and come down the canal into the world. She felt helpless, and raged against medical training that was not sufficient to save this young woman's life.

Coming into the kitchen, all voices stopped as they looked at her, each face a question. But it wasn't to them her eyes went. With an involuntary gasp of breath, they flew to the familiar back of the man standing in front of a window, peering out into the late afternoon sun that flooded the yard.

Sensing the stillness in the room, feeling her presence, he turned slowly, and with a motion that bespoke of controlled anger and pain, looked at her. She took a step back. She had expected to be met with warmth and perhaps love. The man in front of her had neither. There were hard lines around his mouth, and his face was dark and forbidding. His body was rigid, his stance that of a wary gladiator. Hurt clouded her eyes, as she drew in her breath at the change making him once again the cold, vigilant man parceling out his rare, meager attempts at caring. A man who for all appearance had grabbed back any love he might have felt, and with clenched fists, imprisoned it behind walls so thick it would never escape again. He didn't say anything to her; he didn't have to. The hard lines of his body said it all.

"How, how long have you been here?" she gasped.

His eyes, dark and unreadable, moved to the stairs. "Long enough," he answered tersely.

Unaware of the charged current in the air, Anne moved between them, pressing a thick mug filled with hot coffee into her cold hands. Aries bent her head, enticed by the aroma, and automatically took a sip of the stimulating brew. The room swayed, and she stumbled. Jarrett reached her side in a blur of movement and grabbed both of her arms in a grip that made her cry out. Immediately he lightened his touch, but with lingering forcefulness, pushed her into a chair.

"Sit down, before you fall down," he ordered, his voice harsh and cold. "You're exhausted," he said condemningly, "and you need to eat."

"No," she said, stopping Anne from her movement toward the kitchen range. "No, there's not time now. Please Jarrett," her eyes implored him, stilling his sound of protest as they searched for the man that wasn't there.

"He's right, Aries. I'll go back upstairs with her," Doctor Tavish said, and pushed himself up from the kitchen chair. "You sit here and rest for a few minutes. It's a matter of watching and . . ."

"No, it isn't." Defiantly Aries rose to her feet. Tilting her chin, she faced them, each one wrestling with their own private demons and thoughts. She was an outsider, but she had woven her way into their lives. She took a deep breath, and squared her shoulders in preparation to do battle, if needed.

Turning her back on everyone else but Tommy, the one man she'd let make the decision, she said, "I came down here to ask you, Tommy, for the permission to try and save your wife's life."

His eyes widened at her words, and seizing the dim ray of hope, he emitted a low cry of anguish.

"I'll do anything . . . anything to save her. I love her. I . . ." and he lowered his voice, embarrassed by his pleading, "I can't live without her," he said brokenly. "If it means losing the baby, then," he chocked on the words, not daring to say them. Anne put a stricken hand to her mouth, and tears fell from her eyes and down her wrinkled cheeks. "Just tell me," he whispered, "just tell me."

Jarrett turned his eyes away from the painful scene he wanted no part of, a flicker of remembered anguish and pain glimmering in the blue as he relived, with his friend, the agony of helplessness, the inability to save someone you love.

With her heart beating in her throat, the words came out in spurts. "I said try, Tommy. Try," she cautioned. She ignored Jarrett's black look, and moving away from his stillness, turned to Doctor Tavish.

"I'm proposing to attempt to turn the baby." She rushed on, stilling the negative shake of his head. "I've never done it before, I won't tell you I have. But," and her voice lowered, "I've seen my father do it . . . successfully. My hands are small, and would slip more easily into the birth canal, an . . ." She wasn't allowed to finish the sentence.

"Absolutely not," Doctor Tavish roared. "Why you could . . ."

"What, Doctor?" she faced him like an angry badger. Her voice was firm as she threw out the hateful challenge. "What? I could kill her?" There was the sound of indrawn breath as collectively those assembled at the table pulled back from her words.

"Tommy," she said, turning her back on the doctor to face the distraught young man, "it's the only chance. If we let nature take its course, your wife and most likely your baby will die. She's wearing out, getting weaker. If we don't try now, she won't have the strength left to help us." She put her cup down slowly, and resting both hands on the table, held herself still, waiting for his decision. "It's up to you. I can't promise anything—but it's a chance."

The man glanced wildly about the room, looking with supplication at each face, leaving hers, then slowly coming back to it. He took a deep breath, straining it through his lungs, then expelling it as he pierced her with his eyes. She met his look squarely, never flinching, projecting a confidence she didn't feel.

"Okay," he croaked through tightened throat. The one word fell to the floor: he had either saved or condemned his wife and baby.

Aries didn't allow herself to look at Jarrett; instead, she looked directly at Dr. Tavish.

He hesitated, then in a parody of yesterday, he responded in the same words, "I'll be willing to assist you."

Silently, the two of them hurried out of the room, leaving behind three people, bound together with the all-too-real possibility they would lose someone each cared about. Three people fought the long night of blackness each in their own way.

Time was like a vacuum of heavy air, filled with waiting and listening. There was no sound from the room upstairs. No sound in the kitchen. It was as if time and sound had ceased to exist. No one spoke, and no one looked at one another. The time for drawing comfort and support had passed. Now, the need for deep self examination and reserve was necessary to make it through whatever this day brought.

Then, out of the oppressive stillness came a tiny, mewing cry. Another mew, then a full, lusty sound drifted down the stairs, and through the kitchen door. It was the most beautiful sound in the world, and, as if the child realized that, there came loud complaining over all the abuse it had suffered coming into this world.

Tommy started toward the door, then stopped and leaned his head against the doorframe; he stood listening, waiting. The cries had stopped, and fear settled back around them, its wings dipping low, whipping a chill into the air. The bedroom door opened and slammed shut, and a quick, steady tread came down the stairs toward them. Anne moved closer to her son, ready to share his pain.

Aries came into sight, her face a wreath of joy. In her arms she held a small bundle wrapped tightly in a flannel blanket. She stopped short, in front of the man peering at her, waiting and praying. A tiny fist popped free from the confines of the blanket, and waved about accompanied by another angry cry.

"Mr. Simms, I'd like to present to you your daughter. And," she added quickly, "her mother said to tell you she's doing fine, but that you have another redhead on your hands."

The words were no sooner out of her mouth than he gave a whoop of delight, and grabbing her, kissed her soundly on the mouth, kissed his mother soundly, and tenderly, with a great deal more restraint, kissed the wet carrot redhead of his daughter. Then letting out another whoop that rocked the house and caused his daughter to protest loudly, he bolted from the room, and, taking the stairs two at a time, flew to the bedside of his wife.

## Chapter Twenty-five

J arrett spoke only when necessary to Aries, and then only to discuss their leaving. She took her seat beside him on the wagon, the distance between them filled with glacial tension. She was forced to look everywhere but at the chiseled outline of his face as the horse, under Jarrett's frequent snap of the reins, covered the distance to the ranch in record time.

He stopped in front of the house, and still, without uttering a word, came around the wagon and lifted her down. His face was passive, and for all the emotion showing, he could have been helping a stranger. He sat her feet firmly on the ground and started to release her.

"Jarrett," she cried, as her hand rested on the sinewy muscles of his forearm, "please talk to me." Her voice was low, imploring him. "I don't understand." She raised her face to his, as questioning pools of turquoise, flooded with unshed tears.

He looked at her and the only evidence of any response or feeling was the jerk of the muscle at the side of his cold eyes. His lips were a thin line.

257

The pain in her eyes was his undoing, and an ache entered him making him tremble, wrenching him with its inability to be consoled.

His words came with a quiet ferocity. "I won't put myself through that ever again. I won't love any woman that much just to lose her. I can't. I thought I could. I thought that with you I could bury the past, and I did, I did. Then, today, today it all came back, and I knew the moment I drove into that yard and heard those screams, I had made a terrible mistake. I stood there in the kitchen, helpless, helpless like I was . . . Aries, I was married." He took a tortured breath, and pushed her away from him, his hands a tight band on her arms. "She died in my arms trying to give birth to our baby. I failed her. I was helpless," he repeated. "It was then I promised I'd never love again. I'm sorry, Aries. I don't have the words to tell you . . ."

"No," she cried out, her hand raising to her mouth as his words tore at her. "No! Don't say that, Jarrett, don't. Please, don't do this to us. Please don't let the past or what happened today stop you from reaching out." She lowered her voice, and through trembling lips said, "What happened to your wife and mother and to Laurie today, is the exception. Childbirth isn't always that hard, or," and she dropped her voice, "fatal. We're learning more. Her next birth will probably be easier, quicker. It doesn't have to be that way." She emphasized each word, giving them the importance needed to sway him.

"No, Aries, you're right. It doesn't." There was a fatalistic sound to his voice. Then he dropped his hands to his sides, and, turning on his heel, moved away from her. "It doesn't. I'll see to it that it doesn't!"

The days tumbled one into the other. Aries woke each morning with a heavy ache at the flooding realization that she'd lost Jarrett. Her body seemed weighted, heavy with despair, and it was all she could do to leave the security of her room, and go about the duties she imposed upon herself.

At first she thought he'd relent. That seeing her, being around the love she was waiting to lavish on him, would melt that granite-hard resolve. But Jarrett not only distanced himself from her, he slipped back with ease into the role of past, making himself as scarce as possible, only coming in for the rare, occasional meal that he ate in silence. If there was a chore away from the ranch, Jarrett took it. He carried a haunted look, but he protected that with a superior, callous manner.

The summer rushed on, but winter whistled through Aries, chilling her with icy winds. She tried. She woke each morning resolving not to hurt as badly as she did. She resolved not to look for Jarrett, not to listen for his footsteps, or to long for the sound of his voice.

The only person who seemed to reach Jarrett was Timmy. A rare smile crossed the man's face when he listened to the child who never left his side.

It was one of those Montana summer days; a day of sweet smells, punctuated by the lazy hum of a bee, and the patient warmth of the sun as it climbed to its zenith in the sky. It was a day that begged to be enjoyed.

Aries stood out on the porch, raising her face to the sunlight, and with quick resolve, she whistled for King.

The pup, growing into the size of its paws, ran beside her, as they walked toward the beckoning sound of the Wise River. King stopped to sniff at the wildflowers and high grasses, then zigzagged ahead to investigate the lush field leading to the thick brush and willows lining the river.

A chuckle bubbled out of Aries at his puppy antics, his inquisitiveness. She felt freer than she had in a long time. This was what she needed, and she vowed to do more of it, instead of staying so close to the house, waiting.

She lost sight of the pup; he was swallowed up by a thick growth of bushes. She could hear him up ahead, and increasing her pace, she brushed aside the branches of several entwined willows and thick undergrowth, and laughingly calling out his name, plunged into the opening.

"King!" The name froze on her lips. For, there in the clearing, not six feet away from her was a large brown bear. He was up, on all fours, and its massive head stilled as it sniffed the air. She barely had time to register this when, from a thicket at her side, King came barreling into the path. Seeing the bear he gave out an alarmed "woof."

King had never seen anything like this strange animal, but some sense warned him it was something to be reckoned with, and he jumped and danced toward it, changing his tone from a woof to a loud, shrill bark. His feet raised up and down in the same spot, and he neither advanced or retreated. The bear swiveled its head in the direction of the dog, and, as it glanced at the annoyance, its beady, eyes spied the woman standing there, her hand still clutching the willow she'd pushed aside to come through.

A low, warning growl was issued and, in one motion, it raised its mammoth body upright and towered there on its two hind legs.

Aries felt her blood turn to ice; she couldn't move, even though her mind screamed to her to flee.

The bear turned its head on its short neck, and Aries had full view of its long claws. A sour odor reached her, and she gagged with horror. A roaring sound entered her head and her ears clouded over in a feeling of lassitude and disbelief. It was as though she was someone else, watching the horrific scene unfold. Aries was helpless, rooted to the spot.

She wet her too dry lips, and croaked out a whispered, "King."

The pup, hearing its name, turned. That was all the bear needed, and, on legs that seemed too short to hold such a massive body, it took a slow step toward Aries. Then another step, as the distance between them closed.

King gave out with more warning barks, and they mingled with the shrill scream, with a life of its own, that tore from Aries throat.

The bear froze in its tracks, the end of its black nose vibrating as it sniffed out this unwelcome intruder.

The scream freed her, letting the messages from her brain make their way to her leadened feet. *Move*, it cried. *Move*. Obeying this command, she forced her heavy body to put one foot in back of the other as she retreated from the slack-jawed monster in front of her, its massive jaws open, showing tips of long, cruel teeth.

From her throat came small, whimpering sounds of terror, and she inched her way backward, knowing that, should the bear decide to follow, she would be lost. She felt small and insignificant, and realized that one swipe of those razor-sharp paws, one bite with those steel jaws, would leave her dead. She was afraid to turn and run, afraid to turn her back on the death awaiting her. Time was suspended. She knew her fate hung precariously in the air, awaiting the slow senses of the bear.

Another half step back, then another, as heel to toe, she danced this macabre dance with fate.

The bear woofed again, and slowly rotating its head away from her, looked at the bushes just to the side of Aries. There, pushed up against a tree, its small brown rump plopped on the ground sat a cub, looking perplexed and frightened. It gave out a cry sounding much like the cry all babies make for their mothers.

Hearing that, the bear twisted its head back and forth, the

gesture filled with anger, and emitting another loud roar, it took another step in Aries direction.

"No, no," she sobbed. The words were lost in her throat, and she took two more faltering steps backward, knowing that her only hope lay in turning and running. Running as though her life depended on it, for it did. "King," she whispered to the barking dog, "come." Somehow he heard her words, and ran to her, turning every so often to give another, ineffectual bark.

Tensing her body, she bunched her muscles together, and pushed back onto her heels, only to feel her body come to a jarring halt as it slammed into an immovable object.

"Noooo," she moaned as hopelessness washed over her.

Then, a soft breath fell on her ear, and a whispered command, "Don't move." Jarrett. She had no sooner realized that the immovable object included the broad muscles of his chest, when he spoke again, his mouth pressed against her ear, "Don't make a sound, honey. We're going to slowly back away from her. We've got to distance ourselves, let her know there's no threat to her baby." He backed his words with actions, and with his arms wrapped around her, and taking the weight of her body with ease, he slowly, and with great stealth, moved the two of them back, increasing the distance from the two animals.

The cub, seeing a clear path to its mother, gave out another bleat and rolled off its rump and onto its short legs. Losing no time it did a fast, waddling gallop to the safety of its mother's side. Slowly, the ponderous body lowered from its great height, and dropped to all fours. She snorted and sniffed the cub, assuring herself it hadn't been harmed by the humans. Then, as if forgetting they existed, the bear turned and made her way out of the clearing, her brown rump lost to sight as the thicket of wild raspberry bushes swallowed up the pair.

Aries felt her legs give way; cobwebs entered her mind,

accompanied by a floating weightlessness. With an impatient cry, Jarrett put his arm under her knees, and lifted her crumbling body. He held the limp form tight against his chest, and the realization that he could just as easily have been holding her lifeless body, swept over him.

He gave a sob as he buried his face into the warm thickness of her hair.

He carried her back to the house and passed Ted's fearful look as he met them at the edge of the yard. "She's okay," he said, never for a moment relinquishing his hold, "she's okay."

Ted followed him into the house, up the stairs, and into her room. He watched as his son stopped by the side of her bed, and, pulling her tighter against him for a long second, a look of homecoming on his face, held her there, briefly, as if allowing himself this small reward before he laid her with tenderness on the bed. Straightening up, he shook his head in silent despair and said, "Take care of her." Without another word, Jarrett walked from the room.

The bed held Aries, and she let it. Ted brought her a cup of strong tea, and later, a plate of supper. Both rested, untouched, on the table beside the bed. She had protested, telling Ted she'd be down to help him with the evening meal, but she had quickly given in to his orders that she stay in bed and rest. She was fine. Yet, she wasn't. The weakness from her faint had left her, and in its place was a knowledge that she'd never be okay without the love of Jarrett. She felt tears spilling from the corner of her eyes, trailing down her cheeks, and onto the damp pillow.

She had waited for him to come to her, knowing that he wouldn't, seeing the pity in Ted's eyes. And, as night settled around the house, she fought to accept yet another hurt. Once, when Ben looked in on her, she feigned sleep, not wanting to hear the excuses he'd make for his brother.

The house was silent, and the shadowed darkness permeated not only the room, but her very being. Turning her head, she looked out the window into the sparkling diamonds hung in the Montana sky. A shudder swept over her body; she was racked with an overwhelming feeling of hopelessness that blocked out the sound of the bedroom door as it slowly opened and closed. Then she tensed, and before her ears let her hear his steps, her heart recognized his presence. Jarrett drew near the side of her bed.

She opened her mouth to speak, to tell him how welcome, how wanted, he was in this room, in her life, when his calloused fingertips lay gently across her lips, stilling her.

"Shhhh, my love," he whispered into the room. And, without saying more, he again scooped her into his arms, and, as if carrying a rare and precious commodity, he made his way down the stairs and into the night, pausing only when he had her away from the house.

Under the sheltering arms of the big cottonwood, he turned in a slow circle, his face raised to the sky winking through the lacy branches of the tree. "Look, darling" and he motioned upward. It was a clear, brilliant night, and the sky reveled in this nighttime show as the stars, sparkling varying degrees of brilliance, tried to outdo one another, setting the wide Montana sky ablaze with cold splendor.

She tried to look, to see what he was trying to show her, but all she knew was that somehow, someway God had heard her prayers, and she was in his arms again, hearing terms of endearment fall gently from a mouth that was no longer drawn in a tight, cold line. She tightened her arms around his neck.

"Jarrett," she said softly.

"Aries," he cut off her questioning use of his name, "I've tried so hard to not love you. Please darling," he stopped her words again, "let me say this. It should have been said long ago. I thought that by not giving in to this love, I'd not lose you. I vowed I wouldn't let myself be drawn into caring for anyone that completely ever again. I broke that vow, only to have hell force itself back on me a few hours later." His voice became raw with emotion, "I pushed you away, out of my life, but, I couldn't get you out of my heart. Then today I heard King; I heard the fear in his bark." His voice cracked, "I heard you scream, and I ran. I ran, praying all the way, I'd get to you in time. Aries," he stopped, unable to go on. He ground his forehead gently against hers. He raised tormented eyes, and the stars picked up the wetness, making his pupils dark pools of liquid blue. "I could have lost you. I could have lost you in yet another way. I left you there in your room, and I've walked and walked under this blanket of stars."

He stopped talking, and slowly lowered her to her feet, never taking his arms from around her. Placing a finger under her chin, Jarrett tipped her face to his. He took his fill of her, drinking her into his body. Love, heavy and wild, filled Aries, singing through her veins. There was enough for both of them, enough to carry them through any of his fears and worries.

"Aries," the word was still in the vastness of the night, "Aries, I love you. I love you with all my heart. I realized tonight I could lose you, but it's worse living without you. Please say you'll be mine. I need you, my darling. I need you to fill up my life like those stars fill the sky. Marry me, never leave my side. I need you to light my way," he said humbly. He took his hand, and cupped her face, as he breathlessly waited for her reply.

He stood there with his heart in his hands, the love for her written on his face as he asked her to combine her strength, and her love, with his. He was asking her to join him in this dance of life.

Again, her reply was unspoken. Raising her mouth to his, she brushed his lips tenderly, giving him the answer he waited for. Her mouth pledged her love. Crying out, he pulled her into the circle of his arms, and together, the two of them stood silhouetted against the Montana sky, blending as one.

So still they stood, so intent on sharing the gift of love, they didn't notice the sky had deepened until Jarrett looked up, and saw a star positioned directly above them, dominating and blinding the night with its rays. And, he smiled to himself, knowing that there, in the sky, stretching wide across this wondrous expanse of land was his answer, his promise. He tightened his arms around her. From this day forth, he would share her with the night, knowing that her love would conquer any darkness life might throw at them. Knowing that hand in hand they would face each tomorrow with confidence.

The night held its breath as a gentle breeze curled the hem of her gown. Swirling upward, kissing the tips of her hair, it sailed into the heavens, carrying with it the weight and darkness that had enclosed his heart. The stars moved closer, accepting this offering, then giving back to him one of their own. A star more brilliant than any heaven had ever seen. A star to point him, and to guide him. A start to light his path. Aries. His gift. His own Montana Star.